high Hopes

A novel by

KI STEPHENS

To those chasing their dreams, and the ones who cheer them on.

Playlist

CINNAMON GIRL | LANA DEL REY	♥	5:01
MIRRORBALL | TAYLOR SWIFT	♥	3:29
LIABILITY | LORDE	♥	2:52
FREAKIN' OUT ON THE INTERSTATE | BRISTON MARONEY	♥	4:12
FROM EDEN | HOZIER	♥	4:43
TRUE BLUE | BOYGENIUS	♥	4:56
GLUE SONG | BEABADOOBEE	♥	2:15
BABY I'M YOURS | ARCTIC MONKEYS	♥	2:33
SWEET | CIGARETTES AFTER SEX	♥	4:52
SLOW HANDS | NIALL HORAN	♥	3:08
SWEET NOTHING | TAYLOR SWIFT	♥	3:08
THERE'S NO WAY | LAUV, JULIA MICHAELS	♥	2:55
HIGH OFF YOU | ALAYNA	♥	3:54
LIKE REAL PEOPLE DO | HOZIER	♥	3:18
GARDEN SONG | PHOEBE BRIDGERS	♥	3:40
TOUCH TANK | QUINNIE	♥	2:59
NOTHING'S GONNA HURT YOU BABY | CIGARETTES AFTER SEX	♥	4:46
THE ONLY EXCEPTION | PARAMORE	♥	4:28
CLOSE | NICK JONAS, TOVE LO	♥	3:54
I WANNA BE YOURS | ARCTIC MONKEYS	♥	3:04

Chapter One

BIRDIE

I'M NOT sure how long I've been at this. Long enough for my back to ache and my hands to be coated in clay but not long enough to get this vase right. It's always the neck. That's where things go sideways. Too thin, too uneven, too . . . something. There's probably some deep metaphor about life imitating art in there, but I'm too tired to think about it.

The ceramics studio is my sanctuary, especially this late at night. The university shuts down most of the campus by ten, but the lower floors of the arts building? They're a secret treasure.

After-hours access is one of the rare perks of being a 3D4M major—short for Three-Dimensional Forum, which focuses on ceramics, glass, and sculpture. It's a niche and hands-on field of study, housed within a building that hasn't seen a renovation in decades—a relic of an era when the arts received even less funding, patched up just enough to keep the wheels turning.

But it's also full of charm, with its creaky floors and mismatched shelves. And it's mine. Ours, really. I'm sure it feels like home to every artist who spends enough late nights here.

Every shelf is stacked with half-finished pieces, each one a small test of patience, waiting for someone to decide whether they're worth saving or scrapping. Every tool, every lump of clay, every dusty corner holds the marks of people who've tried—and sometimes failed—to make something meaningful.

That's the thing about pottery. You don't get to rush it. The clay knows when you're pushing too hard. It knows when you're not giving it the care and patience it demands. Outside of this room —outside of this craft that feels like both my sanctuary and my life's purpose—you can't always tell when things are about to crack until it's too late.

I lean closer to the wheel now, squinting at the wobble forming at the top of the vase. Damn it. My fingers are slipping. One wrong move and this whole thing collapses. I can't afford to start over— literally.

I need this for the donor event in two weeks. A whole room of rich alumni peering over their glasses, deciding if my art is worth their time, their money. It's a sort of pressure that feels heavy and constant, like a weight pressing into my chest every time I think about it.

I wipe my forehead with the back of my wrist, smearing a streak of clay across my skin. Typical. I could take a break, but I don't trust myself to stop once I'm in this zone. The silence is perfect—no chatter, no noise. Just me and the wheel.

I like the way the world fades out when I'm working. It's a different kind of rhythm, one that makes sense even when nothing else does.

"C'mon, Birdie," I mutter to myself. "Don't blow this."

I know talking out loud to myself is strange, but the habit keeps me focused. Keeps me from staying inside my head too much and spiraling into the self-doubt that always seems to hover just out of reach.

My former friends used to say I take things too seriously, espe-cially when it comes to my art. Maybe they were right, though they never seemed to take much seriously at all—least of all me. But when I'm here, working with my hands, it feels like the only time everything makes sense.

It's not about being quirky or cute or some sort of tortured artist

—it's about getting it right. And sometimes, getting it right takes more focus than people think.

I've got a plan. An actual, real-life plan that includes a paid fellowship and gallery showing. A stepping stone on my way to building a name for myself in the art world. That's the goal, anyway. Not that anyone really expects an art major from Dayton University to hit it big.

Then again, nobody expected I'd still be here at all. I sure didn't.

I press my fingers into the clay, feeling it yield beneath my touch. The tension in my chest eases a little. This is something I can control, something I can shape into what I want it to be.

I push the hair out of my face with the back of my wrist and focus back on the wheel. The steady hum of the motor and the glide of the clay under my hands is almost meditative, pulling me into the rhythm of it. But just when I'm settling in again, a loud crash shatters the silence.

My hands jerk off the vase, and it wobbles dangerously before I stop the wheel with my foot. I freeze, every muscle tensing.

The sound came from somewhere close. Too close. My heart pounds as the distinct thud of footsteps approaches, followed by the creak of a door opening.

I glance around the studio, searching for something to defend myself with in case this is the start of some late-night horror movie. A paintbrush? A wire tool? Fantastic. I could maybe poke someone to death with the tiny carving needle.

There's another heavy footstep, then a pause. Whoever it is, they're getting closer.

Then, the door swings open, and a guy steps into the studio. He's tall—tall enough to make the space feel smaller—with messy blond hair that looks like it's been tousled by the wind or a lazy hand running through it.

He's wearing soccer gear—an athletic jacket zipped halfway, clinging to broad shoulders, and shorts that show off thick, muscular thighs. His presence fills the room, magnetic and confident, like he knows exactly how striking he is and doesn't have to try.

Not exactly the murderous intruder I was expecting.

I blink, trying to calm myself. "Uh, can I help you?"

His mouth quirks into a slight, lopsided grin, and it's unfairly perfect—one of those grins that probably gets people to say yes to anything. "Oh—sorry," he says, holding up his hands as if to prove he's harmless. "Didn't mean to freak you out."

"Well, you did," I mutter, still on edge. "Did you need something?"

He rubs the back of his neck, glancing at the door he just came through. "I think I . . . kicked a soccer ball through a window. We were coming back from practice, and my roommate bet me I couldn't get it over the roof."

"And you missed, I presume?" I ask, tilting my head.

His green eyes are soft and apologetic, and he gives me a sheepish look. "Yeah, badly. The lights were off, so I didn't think anyone was still here."

I stare at him for a moment before standing to dust my hands on my clay-splattered jeans. "Well, it wasn't here. It was probably next door in storage."

He stares at the form now slumping on my wheel. "Sorry. Didn't mean to mess with your . . . clay thing."

I blink. "It's a vase."

"Oh." He stares at it for a beat longer. "It's nice. I mean, you're really good at throwing."

"Thanks," I mumble. I'd wager he couldn't tell the difference between a wheel-thrown mug and a pinch pot if his life depended on it. Still, a compliment's a compliment—even if it's coming from the guy who just shattered a window.

He raises an eyebrow, flashing that grin again. "You're not gonna come with me? What if it's all dark and scary in there?"

I give him an odd look, unsure if he's serious or not. "You're an athlete, right? Tall and strong. I'm pretty sure you can tackle a broom and a few bags of clay alone."

He dramatically glances over his shoulder, then back at me. "You don't know that. I could be one of those 'tough on the outside, scared of the dark' types."

I snort. "Well, even if that's the case, I've still got a vase to fix." I half-heartedly gesture to the slumped form beside me. "I'm afraid you're on your own, pal."

He laughs, and it's a light sound, like he doesn't take himself too seriously. "Okay, fair. But just so you know, I'm gonna fix whatever damage the ball did. Well . . . I'll get someone who knows how to fix it. I'm Liam, by the way."

I pause, studying him for a second. "Birdie."

"Birdie? Like tweet tweet?" he asks, his grin widening. "That's cute."

I narrow my eyes, bemused. "It's a nickname for Bridget. And before you ask, no, I don't fly."

He chuckles again, backing toward the door. "Got it, Bridget-Not-A-Bird. I'll, uh . . . go check on that window now. Prayers I'll survive the scary storage closet." He gives a mock salute before slipping out of the room.

I shake my head as the door clicks shut behind him, the faint echo of his footsteps fading. Typical athlete—overconfident, cocky, and somehow . . . a sense of humor means that makes him not the worst company.

My hands return to the wheel, but my rhythm is gone. The studio feels too quiet now, the stillness heavy and strange. I stare at the misshapen vase, sigh, and then scrape the clay off the wheel before packing up my things.

There's no point in staying here. The vase is beyond saving, and I'm too distracted to focus.

So, I sling my bag over my shoulder and head into the night, locking the door behind me. The walk to my apartment is long, but it's not too bad at this hour—quiet, empty, and peaceful. It feels safe because the campus is well-lit and familiar, though the occasional rustling in the bushes always makes me glance over my shoulder just in case.

Unfortunately, I don't like driving. I avoid it whenever I can, which isn't too hard to do in a big city with a bustling student population. Besides, campus parking is a nightmare I'd rather not deal with.

By the time I reach our place—an off-campus apartment that smells vaguely like coffee and burnt popcorn most days—I'm tired enough to fall face-first into bed, clay-covered jeans and all.

But when I push open the front door, the familiar sound of a blender greets me. Of course. I drop my bag on the floor by the entrance, expecting to see some kind of soupy, alien-like concoction brewing on the kitchen counter, and I'm not disappointed.

"You're back late," calls out a voice from the kitchen. My roommate, Sena, appears from around the corner, clutching her latest smoothie creation—a bright green, questionable-looking mixture of things no one should ever drink after midnight.

Sena is my opposite. She's bright, chatty, and always surrounded by people. She runs track, does theater, and somehow still manages to keep a full social calendar while acing her classes. Being roommates with her is like living with a whirlwind of color and noise.

She's the one who drags me out of my head and into the world. I'm the one who reminds her to study for finals instead of planning another weekend party.

"I had to stay late," I say, wiping my hands on the towel

hanging by the door. "I was in a groove until some guy kicked a ball through a window."

Sena's eyebrows shoot up. "A guy, huh? Was he cute?"

I roll my eyes and make a beeline for the fridge, ignoring her question. "That's not the point. He was . . . fine."

She waggles her brows, grinning. "Fine, you say."

I pop open a can of Diet Coke. "Please, you know I'm not interested in talking to some random guy after the year I've just had."

"Uh-huh." She leans against the counter, taking a long sip of her smoothie and eyeing me carefully. "So, is this fine guy of yours gonna be back to fix the window?"

"He said as much." I shrug, brushing past her toward my room.

"Chin up, sunshine!" she calls after me. "Oh, and by the way, don't forget about our rent this month. It's due next week."

I groan, mentally calculating the amount I'll need to scrape together from my part-time job at the bookstore and whatever free-lance art commissions I can get. Rent isn't outrageous here, but between school supplies and art materials, things are tight.

"I know, I know," I reply over my shoulder. "I've got it covered."

Sena doesn't push. She knows I hate talking about money and how much it stresses me out. Instead, she trails after me and sticks her head into my room, smoothie still in hand. "So, how are things going with the art? That donor thing is coming up, right?"

I nod, glancing at the half-finished sketches on my desk. I was hoping to lie down, sip my Diet Coke, and pretend I didn't have a thousand deadlines breathing down my neck. But, of course, Sena wants to chat now.

"Yeah, it's . . . coming along. Just need to make sure my stuff doesn't completely suck."

Sena shakes her head, smiling. "You'll be fine. Your stuff is incredible. And besides, you've got time to figure it out."

I snort, kicking off my tennis shoes. "If by 'time' you mean two weeks, then sure."

Sena heads back to the kitchen, leaving me on the edge of my bed.

There's a small collection of pieces on my desk—messy sketches, a few experimental pots, the kind of work that never sees the light of day. My stomach tightens a little as I stare at them.

Art is the one thing that's always made sense to me, but lately, it feels like I'm chasing something that's just out of reach. Like no matter how hard I try, I'm never quite good enough. Never quite worthy enough.

I know it's mostly in my head—imposter syndrome, Sena would say—but knowing that doesn't make it any less real. I just need to push through. I've made it this far, right? One more project, one more show, one more piece to prove I belong. Maybe then . . . I'll finally feel like I do.

Chapter Two

LIAM

"Dude, are you seriously wearing that?" Chase shouts from the living room, followed by the sound of a can popping open. "You look like you're about to present a PowerPoint on accounting strategies."

I adjust the tie in the mirror, frowning. Yeah, it's a little tight around the neck, but this is a suit. It's supposed to be uncomfortable. I tug at the collar, willing it to loosen up, but it's no use.

"I'm going to a fancy event, not a bar," I shoot back, pulling on the jacket.

Chase is sprawled out on the couch, feet propped up on the coffee table, phone in one hand and an energy drink in the other. Why he needs 300 milligrams of caffeine just to sit there scrolling through social media is beyond me.

My roommate is the human embodiment of too much. Too much energy, too much confidence, too much everything. Comes prepackaged with his role as a striker—big ego, bigger personality. He's always got some girl on his arm, and if not, he's working on it.

It's weird, rooming with him after last year. That's when it was just me, James, and Hayes—my older brother and his best friend. But they've both graduated now, which left me with the option to either live with Chase or risk getting stuck with a random person.

Chase has his downsides, but at least I knew what I was getting into. Loud nights, a revolving door of visitors, and endless trash talk during FIFA matches. It's not exactly peaceful, but it's better than unpredictable.

Chase takes another swig of his drink of death. "Okay, now we've gone from business meeting to funeral. Loosen up, man."

I look at myself in the mirror again. Dark blond hair's a mess, but that's normal. Suit looks fine, I guess. But Chase is right about one thing—I look like I'd rather be anywhere else. Probably because I would.

The only reason I'm going to this donor thing is because I promised my parents I'd be there. My dad's a high-profile, gallery-famous artist. He has a permanent installation at the Oriel and is one of Dayton's most well-known alums. My mom's not in the arts, but she's a social butterfly at these events. It's her bread and butter.

The two of them donate to the same fellowship every year, and they're both invested in keeping up appearances. So, they expect their son to show up looking respectable, too. Like a man who has his life together and isn't still trying to figure out what the hell he's doing.

"Alright, I'll see you later," I mutter. "Wish me luck."

Chase lets out a laugh. "Good luck? You're a Donovan. You've got this in the bag."

I roll my eyes. "Oh, is that how it works?"

"Absolutely. Just flash that winning smile, and the whole room will eat it up." He smirks, leaning back like he owns the place. "Though, if I was there, no one would bother looking at you. I'm the main event, baby."

I snort. He's not wrong. Ever since he took over the captaincy, our team's been solid. The guy knows how to find the back of the net like nobody's business. But I'll never give him that satisfaction aloud. Not to his face, anyway.

"How did you manage to get your head that far up your own ass?" I ask.

Chase tosses a pillow at me, and I duck out of the way. "Pure skill. Years of practice."

"You sure you don't want to tag along, then?" I ask, only half-joking.

It would be nice to have a buffer, sure, but it would also mean watching him the whole time—monitoring both his behavior and my own. Two inevitable screwups in the making, though honestly, Chase could probably play the game better than I ever could. He's a natural at charming people, even when he doesn't mean to be.

"Hard pass," Chase replies. "Rich people and tiny appetizers? Not my scene. Besides, I've got much better plans tonight." He winks, pulling out his phone to check his messages.

I don't even need to ask what—or who—those plans involve. Chase's roster speaks for itself.

With a sigh, I grab my keys and head outside. My car is parked in the driveway, and I make my way over, shrugging off my suit jacket and tossing it onto the passenger seat before sliding behind the wheel.

As I settle in, my phone buzzes. I glance down at the screen and see a text from my mom.

MOM

Don't forget to smile and try not say anything too awkward! Remember, less is more. Can't wait to see you tonight. XOXO MOM.

I let out a small groan, resting my forehead against the roof of the car for a second. My mom means well—she always does—but the last thing I need right now is a reminder of how much she's banking on me to charm an entire room of donors.

With a deep breath, I slip into the driver's seat and start the engine, the low rumble filling the quiet night. Time to face the music—or, in this case, a room full of strangers deciding how well I play the part.

. . .

THE DONOR EVENT is exactly what it always is: polished, pretentious, and filled with people who look like they were born with a stick up their ass. A showcase at the Ellsworth Gallery, the campus space dedicated to student work.

Normally, it's a quiet place, but tonight, it's transformed for the annual event held for rising seniors in the arts department. The lighting's dim, soft classical music plays in the background, and the whole place feels like it's trying just a little too hard to impress.

The walls are lined with paintings, all framed in sleek black metal, with a few larger installations in the middle of the room—sculptures, ceramics, glasswork—all part of the 3D4M program. Pieces with texture and weight. Stuff you could actually touch, not just stare at.

I trail behind my parents like the dutiful son they want me to be, nodding at the right times, offering the occasional polite smile to anyone who glances my way. My mom's fluttering around, introducing herself to everyone with that perfect smile of hers, already deep in conversation with Dayton's president, Ted Graham.

My father, of course, is standing beside her, exuding calm confidence, the kind that makes people gravitate toward him without him having to say much.

I'm bored and restless, but I know better than to show it. This is one of those nights where appearances matter more than anything else, and the last thing I need is a lecture about my "attitude."

When my gaze settles on a vase in the far right corner of the room, my mind jumps right back to that night in the studio. It's not even the same style—this one's taller, with sleek lines and glossy finishes—but it doesn't matter.

All I can think about is kicking that damn soccer ball through the window and meeting Birdie. Her light brown bob, a little messy around the edges, and the fact that she's on the taller side for a woman were the first things I noticed. But it was her kind hazel eyes—steady and serious—that really stuck with me.

There was something about the way she looked at me, like she was rattled by my presence in her carefully curated life. A disruption she hadn't planned for but was determined to handle anyway, with that steady, no-nonsense energy of hers.

I went to the arts director the next day, offering to pay for the window. Mrs. Ellis just waved me off, saying they had a budget for incidentals. I wasn't about to beg the woman to take my money. Still, I kind of wonder what Birdie would have had to say about it— if she knew I got away with the escapade scot-free.

Another perk of being a Donovan, I'm sure.

My mom tugs on my sleeve, breaking me from my thoughts. "Liam, honey, come over here and join us. President Graham has a question for you."

I blink and follow her to a small circle of suited guests, all mid-conversation.

"I hear your season is off to an impeccable start, Liam," Graham says. "How's Coach Harris been treating you all?"

I open my mouth, fully prepared to give the usual nod-and-smile response my parents expect. A safe, polished answer to keep things simple. But something tugs at me. Something that makes me want to say what I'm actually thinking instead.

"Coach is solid," I reply. "Keeps us running drills until we're about ready to faint, but hey, that's his job, right? Better than the end of last season when he had us playing puke-and-rally. Too many losses can really mess with a man's head." I grin, fully aware I'm saying too much, but I can't seem to stop. "We're all lucky he hasn't brought out the tactics cone yet."

Graham raises a skeptical eyebrow, glancing briefly at my dad for context. "Is that like a . . . motivational tool?"

I snort. "Yeah, we sit on it if we screw up a play, and the rest of the team has to yell at us. It's pure humiliation, but I guess it works."

The president chuckles politely, but I can feel my mom's hand on my wrist, her fingers pinching in that subtle way that says stop talking, now.

I glance down at her hand, then back up at President Graham, giving him a tight, brief smile. "Anyway, Coach is good. Thanks for asking."

I shake off her hand, clenching my fist as I step back. It's a small gesture, but one that makes my skin itch with irritation. It's suffocating. A reminder that I'm supposed to fit into their mold, even when it feels like wearing a suit two sizes too small.

Without another word, I turn on my heel and walk away from the group, leaving my mom to handle the rest of the small talk.

I know they mean well, but they expect me to be a different version of myself at these things. The version they've carefully molded over the years. The man who's the perfectly neurotypical poster child of their success.

I'm not that guy. I don't want to be him, and I'm not great at pretending otherwise.

I wander around the room, weaving between guests and peeking at the art pieces on display. I don't know much about art. It's always felt like something distant, something my parents understood and appreciated, while I kept it at arm's length rather than risk feeling out of place. But it's quiet over here, just the way I like it.

And there's something familiar about this corner.

Birdie, standing next to a collection of pieces—small vases, bowls, and what looks like an abstract sculpture of some sort. She's wearing a dress, simple but nice, nothing flashy. Her short hair's pulled back, and she looks . . . different. More put together, I guess. Not covered in clay like she was in the studio, but still the same sort of intensity in her eyes.

The kind that makes you feel like she's fully present, like she's seeing things most people don't.

I don't think much about it; I just head straight for her.

She's busy talking to some older woman, probably another donor, nodding and smiling politely, but the second she spots me out of the corner of her eye, recognition dawns. Her smile tightens slightly, and after a few more pleasantries, the woman pats her arm and drifts off, leaving us alone.

"You're here," I say as I approach, flashing a grin. "I was wondering if you would be."

She raises an eyebrow. "Your deductive reasoning is unparalleled."

I chuckle, letting the sarcasm roll off me. "These yours?" I gesture to the pieces—small, delicate vases with uneven, organic shapes, bowls that look like they were pulled right out of the earth. And then there's the abstract sculpture—jagged, almost chaotic, like someone captured movement in clay.

"Yes," she says curtly. "No soccer balls allowed near them."

I laugh, holding up my hands in mock surrender. "Noted. Don't worry, I left the ball at home." Then I turn my attention back toward her pieces. "So, these are pretty . . . different."

She cocks her head. "*Different* how?"

Right. People don't like to hear the word *different* when it comes to their art, their personalities, their anything. *Different* means out of place, and out of place means wrong. "I don't know. I'm not an art critic. I just know I like them."

A quiet giggle escapes her. "High praise."

Before I can add anything else, that tentative, soft smile of hers fades into oblivion. She looks right past me, eyes going wide, posture stiffening.

I turn to find what she's staring at, and sure enough, it's my dad —heading straight for us, all calm and collected. He's on a mission, it seems, and that mission is to assess the situation like he's sizing up a potential investment. Or possibly just to scold me for wandering off.

I swivel back to Birdie, and she's already waving me off, a flicker of panic in her eyes. "You need to go," she mutters, voice low and urgent. "I need to impress these donors if I want a shot at winning the fellowship. That guy behind you, he's a major part of the selection committee, and I already know he's a stickler for formality."

I blink. She doesn't know we're related, of course, because how would she? But it's almost funny how dead-on she is about his vibe. "You mean the tall guy in blue? He looks a little lost here, doesn't he?"

"Just another out-of-touch donor. Made it big, and now he wants to feel all important again." She huffs, her eyes darting back and forth between us. "But his money talks, and I kinda need him to like me. So, sorry, not sorry, but I need you to leave. Like right now."

I snort and then flash her a quick, sarcastic bow. "Your wish is my command, Bridget-Not-A-Bird. I'll make myself scarce."

Her eyes narrow, but I catch the slightest twitch of amusement in the corner of her mouth. Before my dad can get any closer, I scurry off, slipping through the crowd like I've got somewhere to be. The last thing I need is him cornering me for oversharing with the president earlier.

As I head out of her line of sight, I glance back for a second. She's already in full-on charm mode, that same forced smile in place. A mask I know all too well. And my dad? He's stuck listening to her pitch now.

It's a weird thing, watching someone else play the same game I've been stuck in my whole life. It's unnecessary pomp and circumstance. A performance for a man who's likely already made up his mind.

Right now, I guess I should just be thankful it's not me standing there, putting on another show for his approval.

Chapter Three
BIRDIE

THE ROOM IS TOO BRIGHT. Not in the literal sense—the lights are dim, the kind meant to flatter the artwork and the people milling around—but it feels like all eyes are burning straight through me. I adjust my posture, standing a little straighter, the polite smile on my face feeling more forced by the second.

I've done this before. Plenty of times, actually. Talking up my work to donors, explaining my artistic process like it's some magical thing instead of hours spent covered in clay, cursing under my breath when the wheel gets away from me.

But tonight's different. This time, it actually matters. It's not just about making a good impression—it's about landing the fellowship. Without it, my next year at Dayton will be rough. The tuition, the art supplies, the cost of living—it's all riding on this. Without the fellowship, I'd be scrambling for commissions just to stay afloat.

Or worse, picking up more shifts at the bookstore, which would eat up the time I need to work on my pottery. Less time for pottery means fewer pieces to sell, and fewer sales mean more shifts. It's a vicious cycle I can't afford.

Which is why it's a terrifying honor that David Donovan is gracing me with his presence now. I don't have time to overthink or panic. The man is one of the biggest names in contemporary sculpture, with installations in galleries all over the world.

He's a Dayton legend. The real fucking deal.

But he's not just a famous (albeit out of touch) artist—he's also a big part of the selection committee for the fellowship. And right now, he's staring intently at my work.

My gaze drifts over to the collection of vases and bowls I've set up—delicate, earthy pieces that are supposed to show my growth as an artist. They feel so me. Raw, unpolished, and unapologetically honest. Pieces of me that tell a story I'm still learning how to articulate.

But standing here, surrounded by people dressed in clothes that cost more than my entire art studio's supply budget, it seems like maybe "unpolished" isn't what anyone wants tonight.

And if the slightly detached look on David Donovan's face is any indication, I might already be losing him. "Mr. Donovan," I say, "Thank you for giving me your time tonight."

He glances up, giving me a polite nod. "This is your work?"

I nod quickly, my palms suddenly clammy. This is it. The moment I've been preparing for, and somehow, it still feels like I'm standing on shaky ground.

"Yes, they're mine. Bridget Collins," I tell him, extending a hand for him to shake. "I've been working on pieces that explore organic texture and form, keeping them raw and tactile. I want them to feel almost like something you could find in nature."

He studies the vases for a too-long moment, and I try not to fidget, even though everything inside me is screaming to do something. Say more. Do more.

Be impressive, Birdie. This is the only thing you have going for you.

He narrows his eyes. "So, how do you know my son?"

I rear back. "Your . . . son?"

"Yes," he says, a touch of amusement in his voice. "The young man who ran out of here as soon as he saw me coming."

I freeze and awkwardly clear my throat. "*Liam* is your son?"

David chuckles. "Yes. Did he not mention that?"

No. Definitely not. The same Liam who waltzed into the ceramics studio, informed me about a broken window, and then flashed me that ridiculous grin of his? For whatever reason, he didn't think it was worth mentioning that his father was a world-renowned artist and the head of the committee deciding my future.

I laugh nervously. "No, we er, we just recently met. He . . . well, he was chasing a rogue soccer ball into the ceramics studio."

"That sounds a lot like my son," David says with an amused smile. "Always a bit too energetic for his own good."

My stomach twists. I've just thrown Liam under the bus, and now I'm scrambling to figure out how much worse I've made things.

"Anyway," I say, attempting to steer the conversation back to safer ground. "I'm really passionate about exploring the connection between the imperfections of nature and how we view art. These pieces reflect that—trying to keep them as raw and real as possible."

David nods, disinterested. "Is this your first exhibition?"

"My first of this size," I say quickly. "It's been a goal of mine since I entered the program. The fellowship would allow me to focus entirely on my work next year. Hopefully, I can enter a few showcases and make some larger-scale pieces like the ones you have at the Oriel."

The Oriel is a prestigious gallery with gleaming white walls and polished floors. A cavernous space with sculptures so massive they feel like they might swallow you whole. It's the kind of place most artists only dream about.

"That's good," he says. "It's important to have lofty goals. And your work certainly has a . . . unique perspective. That's something we look for."

I resist the urge to wince or ask for clarification. Unique, I think, might be better than "different," as his son so helpfully pointed out, but still not quite the validation I was hoping for. "Thank you. I appreciate that."

He gives a tight smile. "Well, good luck with the selection process, Miss Collins."

He walks away before I can respond. Just like that. No further questions, no actual critique. But at least I didn't have to endure a full deconstruction of my work.

As soon as he's out of earshot, I slump my shoulders and exhale sharply. I'm sufficiently rattled, thoroughly drained.

I glance at my collection one last time, trying to remind myself that unique doesn't mean bad. It's just not the glowing praise I'd hoped for.

But this is fine. Really. Totally fine.

Right?

I SHIVER as I push open the door to Lucky's. It's an off-campus bar frequented by athletes, a bit cramped and loud for my style. But it's better than the stiff, overpolished atmosphere of donor events. There's no soft classical music here—just top forties and the warm, worn-in smell of beer and cheap liquor.

"Birdie!" a voice calls out from one of the high tables, and I spot Sena waving me over. She's sitting with a few other theater majors, her usual crowd, a half-empty glass in front of her.

I smile as I make my way over, already feeling the tension start to melt away.

"Hey," I say, sliding into the booth beside her. "How was your night?"

"Great! And yours?" Sena raises an eyebrow, offering me a sympathetic look. "Let me guess—full of pretentious compliments and not-so-subtle critiques?"

I laugh and rub the back of my neck. "Pretty much. How'd you know?"

"Because that's every arts event ever." She lifts her glass in a mock salute. "The glamorous world of struggling creatives."

I grab the drink that's already waiting for me—a whiskey sour. Sena knows me well enough by now, and she must've guessed I'd need this tonight. "Here's to the good life," I say, clinking my glass against hers before taking a long sip.

Sena snorts. "Yeah, I've got lines I still haven't memorized for next week's performance. I'm running on fumes here."

Sena will always say she's falling behind but then kind of pull a miracle out of her ass at the last minute. It's that effortless, easy-breezy confidence she has, the kind I could only dream of.

"Which is why it only makes sense that you're out drinking at a bar."

"Hey!" She swats me on the arm. "I needed a break from the stress."

"Same," I admit, pulling a stray piece of clay from under my nail and flicking it onto a napkin. "I think we both earned it. But, in my defense, at least you didn't have the son of a major donor show up and pretend to care about your art."

Her eyebrows shoot up. "Wait, who are we talking about?"

I briefly relay the details about Liam—how he waltzed over to me, acting all aloof and clumsily charming, and how his famous dad showed up right afterward. I keep it short, brushing past the parts that don't matter.

I don't need to blabber on about Liam and his rich daddy. Not here, not now. Not when I'm surrounded by people who actually care about art and expression, not status or money. It's all Sena's people here, theater majors, the kind who live for performance and lights.

So, instead, I ask her friends about their upcoming show, and they dive into animated chatter, bouncing off each other like a well-rehearsed scene. I like the way they feed off each other's energy, their passion spilling out like a shared secret.

Hanging out with them has been easy lately. They're self-involved in the best way—totally absorbed in their own worlds, their own stories. And I don't need to explain myself or prove anything to them.

"Let's go dance!" Sena takes my hand and attempts to drag me out with the rest of them.

It's tempting, the idea of losing myself in the music and the movement. I used to love dancing, used to get caught up in the energy of it, the freedom. But lately, I just can't bring myself to move like that anymore. It feels too vulnerable, like exposing a part of me I've been keeping locked away.

I smile but shake my head. "You guys go ahead. I'll hold down the fort here."

Sena's face twists into a playful pout, but she doesn't push. Even though we've only been friends and roommates for a few months, she's already figured out when I'm not in the mood.

"Suit yourself," she says, giving a little wave before disappearing into the crowd.

I take another sip of my drink, watching them blend into the sea of bodies on the dance floor. Their carefree energy fills the space, and something sharp clenches inside my chest. I shouldn't be here, should I? Laughing and drinking, pretending like everything's fine.

Living, moving forward, while Emily's just . . . gone.

I blink, the sudden weight of the thought making it harder to swallow my drink. The accident plays in my mind like an old film reel—the screech of tires, the crunch of metal, the way time slowed to nothing in those few terrible moments. Four broken ribs, a shattered collarbone, and a head injury that left me unconscious for days.

I made it. The other driver didn't.

I was home for winter break, heading back from a friend's house, and her car came out of nowhere. T-boned the passenger side of my old Toyota. The force of the impact spun us into oncoming traffic. By the time all the noise stopped and I could finally make sense of what had happened, it was too late.

I was injured, but she was gone.

They said it wasn't my fault. That the other driver was speeding. She ran a red light and lost control. But it doesn't matter, does it? It still haunts me just the same.

I met her parents after the accident. She was a senior in high school, they said, Dayton-bound like me. A bright-eyed girl with her whole life ahead of her.

They were afraid I'd sue, like I had any energy to think about lawyers or lawsuits when I was still trying to wrap my head around the fact that I survived, and she didn't.

I hadn't even known her name until I read it in the accident report—Emily Matthis. What a sweet name for a girl who barely had the chance to live. She was a stranger, but she shouldn't be dead. And I shouldn't be here, pretending like everything's okay.

But it's not just the guilt of being here, of still having a life to live when hers is gone. It's the fact that I don't know how to move forward, even though I have to. It eats at me, slowly but surely, until I wonder if I even deserve to be moving forward at all.

A year ago, nobody expected I'd come back to school. Not with the way I reacted. Not with the way I shut everyone out and let myself spiral.

My old friends quickly lost hope of me bouncing back. They were confused as to why I couldn't be the same vapid, carefree Birdie they used to know. They wanted me to be more self-absorbed, I guess. Shallower. More oblivious. To care about parties and boys and fitting in the way I did before.

But after the accident, I stopped caring about anything other than my dad and my art. And pushing forward with ceramics was really more about surviving. About doing the one thing I know how to do in a world that feels so far out of my control.

Now, nine months later, seated on a rickety barstool at Lucky's,

I take another long sip of my drink. The cool, sour liquid does nothing to ease the tightness in my chest. I glance up at the dance floor, at the blur of moving bodies, and the familiar pull of isolation tugs at me.

I should be grateful. I should feel lucky. I made it out alive. But all I can think is that Emily Matthis didn't. So no, I'm not in the mood to dance tonight. Maybe next week. Next month. Maybe never, if the guilt and uncertainty keep clinging to me like this.

Chapter Four

LIAM

LATE SEPTEMBER in North Carolina still feels like the middle of summer, with humidity thick enough to choke on beneath a burning, brutal sun. Sweat runs down the back of my neck, and the grass feels like sandpaper beneath my cleats.

I feel every sensation on my skin like it's turned up a notch—the sticky cling of my jersey, the sting of salt from sweat dripping into my eyes, the grit under my fingertips when I catch myself on the ground. It's distracting if I let it be.

Today, we're running drill after drill, no mercy, just sharp whistles and gruff commands from Coach. "Come on, Donovan!" Harris yells. "Move your damn feet!"

I'm already a step ahead—sprinting, dodging, weaving between cones like my life depends on it. Chase is on my heels, breathing down my neck, probably grinning like a little kid because that's how he is. He'll chase you down for the thrill of it.

We're neck and neck by the time we reach the end of the field, my breath coming in ragged gasps. Chase elbows me, just enough to throw me off-balance, and then bolts ahead, laughing as he does.

"Cheap shot, man!" I shout, trying to catch my breath.

"That's called winning," he tosses over his shoulder. "You should try it sometime."

I flip him off, but a grin tugs at my lips. Chase is annoying, cocky and sure-footed, but damn if he isn't one of the best strikers

I've ever played with. Fast, ruthless, and always two steps ahead, both on and off the field.

As we jog back to reset for the next drill, I see Santi and Amir messing around near the goalposts, taking turns launching shots into the net. Santi's the kind of player who's always talking trash, but he's got the skills to back it up, and Amir's the quiet type—solid as a rock, a defensive wall that's impossible to break through.

Chase sidles up to me, nudging my shoulder. "You're slow today, bud. Late night? I saw your light on when I got back."

I was up late finishing a civil engineering assignment. That's what happens when you put things off until the last minute. Some people lose it under pressure. Me? I can't focus until there's a tight deadline staring me down like it's daring me to fail. But at least I get things done, even if I have to practically set fire to my brain to do it.

It's a hellscape up there. Calculations, diagrams, and deadlines all fighting for space in my mixed-up head.

I grunt, rolling my neck to shake off the tension. "Classwork."

"Don't you usually just wing it?"

"I mean, I usually stare at my screen for a few hours before pulling an all-nighter the night before it's due. If that's what 'winging it' is, then yeah."

Chase snorts. "Brutal, buddy."

Before I can respond, Coach's whistle shrieks again. "Alright, guys, small-sided game. Five-on-five. Let's go!"

Chase flashes me another grin, and this time, it's all shiny, perfect teeth and unshakeable confidence. "Guess I'm kicking your ass today."

"Bring it," I mutter, jogging over to my side of the field.

The game is fast-paced—tight spaces, quick decisions, constant movement. I'm a winger, so my job is to keep the ball moving, to weave through defenders and set up crosses. But today, I'm distracted. My mind keeps drifting back to all the things I don't usually like to think about.

School is a relentless one. The civil engineering assignment I barely finished on time. The pressure to balance it all. The donor event with my parents and the way my dad chewed me out afterward.

I couldn't bring myself to act the part. To play along like everything was fine.

"You embarrassed me, Liam," Dad had said, his voice low and full of disappointment. "Running away from me in front of a prospective recipient. Leaving halfway through the event without a word to your mother or me. Do you think that's funny?"

What was I supposed to say? I didn't want to be at the event in the first place. I tried my best, but I knew it the moment I stepped out of line. Why should I pretend like I belong in those rooms, making small talk with people who wouldn't even look twice at me if my last name weren't Donovan?

The ball comes flying toward me, forcing me back to the present. I take off, sprinting down the sideline, heart pounding in my chest. Santi's coming up fast, trying to block me, but I duck around him, sending the ball sailing toward the goal just as Chase comes barreling in.

He heads it into the back of the net. Goal.

Chase pumps his fist, flashing me a triumphant grin, but all I can do is nod and jog back down the field. Practice is winding down, and exhaustion's starting to creep into my bones. I glance toward the arts building, my gaze lingering on the window I shattered with that damn ball.

It's patched up now—fresh glass, not even a scratch. I wonder if Birdie's in there, spinning clay on her wheel, cursing under her breath when things go wrong. I wonder what she thought when she realized that "out-of-touch artist" was my dad.

Maybe she was confused or embarrassed, but she shouldn't

have been. She was right, after all—my dad does want to feel important. He wants to feel like he's still relevant, like his work matters. Always has.

A man who chases validation but can't be bothered to spare any for his own sons.

"Donovan!" Coach's voice cuts through my thoughts, and I snap back to reality. He waves me over. "Get your head out of the clouds and come over here!"

I jog toward him, wiping the sweat from my forehead with the back of my hand. My legs feel heavier than they should, my focus still half-scattered.

Coach Harris gives me a look I don't waste time deciphering. "Had an interesting chat with Ted Graham the other day."

Oh, right. Here we go. I know I shouldn't open my mouth when it comes to team dynamics, but it wasn't done in an effort to tattle. I was trying to be relatable, I think. Or maybe I was trying to take the attention off myself and shift the conversation.

"Apparently," Coach grits out, "you've been telling our president that I use barbaric shaming tactics to keep you all in line."

I tilt my head. "I wouldn't say it's barbaric. In fact, I think it's character-building. A real bonding experience. Graham must have misread me."

He raises an eyebrow, but I just shrug. It's not a lie. I didn't bring it up to rag on my coach—I just thought it was funny at the time. The team jokes about it constantly.

Coach grunts. "Well, next time you're chatting with the man who signs my checks and a room full of donors, keep your loose lips in check." He claps me on the shoulder, hard enough to sting. "You made me look bad, Donovan."

There's that disappointment again. Somehow, I manage to make grown men look bad without even trying. A real feat for a college kid barely scraping by.

"Sorry, Coach," I mutter, rubbing the back of my neck again.

He laughs gruffly. "Just keep it on the field, alright? You've got too much talent to be talking yourself into trouble."

"Got it." Lips sealed, for now.

It's not like I even enjoy talking that much. I don't particularly love the sound of my own voice or the attention it can draw. But sometimes, it's like my thoughts spill out before I have a chance to lock them down.

I just say what's on my mind, no filter, no second-guessing, and it's hard for me to understand how other people can hold it all in. Must be exhausting keeping every stray thought caged up inside.

It's a constant battle, I think. A pointless fight I'm designed to lose.

It's a week later, and I'm sprawled out on the grass of the practice field, the first crisp night of October finally cooling things down. My shirt clings to me, drenched in sweat, but I don't care.

I like being alone out here. When I'm practicing by myself, pushing harder than I need to, everything feels predictable. Outcomes are controlled. Effort and results are balanced. It makes group practice easier—shutting off my brain, not thinking about the thousands of overlapping sensations or the act of playing itself, but just doing it.

I stare up at the sky, dotted with stars, and let the light breeze wrap around me. The faint glitter of light against the black makes me feel like maybe things aren't as overwhelming as they sometimes seem.

Then there's a clatter, sharp and sudden, cutting through the silence.

I sit up, my muscles groaning in protest, and glance toward the arts building. Someone's standing outside, their figure just barely visible under a single flickering light.

I push myself up, curiosity tugging at me, and jog over.

"Shit, shit, shit," the girl mutters under her breath.

She's crouched down, picking up the shattered remains of what looks like a clay pot. Soft brown hair, two beaded pearl clips. A frazzled but determined demeanor.

It's Birdie Collins, of course. She's kneeling in the dirt, her hands trembling slightly as she tries to gather the broken pieces.

Without thinking much of it, I drop to my knees beside her. "Need a hand?"

Her focus stays locked on the scattered shards as she mutters, "It's fine, really. This piece was crap anyway." Her hands move quickly, sweeping up the fragments like she's trying to erase the evidence before anyone notices—like she can make it disappear if she moves fast enough.

But then her eyes flicker up, and they lock on mine. Her expression shifts, the smallest flicker of recognition crossing her face. For a split second, I can see the wheels turning in her head before she deadpans, "Liam Donovan. What are you doing here?"

I quirk an eyebrow. "Oh, we're full naming now?"

She snorts, brushing her hands off on her jeans before sitting back on her heels. "You"—she wags a finger in my face—"you let me say all those things. Ran off and didn't even bother telling me who your dad was."

I shrug, leaning back slightly. "Neither did you."

Her eyes narrow, but there's a glint of something—maybe amusement, maybe something else—before she shakes her head, dropping her gaze back to the mess at our feet. "Touché."

I wince. "You could probably . . . glue it back together? What's that thing where you put the gold shit in the cracks?"

I know about this technique—Dad used to go on about it during one of his metaphor-heavy talks. 'It's about embracing the flaws, making something even more valuable than it was before.'

"Kintsugi, and it's urushi lacquer." She keeps her focus on the broken pot for a second before letting out a long breath. "It's fine. I didn't like this one that much."

I watch her for a moment. "Yeah? Looked pretty solid to me. You sure you didn't just lose your temper and take it out on this poor, unsuspecting pot?"

She laughs under her breath and gives me a sidelong glance. "I never lose my temper."

"No?"

"No." She taps her temple. "This thing up here, it's like a steel trap. Perfectly tempered at all times."

I grin. "Right. I can tell by the way you were sweating bullets at the donor event on Saturday. Screams calm under pressure."

She rolls her eyes. "If I was going to throw something in a fit of rage, I'd pick something a little more satisfying to break." She gestures noncommittally to the remaining shards. "This one was already on its way out."

I glance at the pieces, then back at her. There's something in the way she talks—so casual, like everything's under control—but the way she was muttering under her breath a minute ago says otherwise.

I've only known her a few days, but even I can already tell she's not the type to let anyone see her slip, not easily.

"So, kintsugi, huh?" I say lightly. "It's meant to make things more beautiful, isn't it? The cracks, the imperfections. Wouldn't it be the perfect fix for a broken piece like this?"

She snorts. "Did your dad teach you that?"

I hold up my hands in mock surrender. "I try not to listen too hard when my dad talks." Most of it's just noise—art metaphors, life lessons I'm supposed to care about but don't. But this one . . . it kind of stuck with me. "But if you can fix something and make it better, why not try?"

She's quiet for a long while, like she's considering my point, her gaze flickering over the broken pieces in her hands. But then she murmurs, almost to herself, "It doesn't always work that way."

I shrug, letting it go. "Okay."

She tilts her head. "Okay?"

"What? Did you want me to argue with you about it some more? You're right. Some things are meant to stay broken. Some things can't be fixed with a bit of gold-dusted glue. I'm not here to change your mind."

She flashes me a sideways smile. "Do you always do that?"

"Do what?"

"Just . . . let things go like that? Most people would have tried to convince me. Push me to see their point."

"Not my style. I say what I think, you say what you think, and we move on. Doesn't mean I have to keep hammering at it. I'm not here to win some devil's advocate debate."

Her smile lingers for a second, and then she nods, almost to herself. "That's . . . kind of chaotic. Kind of refreshing."

I wink. "I aim to please."

She laughs gently. "You're strange, too. I like that."

"So are you," I say, because it's the truth. She's honest in a way that most people aren't. Guarded, sure, but there's something else there, too. Something that pulls you in, like she's constantly holding back a storm but doesn't let it show. Plus, she's quite beautiful. "And you're really pretty."

Her cheeks go pink. "I—I'm not even sure what to say to that."

"Well, since we're exchanging compliments, you could tell me I'm pretty, too."

She lets out a laugh, one of those short, surprised ones that bubble up before she can stop it. For a second, it looks like she's trying to figure out if I'm serious. And then, with a little shake of her head, she says, "You're pretty, too, Liam. The prettiest disaster I've ever met."

I smile. "I'll take it."

Chapter Five
BIRDIE

THE PRETTY LITTLE envelope sits on the edge of my desk, taunting me. It's thinner than I imagined it would be, a single crisp piece of paper enclosed inside the smooth, cream-colored card stock. I don't know why I expected something grander, something more—after all, it's just a letter.

A letter that could change the course of my entire life.

With shaky hands, I tear it open and pull out the folded sheet inside.

Miss Bridget Collins,

We are pleased to inform you that you have been selected as one of the five finalists for the prestigious Dayton Fellowship in the Arts. As a finalist, you are invited to present a detailed proposal for your intended body of work, which will be evaluated by a panel of faculty and esteemed artists. The selection process will involve an interview and studio visit, where you will have the opportunity to discuss your artistic vision in depth.

If chosen as the recipient, you will receive a stipend of $15,000, as well as the opportunity to participate in a summer mentorship with renowned artists David Donovan and Claire Mahler. The fellowship will culminate in an exhibition at the Oriel Gallery, where you will have the opportunity to showcase your completed works.

Best regards,
Margaret Ellis
Arts Director
Dayton University

My breath catches as I read it again, slower this time, trying to let the words sink in. I'm one of five. I'm in the running for this fellowship, the single thread of hope I've been clinging to. The award amount would be just enough to cover a year of tuition.

And I desperately need it. Desperately enough to feel like everything rides on this.

I was raised by a single dad who's been gracious enough to help with my medical bills since the accident, but there are still outstanding costs—the physical therapy copays I've been covering, the ever-mounting credit card debt, on top of everything else with school.

Not to mention the money I donated to the Matthis family to help with Emily's funeral expenses. A small gesture to show that I held no contempt for her, to make sure they knew I wasn't planning on suing.

All I've ever wanted since the accident is for all of us to find peace.

And the mentorship? I've admired Claire Mahler's sculpture work since I was a preteen. Unlike the other big names, she's always felt grounded, approachable. Her work reflects it, too—raw, unpolished, but somehow more human because of it.

Watching her rise in the art world has been like seeing the path I've always wanted to take. She wasn't born into success. She fought for it, piece by piece. And now, the thought of potentially working with her? It's almost surreal.

My heart does this weird stuttering thing in my chest, and I grip the letter tighter, like holding it will somehow cement it into reality. *One of five.* This isn't a dream—it's happening.

All those late nights in the studio, the hours spent hunched over the wheel, the constant fear that I wasn't good enough . . . it might all actually pay off.

I have a real shot here.

But what if I blow it? What if I can't handle the pressure of competing against the other finalists, artists who are just as hungry and talented as I am? Four other people are fighting for this just as hard, and only one of us will win.

The pressure to perform, to be perfect, has already overwhelmed me. And on top of that . . . there's the whole *David Donovan* of it all. I'll have to work with the man if I win. The stern-faced father of the man who just waltzed into my life with that careless grin of his.

Pretty boy Liam. I wonder what he'll think if I win, if I end up working with his dad after all. I wonder if he'll even care.

From what little I know about him, he's made it clear he doesn't get along with his dad. Or, at the very least, they have some strange oil-and-water dynamic. A bit of a prickly yet begrudgingly loyal situation if I've clocked it right.

But, complicated or not, he still knows his dad, knows how he operates . . . what he looks for in a fellowship recipient. Maybe he could give me tips on how to impress him. What the illustrious David Donovan really wants in a protégé.

Liam seemed eager enough the other night—he called me pretty, for God's sake. Maybe he'd be willing to help me out. It wouldn't hurt to ask, right?

A part of me cringes at the thought of relying on someone else to get ahead, but it's not like I'd be asking him for a handout, just a little insight. A teeny tiny home-grown advantage.

The problem is, I'm not sure what I could possibly offer him in exchange. What does a guy like Liam Donovan need from someone like me? His family is wealthy, he's a soccer star, and he's ridiculously good-looking in that effortless way that's almost infuriating. He's got everything in his life going for him.

And I'm the girl who spends most of her time covered in clay, barely scraping by.

Still, Liam doesn't strike me as the type who's too concerned with what's in it for him. He didn't exactly stick around at the gallery event to win points with his dad. If anything, he looked just as out of place there as I felt. Maybe that's something we have in common—hating the pretense, the forced politeness, the endless schmoozing that comes with the art world.

I lean back, staring at the letter in my hands, the weight of the decision settling over me. If I want to win this thing, I need every advantage I can find. And Liam? Conspiring with him might just give me the edge I need.

I WAIT for Liam after practice on Friday night, pacing the edge of the field, arms crossed against the evening chill. It's a weird sort of feeling, being stationed out here. Almost like I'm waiting for my boyfriend after a game or something. But I haven't had a boyfriend in years, and Liam Donovan is definitely not that.

I tug my sleeves down, watching as the team finishes their final laps. The soccer guys are all sweat-slicked and flushed from exertion. They look good. Mouthwateringly good. They're laughing, shoving each other around, and even from here, I can see the easy confidence in the way they move, like they own the field.

A couple of them eye me as they jog past, probably wondering what the hell I'm doing out here. Am I a groupie, a stalker, or just a random girl who wandered too close to their territory? I ignore it, pretending to be absorbed in my phone.

When practice ends and Liam finally spots me, he smirks. That kind of smirk that suggests he's not entirely surprised to see me, but he's still amused by it. He gives a quick nod to his friends and says something to them under his breath, waving them away as they file off the field.

He jogs over to meet me, sweat glistening on his skin, his shirt sticking to every line of muscle. "Waiting for me, Birdie?"

I snort. "Obviously."

"It's because I called you pretty, isn't it? Careful now—you can't fall in love with me over a single compliment."

I elbow him lightly. "Are you that full of yourself?"

"Someone has to be." He grins wider, leaning back on his heels. "What can I do for you?"

"I was wondering . . ." I glance at the ground, already regretting how awkward this is about to sound. "If maybe you needed help with anything?"

He stares at me, wide-eyed and mystified, like I've just offered to clean his cleats with my bare hands. "Help? With . . . anything?"

"You kn-know," I stammer. "Some light cleaning, laundry . . . um, homework help? I could make you a set of mugs or something."

He raises an eyebrow. "Mugs? Really?"

I groan. I put myself in this ridiculous position, and now I can't even dig myself out gracefully. Subtlety is not my forte. But more than that, asking someone for help feels like admitting defeat.

"Yeah, I've been practicing with the thumbprint technique," I say. "They're supposed to be much more ergonomic, and I figured —hey, useful, right?"

He taps his foot, waiting. "Just come right out with it, okay? Tell me what you want."

I suck in a breath. "I'm officially a finalist for the arts fellowship. And your dad's on the committee, so . . . I was wondering if you could, you know . . . help me impress him."

He stares at me, slowly scratches the back of his neck, and for a moment, I swear he's about to laugh. I know I'm out of my league here. It's humiliating, plain and simple.

These highbrow people—art world elites with their galleries

and trust fund kiddos—are so far out of my wheelhouse it's almost laughable. I grew up in a world where impressing someone meant melting a slice of cheese over a pan-fried burger and cracking open a cold beer.

My dad's blue-collar through and through, the kind of guy who measures success in hard work and calloused hands, not fancy titles or expensive art shows.

But Liam? I never would've assumed he belonged to that world, either. Not when we first met, not even now. There's something about him that feels like he's caught between two places—like he's equally out of step at those gallery events as he would be in my dad's garage.

A wry grin pulls at his lips. "Believe me, if I knew how to influence my dad and win his favor, I'd do it myself."

"Please," I say, giving him the biggest puppy-dog eyes I can manage. "There's got to be something you can do. Maybe just some insider knowledge? What he likes, what he hates, how he thinks . . . anything, really."

He rolls his eyes. "Look, Birdie, I wish—"

Before he can finish, frustration boils over, and I turn on my heel to leave. I don't need this—don't need to stand here and beg for scraps of information. But before I can take more than a step, his hand gently wraps around my arm, stopping me.

"Okay, okay, just wait a second," he says, his voice softer now, almost pleading. "I make no promises, but I can try my best to help you."

I turn, and his hand falls away. "Thank you so much. Really. I'm still working on my proposal, but maybe you could take a look at it when I'm finished? From there, we could brainstorm or something. I don't know, I just—"

"How about I read over what you have now, and we'll go from there?"

Of course, he's making it sound easy, like I haven't already started to pour my heart and soul into this. Like I haven't spent sleepless nights agonizing over my art in the first place.

But maybe to him, it is easy. Maybe the strained relationship with his dad has taught him how to navigate this world without flinching. I guess that's what comes with the confidence of never needing, or wanting, anyone's approval.

I sigh. "And you're sure there's nothing I can do for you in return?"

His gaze shifts, sweeping over me from head to toe in one long, deliberate look. Green eyes sharp with mischief, perfect mouth curling like he's already got some clever thought brewing. It's unnerving, it's electric, all sorts of distracting.

An involuntary shiver runs down my spine, even though I tell myself not to react. His lips quirk into a faint, knowing smile, and when he finally speaks, his voice drops, low and smooth. "I'll let you know if I think of something."

I swallow hard. "Right. Well . . . just make it reasonable, yeah? Quid pro quo. No weird or borderline illegal favors."

He taps me on the tip of my nose. "Don't worry, I'm a very reasonable person."

I snort. "Debatable."

"You haven't known me long enough to make a comment like that."

"I'm making an educated guess."

He steps a little closer, just enough to make my pulse spike. "Guess you'll have to spend more time with me to find out for sure."

My cheeks flush. "Is helping me impress your dad just a ploy to get me to hang out with you?"

He laughs, a low, easy sound. "Maybe it's a win-win."

I shake my head. "I've got a bit too much on my plate to play games here, Liam."

"No games," he says, still grinning. "Just business."

Business. Sure. Except nothing about this grinning, golden-haired man feels like business. It feels unpredictable, and messy, and dangerous, like getting too close to something you can't fully control.

I pull out my phone and hand it over to him. "You should put your number in, then, for *business* purposes."

He takes my phone, types in a few words, and then hands it back, still smirking like he's in on his own private joke. I glance at the screen, expecting something ridiculous, and sure enough, he's saved his name as "Liam (your only hope)."

I roll my eyes and pocket the phone before he can see me smile. "Real mature."

"Always," he replies.

"Right," I say, stepping back a bit, trying to regain my footing in this weird push-pull dynamic we've got going on. "Well, thanks for agreeing to help . . . Whenever you think of something I can do, just let me know."

"I will." His voice is casual, but there's a glint of something in his eyes that makes my stomach flip. "Oh, and Birdie?"

His messy blond hair falls over his forehead as he leans slightly closer, like he's about to share a secret. "You really are pretty, you know? Alarmingly so," he says roughly. "Just—I find it a bit distracting looking at you, talking to you, that's all."

It's a trite sentiment. I know it is. But it stops me in my tracks anyway.

It's not like I haven't heard it before. Men always try flattery as an easy in. But something about the way he says the words, like it's not just a throwaway compliment but a *fact*, leaves me speechless. This isn't a man fishing for approval or trying to get in my pants. There's no hidden agenda in his voice, just a blunt sort of honesty.

I give him a quick smile, trying to shake off the unexpected flutter in my chest. "Thanks. Er, I'll keep that in mind next time you're tongue-tied."

"Small mercies," he says and then gives a two-finger salute.

I finally turn to walk away, trying to focus on anything other than the heat crawling up my neck. But as I step back onto the path, my heart pounds in my ears, my pulse betraying me. I was right.

Inviting Liam Donovan into my world means opening the door to something messy, something unpredictable. And I think some strange, reckless part of me might actually want that.

It's not about letting my guard down, moving on, or letting go. It's just him. Just Liam.

Chapter Six
LIAM

CHASE and the guys are scattered across our living room, eyes glued to the screen, yelling at every pass and tackle like they've got something personally riding on it. The Bobcats are playing the Outlaws. It's a mid-season game with zero stakes, but everyone's acting like it's the goddamn Super Bowl.

I'm sitting on the edge of the couch, and I'm finding it hard to pretend like I care. It's mind-numbingly dull. I'd rather be playing football than watching it. Never understood the appeal of sitting around, yelling at a bunch of guys doing something I could be doing myself.

The only reason I'm down here right now is because Chase begged me. Said something about tradition, bonding, whatever. So here I am, feet up on the coffee table, scrolling through my phone to kill time while they're all losing their minds over some missed field goal.

I don't play sports because I want to be part of some bro-ey culture. I play them because I like running around and being good at something physical, something straightforward.

"You see that?" Chase shouts, slapping me on the shoulder. "Fucking disgraceful, man!"

I grunt, barely glancing up. "Yeah. Brutal."

"You're the worst fake fan I've ever seen," Chase laughs, tossing a barbecue chip directly at my face.

I catch it in my mouth with a half-hearted wink. My phone

buzzes as Chase snorts and shakes his head, muttering something about my priorities. I glance at the screen. It's my brother, James, calling, and the sight of his name sends a pang of something sharp and familiar through me.

Without thinking, I'm off the couch, pushing past empty pizza boxes and Solo cups, heading for the back door. Once I'm outside, I shake out my hands and let the tension bleed out of my shoulders.

"Hey," I say, leaning against the railing. "What's up?"

"Hey, bud," James replies, his tone easy but carrying that subtle edge I've learned to pick up on. "Just wondering how things are going. What are you up to?"

My stomach dips. It's been months since we've talked—like, really talked. He's been busy with the season, grinding through his first year in the minors as a third baseman. Between practices, travel, and trying to keep his spot on the team, I haven't wanted to add to his plate.

Meanwhile, I've just been . . . here. Doing the college thing. Soccer. Dealing with our parents. Same old.

"Not much. Watching the Bobcats game with some of the guys," I say. "How was the end of the season?"

James lets out a low chuckle. "Tough as hell. Got my ass handed to me more times than I care to admit. But I'm still here, so that's something."

I laugh. My older brother has always been the kind of guy who'll throw himself into anything full throttle, even when the odds are stacked against him. Whether it's baseball or life, he plays like a wild card.

"What's wrong? Are you still swinging your curveballs directly into the dirt?"

James snorts, but my mind flickers back to us as kids. Him teaching me how to hit in the backyard, the two of us swinging at imaginary pitches until the sun went down. He was always so sure of himself, even back then—confident in a way that felt unshakable.

"Yeah, yeah." There's something off in his voice. I can't put my finger on it, but I know I don't like it. "How's the season treating you? Harris still being a hard-ass?"

"It's good so far," I say, pacing the deck. "Living with Chase is helping keep me focused. He's serious about going pro, getting scouted, all that."

Chase's lifelong dream is to secure a Generation Adidas contract and leave school early. It's one of the most coveted opportunities in college soccer—a deal that guarantees a fast track to the MLS, skipping the draft entirely. He talks about it like it's already locked in, just waiting for the paperwork to clear.

In reality, only a handful of players get offered one each year—maybe a dozen out of thousands across the country. The chances are slim, but Chase carries himself like he's one of the chosen few, like failure isn't even on the table.

"That's awesome, man. You thinking about soccer after school, or are you still on the civil engineering track?"

There's a long pause, like he's waiting for me to say the right thing. His silences are weighted, always full of something unsaid, and it's hard to decipher whether he's holding back judgment or trying to give me space.

My brother isn't the steady, play-it-safe type. He believes in having ambitions, sure, but he's always encouraged me to pursue whatever I want, even if it's a risk. That's why he pushed me to chase collegiate-level soccer in the first place, no matter what our parents thought.

"I'm really not sure yet," I admit. "Mom and Dad are still pushing for the latter. You know how they are."

"Yeah, I know." His voice tightens, and it's clear what he's thinking—our parents, with their endless expectations, pivoting us toward their idea of success. James took a different route, refusing to fall in line with their version of a "stable" future.

It's funny, considering they didn't follow any kind of traditional path themselves. Dad's this big-shot artist, while our mom's a public speaker. She lectures on "The Psychology of Charisma and Influence," which, in my mind, is just a fancy way of saying she's a master manipulator. Well-versed in the art of wrapping people around her perfect finger.

And yet, professional sports? Not a "real career" to them. Makes no sense.

I shake off the thought, not wanting to get sucked into the usual rabbit hole of resentment and frustration over their hypocrisy. "I met a girl, by the way," I tell him, changing the subject. "An arts major."

I don't know why I bother bringing it up. Birdie isn't a girl I'm seeing. She's not a hookup or even close to being that.

"Oh yeah?" He clears his throat. "Didn't think you'd wanna get mixed up with the artsy type."

"Eh, it's not really like that. She's applying for Dad's fellowship, and I'm helping her out with the application."

"Helping her out?" His tone shifts, something guarded creeping in. "And what's she offering you in return?"

I frown. "Why's it matter?"

He lets out a low hum, the kind that makes my stomach knot up. "Just be careful. Some people will do anything to get what they want, especially when Dad's involved."

I bristle. "I know I'm not great at reading people, but that doesn't mean I'm some easy target."

"Didn't say you were," he says quickly. "Sometimes you don't see things the way other people do, and that can make things tricky."

I grit my teeth, the familiar frustration bubbling up. I'm a twenty-one-year-old man, not some clueless, naive kid. Just because I don't play the same games as everyone, forget social niceties once in a while, doesn't mean I can't see through bullshit when it's there.

"Why are you acting like Dad?"

James has made a lot of offhand comments over the years—telling me to think before I speak, hitting me upside the head, putting me in my place, typical big brother stuff. But he's never made me feel less than for being the way I am. I don't know why he'd start now.

He blows out a long breath. "I just don't think—"

"I know what I'm doing," I cut in, eager to shut this shit down.

Birdie's been clear about her intentions. She's looking for a way to get ahead, an easy in, and I'm fine with that. I know she's not interested in getting to know me for me, and honestly, it doesn't bother me in the slightest. At least she's not pretending it's something else.

And it's not even about *her* specifically; it's about people always assuming I'm a step behind. The fact that my parents—and now James—think I need looking after, that I'm somehow incapable of handling myself. I'm tired of it.

"Alright, alright," James mutters. "Just keep your head on straight, okay? I don't want you getting screwed over."

"Yeah, sure," I say. "I'll try not to trade in my trust fund for magic beans."

He snorts, but it's forced, more out of habit than humor. We chat for a few more minutes, mostly surface-level stuff about baseball and the rest of his season. Common pleasantries that make me want to bang my head against this railing.

When we finally hang up, I sit there for a minute, staring out into the yard, trying to shake off the weirdness. James is being needlessly overprotective. It's a new development that's come out of nowhere, like he's suddenly decided I need *more* people telling me I'm deficient when I'm not.

I ignore social cues, so sue me.

I know who I am. I know what I'm capable of. And I don't need my big brother telling me otherwise.

I'M LYING in bed on Monday night, tossing a half-empty water bottle in the air, letting it fall back into my hand, over and over. It's something to do, at least, while my brain runs circles around itself. It's late, too late to be awake, but I can't shut off.

Too busy with my big brain and my even bigger impulse control issues.

My phone buzzes on my nightstand, and I grab it, squinting at the bright screen.

> **BIRDIE**
> You awake?

> **LIAM**
> What's up?

> **BIRDIE**
> I'm working on my proposal and completely stuck. my brain is fried.

> **LIAM**
> want me to come over? help you work through it?

The words are out before I can think twice. A little too eager, maybe. But whatever. It's not like I'm doing anything useful. If I could sleep, I would, but this tossing-and-turning routine isn't doing me any favors.

> **BIRDIE**
> right now? isn't it kind of late?

LIAM

it's late, yeah, but who's keeping track? I'm wide awake. I could be there in ten minutes.

A long, stilted pause. I toss the bottle up again, catching it without looking. Maybe this was a bad idea. But before I can over-think it, her message pops up.

BIRDIE

okay. sure. I live off nile in the oak lane apartments. 304. just . . . don't wake the neighbors.

LIAM

quiet as a ninja. be there soon.

I'm already out of bed, pulling on a hoodie and grabbing my keys. As I head out the door, my pulse picks up, thrumming with a weird mix of nerves and excitement.

I'm not sure why—it's just helping her with a proposal, right? But something about the fact that it's late and unplanned adds this unexpected edge. Anticipation, maybe. Or just a rush of doing something on impulse.

Ten minutes later, I'm standing in front of Birdie's door. I raise my hand and tap my knuckles twice.

When the door creaks open, she blinks at me, a little surprised but not unhappy. She's wearing pajama shorts and a loose sweat-shirt, her short hair half-up, with strands falling messily around her face. There's something unguarded about the way she looks.

She's stripped of pretense here, comfortable in her own skin. No sharp remarks or forced politeness, just Birdie. I like it.

"Hey." I glance over her shoulder to the living room beyond her. Her tattered blue couch is littered with notebooks, a half-empty mug of coffee, and a scattered pile of pens. She's clearly been at this for hours, absorbed in her work. "You really needed me, huh?"

She huffs. "You're here because you begged me."

"If that's your version of begging, you've got some pretty low standards."

"Funny, I've been told the exact opposite." Her eyes flicker, something unreadable passing through them before she turns, walking further inside and leaving the door open behind her.

I stand there, rooted to the spot, for a good thirty seconds. It's a wonder why I'm hesitating now. I insisted on coming over to help, but now that I'm here, there's this strange feeling wriggling its way inside me—anticipation laced with something heavier I can't quite name.

"You coming?" she calls over her shoulder. "I don't have all night."

I like the way she says it—casual, a little snarky, like I'm not standing here at midnight ready to help her get a leg up on my dad. Like this isn't something most people would think twice about, inviting a virtual stranger into their home.

It's refreshing. She doesn't make things weird, doesn't get all uppity about every little move. I don't have to guess where I stand with her, and that's why helping her out seems like the right thing to do. The only thing I can do.

Chapter Seven

BIRDIE

It's three o'clock in the morning, and there's a giant man I hardly know sprawled out on my couch. Large limbs tangled beneath a threadbare blanket. Golden hair peeking out from the edge of the pillow he's half crushed. Dark lashes fanned across sun-kissed cheeks. It's oddly peaceful and wholly disarming.

We spent the last few hours cutting and primping my proposal, Liam offering suggestions and ideas that, I have to admit, seem pretty damn helpful.

He has this way of zeroing in on the essentials—like when he suggested focusing on the contrast between my raw, unpolished pieces and the more delicate, floral designs I like to weave into my work.

He says it's that juxtaposition that makes the pieces stand out. "Anyone can do pretty or messy, but you? You do both at once. That's what'll catch their attention."

And for some strange reason, I trust him.

His dad's work is all about layers of meaning. Art that doesn't just sit on the surface but pulls you in, makes you think twice. I know my work has that same potential, that balance between natural textures and intricate details. There's a rawness to it, an honesty. Something you can't fake.

Liam thinks I should lean into that more, play it up in my proposal. He says if there's one thing donors like, it's a clear narrative—a reason to care about the artist as much as the art.

And his ideas just make sense. Using smaller, unfinished pieces to demonstrate the shift from rough to refined. Highlighting key themes the selection committee will be looking for—a body of work that isn't just aesthetically pleasing but that tells a story, that showcases the full breadth of my technique.

Liam's unfiltered, blunt way of speaking means no sugarcoating, no dancing around what needs to be said. And that's exactly the kind of help I was hoping for. The kick in the ass I needed to finish this strong.

I'm glad I asked for his help. He's been nothing but patient and surprisingly thoughtful. Though, somewhere around hour two, the caffeine wore off, and while I was in full-on work mode, he was fading fast. He fought it at first, but eventually, even his endless energy couldn't keep up.

Silence followed. I turned to find him completely out—head back, mouth slightly open, fast asleep. So, I grabbed a blanket from the back of the couch and tossed it over him. No use waking him up for something that can wait until the light of day.

Now, I'm tiptoeing down the hallway, heading for my bedroom. The apartment is quiet and still, the kind of silence that feels almost sacred at this hour. Just as I'm about to slip past Sena's room, her door creaks open.

With her messy bed head and oversized pajamas, she sticks her head out, eyes bleary but curious. I stop in my tracks. Without a word, she grabs my wrist and yanks me inside.

"You have a man out there?" she whispers, voice full of scandal.

I roll my eyes, tugging my wrist free. "Kind of?"

Her eyebrows shoot up. "What's that mean?"

I sigh, rubbing my temples. "There's a man, yes, but he's just helping me with my proposal. He's . . . the son of that donor I told you about."

"And he's helping you with your proposal," she awkwardly parrots, blinking twice. "So, you're . . . using him, then?"

My nose scrunches. "No, you drama queen. I asked him for help, and he was open to it."

"And now he's here, in the middle of the night." She gives me this knowing look and waggles her eyebrows like she's living in some ridiculous soap opera. "You sure you're not trading him some *favors* in return?"

I shove her shoulder. "God, no. It's not like that. Stop being weird."

She snickers. "Whatever you say."

I quietly slip out of her room and into my own, closing the door behind me with a sigh. I could write Sena's accusations off as ridiculous, but even I can't deny she has a point.

If I were to hook up with anyone these days, it would probably be him. He's handsome, goofy in a way that puts me at ease, and just the right amount of charming without being a total schmooze.

The thought isn't exactly unwelcome—it's just not why he's here.

I flop onto my bed and stare up at the ceiling, my mind too wired to sleep, the house too quiet without Liam rattling on beside me. And Sena's comments keep on stirring inside my head.

What am I really doing here? I asked Liam for help, and he agreed. I didn't blackmail him; I didn't coerce him by offering empty promises or favors in exchange. But does that automatically mean I'm not taking advantage?

We've only spent a little bit of time together, but I already know that I like being around him. He's helpful, sure, but he also has this way of making everything feel lighter, easier—like I don't have to try so hard to keep it all together.

Maybe that's why I feel a little guilty, why I let Sena's teasing dig under my skin. She's good at pressing, cutting to the core in a way that feels almost too accurate, like she sees through all my excuses and bullshit straight to my core.

That's how I ended up living with her in the first place. After the accident, everything shifted. My entire life flipped upside down, and nothing felt the same anymore. I pulled away from everyone I'd known for years, retreating into myself.

My friends didn't understand why I was shutting them out, why I couldn't just "move on" the way they all insisted I should. "It wasn't your fault," they'd say, like that somehow erased the guilt gnawing at my insides. Like it made a difference to Emily's parents, her family, her friends.

They didn't get it. I'd catch their exasperated looks whenever I refused their invites to parties or when I stopped responding to group texts. It wasn't that I didn't care about them anymore, but after the accident, I felt like I was existing in a different world.

A world where I was constantly haunted by what happened, and they were free to live without that weight. Eventually, I stopped trying to explain. I stopped talking to them altogether.

And I realized I didn't miss them all that much.

So, when Sena came into the bookstore last spring to order a play anthology for her directing class, I was intrigued. She was grounded and self-assured. And I wanted to know more. I asked her what interested her in directing, and she just said, "I like being in charge. Obviously. And I'm damn good at it, too."

It was funny. Blunt. The kind of open levity I was missing in my old relationships.

She came back the next week to pick up her book and asked me to tape up a flyer on the community board:

Theater major in search of roommate. Here for a good time, not a long time. Must be chill and punctual.

I jumped on it without even thinking. It was an out—a chance to disappear from everything that felt suffocating. To put the final bit of distance between myself and the life I once lived.

And here we are now—two random girls thrown together by circumstance. She pushes me out of my shell, and I haphazardly allow it. To some degree. It's easier, I think, to listen to someone who doesn't know your past. Who doesn't try to fix you or make you explain it all.

Someone who isn't worried so much about appearances. Because they don't need to *look* like they have it all figured out, they just *do*, effortlessly.

I roll over, pulling the blanket up to my chin, letting the weight of the night settle over me. If I can't change the past, then I'd quite like to stop running from it. For now, I suppose my disappearing act will have to do.

WHEN I EMERGE from my room the next morning, my hair's a mess, and my oversized T-shirt just barely covers my ass. Liam is still lying on our couch. I freeze when I see him, blinking away the sleep from my eyes.

He looks different in the daylight—more peaceful, almost misplaced, sprawled across the couch with his long limbs claiming most of the space. His messy hair falls into his eyes, and a faint dusting of stubble shades his jaw.

I bite back a smile as I watch him stir, shifting under the blanket I'd tossed over him. He looks so . . . comfortable here, like he belongs.

I inch closer, trying not to wake him as I head to the kitchen for some coffee. The apartment is blissfully quiet—Sena's already left for her usual early morning catch-up with her theater pals, something about "creative brainstorming."

I would feel bad for waking her up in the middle of the night, but she always says theater people thrive on chaos. If anything, I probably gave her some fresh material for her next improv session.

Liam stirs, his face scrunching briefly before relaxing again. He stretches those impossibly long arms, groaning as he rubs a hand across his face. "Mornin'," he mumbles, his voice thick with sleep, cracking an eye open to look at me.

"Morning," I reply, moving toward the coffee machine. "Didn't mean to wake you."

"You didn't." He sits up and runs a hand through his blond hair. "What time is it?"

"Just after eight." I pour myself a cup of coffee, taking a slow sip before offering, "You want some?"

"Nah, I'm good." He gives me a lazy grin. "You need a ride to campus?"

I cough, caught off guard. "What was that?"

He stands, stretching again, his shirt riding up just enough to reveal a strip of toned stomach. I quickly look away, pretending to focus on something outside the window.

"I said, I can give you a ride. Since we're both headed there." He scratches the back of his neck, yawning. "I'll just pop by my place, brush my teeth, wash my face . . . you know, make myself look less like I just rolled off your couch."

I laugh nervously and tug the hem of my T-shirt over my barely there shorts. "I usually ride my bike or walk, so . . . thanks, but no, thanks."

His brow furrows slightly, a playful smirk tugging at his lips. "It's been pretty cold lately. You really wanna bike it?"

"It's fine," I murmur. "It's a quick ride."

Truth is, I really, really don't like car rides. Not driving, not riding with people I barely know, and definitely not being a passenger with no control. The thought makes my chest tighten a little.

"Suit yourself."

I clear my throat, trying to shake off the unease. "Thanks again for helping me last night. I'm almost done with the proposal. And I'm feeling a lot more confident now, too."

"Don't mention it," he says, shoving his hands in his pockets, still watching me. "You did all the heavy lifting."

"I'd give you a hug goodbye, but you know . . ." I gesture vaguely to my chest. "Braless, pantless, haven't brushed my teeth yet. And I don't really like hugs, either. My old friends used to say *Collins is like a cactus.*"

"Sharp, unapproachable, and thriving in dry conditions?"

"Exactly," I say, deadpan.

His lips twitch with the beginnings of a smirk. "It's okay," he says, "I'm not usually a touchy-feely sort of guy, either."

"Really?" I snort, rolling my eyes. "Isn't physical touch, like, every guy's love language?"

"Didn't realize we were talking about *love* here."

My face flushes, and I instantly regret the joke. "I just mean . . . most guys I know like to be touched. In some manner of speaking."

He grins, tilting his head. "Oh, I like to be touched, Birdie. But I'm selective about who gets the honor."

I groan and throw my hands up. "Why do I even try?"

"Because deep down, you like me." He shrugs, his expression so casual it almost feels like he believes it. "And because I'm the only guy who'll show up at midnight to fix your broken proposal."

I roll my eyes. "I'm pretty sure you just fell asleep on my couch and let me finish up the real work."

"Falling asleep was part of the process," he says, all mock seriousness. "You know, moral support."

"Moral support," I repeat, deadpan. "Right. I'll remember that the next time I'm stuck waffling alone at 3:00 a.m."

"Please do." He shoots me another grin, his hands still tucked in his pockets, as if he's entirely at ease despite my awkward fumbling. "Anyway, I'll get out of your hair. But seriously, if you ever need help—or a *ride*—you know where to find me."

He tips his chin, and I hesitate for a moment, watching with reluctant fascination as he heads toward the door. There's something about his easy confidence that leaves me both exasperated and . . . intrigued. The kind of charm that feels effortlessly disarming, like he doesn't even realize the effect he has.

As the door clicks shut behind him, I shake my head, trying to ignore the lingering warmth in my chest.

"*Call me for a ride,*" I mutter under my breath, mocking him despite the quiet, undeniable smile tugging at my lips. "What a generous guy."

Chapter Eight

BIRDIE

IF ONLY I could skip class and work in lieu of more studio time. The written portion of my proposal is nearly complete, thanks to Liam's feedback. My sample pieces are ready to go, pieces that feel like they've been molded from the guts of my frustration, my late nights, and the quiet ache I can never quite shake.

I should feel relieved. But there's still so much left to do. I need to prepare a verbal presentation, create a visual slide deck that'll capture the essence of my work, finalize my artist statement. Plus, I need to add a few newer pieces to showcase the theme.

The problem is, I've been running on fumes all week, and my shifts at the bookstore haven't helped.

I clock in at 4:00 p.m. with a resigned sigh. It's like I'm moving in slow motion, mechanically shelving books, ringing up customers, answering questions that feel like noise buzzing around my head.

Every task is dragging, and it's hard to care about whether the new release section is properly aligned when all I can think about is my studio work. My mind keeps wandering back to the pieces I've left unfinished.

I'm sure Liam would tell me I'm overthinking again, that I should just let it all come together naturally. But I can't shake the pressure.

I glance at the clock. Only two more hours of this. My fingers ache to get back to the clay, to let the tension in my body melt away into something tangible. But for now, I'm stuck here.

Another customer approaches the counter, and I force a smile, barely registering them as I ring up their order. I swipe the book across the scanner, watching the red light flicker, hearing the soft beep that's become part of the soundtrack to my life in this place. But it's all automatic. I'm not here, not really.

"Excuse me," the customer says, clearing their throat. The polite, expectant tone cuts through my daydream, and I blink to focus on the person in front of me.

To my not-so-pleasant surprise, I know the guy. Ben Wilkes. A ghost from my past with effortlessly floppy brown hair and a killer smile that could charm the paint off a wall.

"Hey, Birdie," he says, as smooth as ever, his voice carrying that familiar note of casual confidence. "Long time, no see."

Ben and I shared art history class during my freshman year. He slid effortlessly into my little circle of friends, the kind of guy who was impossible to ignore. We connected. Kind of. I was mostly interested in him because I felt like I had to be. He was handsome, he was charming in a practiced way, and most importantly, he was there.

My friends were dating, "talking to" all sorts of guys with easy grins and shared playlists. And I wanted to fit in, to be part of whatever they had.

But that was a different version of me. Before the accident. Before everything changed.

"Yeah, hey," I manage, forcing a tight smile. "It's been a while."

He gives me an awkward look, scratching the back of his neck like he's not sure what to say next. Then, "How've you been?" His voice is light, but there's a certain softness to it, like he's tiptoeing around the subject. His eyes sweep over me, probably looking for signs of the person I used to be, the girl he remembers.

She wasn't my favorite person. Too caught up in fitting in, being agreeable, and pretending everything was fine when it wasn't.

"I'm fine," I say sharply.

The barely veiled sympathy is clear in his gaze, and it grates on me. "You still living over on Blythe?" he asks.

"I'm off campus now. It's quieter."

"Oh," he says, his cheeks coloring slightly. He shifts his weight, looking like he's unsure whether to leave or keep going. Then he blurts, "Are you seeing anyone?"

"No," I reply, my voice flat.

His face brightens. "We should meet up for coffee sometime. I owe you one. My treat."

The way he says it, like he's extending an olive branch or trying to make up for something, sends a wave of irritation through me. I remember how easily things crumbled between us when I pulled back last year, how he stopped texting when I stopped being the fun, carefree Birdie he'd once been drawn to.

I wonder if he's still hanging out with the friends I walked away from—those biweekly dinner parties, their paint-and-sip nights, the midnight campus strolls I used to be a part of.

There were five of us back then. We used to trade secrets over cheap wine, cram for exams at the last minute, and dream out loud about the futures we thought we'd have.

And then the accident.

After that, it was like the ground opened up beneath me, and I was just falling, falling, falling, while they stayed anchored in their perfect, uncomplicated worlds. I didn't belong anymore.

I swallow hard and hand Ben his receipt. "Maybe. I've been pretty busy lately."

"Yeah, I get it," he says, still smiling, but it's slipping, put off by my distance. "Anyway, I'll text you sometime."

I nod, already turning away, and then he leaves, finally.

By the time my shift ends, I'm exhausted—not physically, but emotionally. Ben's face lingers in my mind, and so does the weight of everything that fell apart. It's not that I want my friends back—

they were fair-weather at best—but I miss the version of myself who didn't feel like this, so heavy and out of step.

I want to tap out, go home, and rot in bed. But I know better than that. If I stop moving, even for a second, I might never start again.

Instead, I head to the studio, where I can channel all this frustration, this disappointment, this lingering grief into my work. I need to mold these feelings into something tangible, something that'll speak for me in ways I can't.

It's dark by the time I step inside, but I can already feel the relief creeping in. This is where I can shed everything else. This is where I can breathe again.

I set up my station, pulling out a slab of clay and kneading it with a little more force than necessary. My muscles are sore, my fingers aching from the day's work, but there's something cathartic about the repetitive motion. About the way the clay gives under my hands, as if it understands, as if it's taking all the frustration and molding it into art.

There are a handful of pieces I still need to finish, and I have to get them right if I'm going to stand a chance at winning this fellowship. The pressure gnaws at me—constantly reminding me that this has to be perfect, or at least close enough to it. If I mess this up, I'm not sure what my fallback will be.

A minimum-wage job, less time for art, and mounting financial stress, most likely. Not exactly the vision of stability for a girl who's struggling.

I stare at my half-finished sample on the table in front of me. Another large vase—it's unpolished, and I like that it feels like two sides of me merged into one—delicate but intentional. Jagged yet purposeful. But something is missing, and I can't figure out what it is.

I wipe my hands on my jeans and pull out my phone, typing out a quick text to Liam.

> I can't match the vibe I'm going for. everything looks wrong. it's like I'm too close to it and can't see straight :(

While I wait for a response, I grab a needle tool and carefully carve more detail into the floral pattern along the edges. The tension in my chest loosens, just a little, as I focus on making each line intentional, sharp yet soft, like a whisper that leaves a mark.

I set the bat aside and turn to the next lump of clay, letting the frustration roll out of me. I pump out three more pieces in quick succession—another vase, a bowl, and a shallow dish—but none of them are quite right, either. I can feel it, in the way they sit on the table, in how my gut twists when I look at them. Each one is a little off, a little too *something*.

I wrap them in plastic, ready to call it quits for the evening. My own little Goldilocks moment—one's too messy, the other's too clean, the last is just plain boring. None of them feel like me.

As I stand there, staring at my creations with growing dissatisfaction, the door to the studio creaks open behind me. I turn, and in walks Liam, his lazy grin firmly in place. He's carrying a grocery bag, and I can only assume he's up to something unnecessary but well-meaning.

"You're still here," he says as he saunters over. "I was hoping I'd catch you."

I haven't seen him since Tuesday morning when he left my place and I dodged his offer of a ride. It's now Friday, and I know he usually has late practices on these nights. Either that or an actual game.

I sigh and set down my tool. "Shouldn't you be at practice or something?"

He drops into the chair beside me. "Canceled. Coach Harris is giving us a recovery day." He tosses the bag on the table. "Thought you could use a pick-me-up."

I glance at the spilled contents—an energy drink, popcorn, sour candy, and something that suspiciously looks like a protein bar. "You realize I'm not training for a marathon, right?"

He leans back and folds his arms behind his head. "You're working yourself harder than I am, and that's saying something."

I think there's an innuendo in there somewhere, but I'm too bedraggled to bother with it. Instead, I let out a small, exhausted laugh and shake my head.

The last week has been a constant blur of studio sessions, writing late into the night, and poring over every detail of my proposal. When I'm not in class or sleeping (which, let's be real, is barely happening), I'm here, in the studio, trying to mold clay into something that will impress a committee of people who've been judging art longer than I've been alive.

As if that weren't enough to keep me teetering on the edge of burnout, I signed up for this intimidating peer critique on Sunday at NCU, hoping to get an unbiased, outside perspective. I just need to know if what I'm creating is good enough—if it's worth including in my fellowship proposal or if I'm missing something entirely.

"It's crunch time," I say as I brush a stray hair out of my face. "No slacking."

"How's it coming along?"

I stare hopelessly at the half-finished vase. "It's getting there. Slowly."

He leans forward to inspect my work. "You know, I think you could make the contrast even more extreme here. Maybe exaggerate the edges and make the smooth parts even sleeker. Push it further."

I slowly blink and purse my lips, tilting my head to envision it.

He's right. Again. He's so casually good at this. It's like he doesn't have to think twice before throwing out ideas that shift my perspective, that unlock something I hadn't even realized was stuck.

I pick up my tool and carve deeper into the rough edge, the motion deliberate and confident. It feels like breaking through a wall.

"God, how do you do that?" I mutter, half to myself. "You make it so easy."

He chuckles, grabbing the popcorn and tearing it open. "I'm just throwing out thoughts. You're the one making them come to life." He tosses a kernel in the air and catches it in his mouth with a casual flick of his head. "Just so you know, I do freak out about my own shit on occasion. I'm not always so calm and cool and sexy."

"I think you mean collected," I say, smirking.

"No."

I glance over at him, eyebrow raised. "Right, and what do you have to freak out about?"

"You know, figuring out if I'm gonna go for the draft next year or stick with engineering instead." He tilts his head back, eyes on the ceiling. The long, graceful column of his neck stretches as his throat bobs. "There's a lot riding on that decision."

It takes me a few moments to process that. Liam hasn't talked to me much about school—we've been so focused on me, on my proposal, my work, my frustrations. But now that I know his major, it oddly fits. Engineering has that balance of structure and creativity, much like him.

"Do you . . . want to be an engineer?" I ask.

He sighs. "Not really. I do like the problem-solving part of it, though. The logic. The predictability of it all. And it's a good fall-back, right? Safe."

"Safe doesn't exactly scream Liam Donovan to me."

He laughs, loud and sudden, like he wasn't expecting me to say that. "Yeah? And what does?"

I glance at him, considering. "Just . . . you don't strike me as the type to settle for safe. You're more like the guy who runs headfirst into chaos just to see how it plays out."

He grins, wide and bright. "You think you've got me all figured out, huh?"

"Maybe a little."

He watches me, his gaze steady and intent, like he's studying me the way he studies my work—eyes lingering as though searching for hidden details. It's unnerving how intense his focus is when it's on me, how it makes my pulse quicken, my stomach flutter.

"You're not wrong," he says softly. "I like taking risks. But I guess with this . . . choosing soccer . . . it feels different. Like, if I screw it up, I'm stuck. And I don't want to make the wrong choice."

I pause, contemplating his words, the weight they carry. I've seen that same uncertainty in myself, the fear of choosing wrong, of messing up something that feels so big it could change everything.

"Do you think you'd regret not going for it?"

His eyes flick back to the ceiling, and for a second, I wonder if I pushed too far. But then he sighs and says, "Yeah. I think I would."

There's a weight to his words, something deeper that I don't know how to unpack. I'm compelled to say something, to offer advice or tell him it'll all work out—but I hold in my consolation. He doesn't need empty reassurances. He just needs someone to listen.

"Then it seems you've got your answer."

"And what about you?" he asks. "You ever think about what happens if you don't get the fellowship?"

Have I thought about it? Only incessantly. I've been trying not to spiral into worst-case scenarios because dwelling can be dangerous. That kind of thinking is a rabbit hole I'm not ready to fall down. But I can feel the panic creeping in at the edges, the what-ifs I've been trying to keep at bay.

"Yeah," I say quietly. "All the time."

"And?"

"And . . . I don't know. I guess I'd figure something out. But I really don't want to think about it."

He leans forward, resting his elbows on his knees. "You'll get it, Birdie. I know you will."

Maybe he didn't need platitudes, but he was right to offer me some. Praise and encouragement aren't things I've heard much of lately.

Plus, the way he says it, like he truly means it, makes my chest tighten. It's not just empty words with him, not some throwaway reassurance. It settles under my skin, deep in my bones, in a way that nothing else has lately.

And I believe him.

"Thank you."

He stands, stretching again, and I try not to notice the way his shirt rides up, showing that strip of skin I've been pretending not to look at since we met. He's built—lean muscle, taut stomach, the kind of body that looks like it belongs in a sports magazine, not casually leaning against my worktable.

The worst part is, it seems like he either doesn't know or doesn't care that half the people around him are probably thinking the same thing I am: he's hot as hell. If I were bolder—or significantly less focused on the fellowship—I might joke about offering him sexual favors in return for his help. But that would be crossing a line I don't even want to toe.

"So, what's next on the agenda?" he asks, pulling me out of my thoughts. "More clay, or do you want me to take some photos?"

"Photos?"

He nods, already reaching for his phone. "Yeah, you said the committee will want to see the process, not just the finished product. Plus, I like photography. It's a hobby I've been messing around with, and it might help showcase your work better than just tossing it all in a folder."

I hesitate for a second before nodding, grateful for the suggestion. "Okay. Yeah, that actually sounds perfect."

As he snaps pictures, I steal a glance at him from the corner of my eye. His brow is furrowed in concentration, and there's something about the way he's so serious in moments like this that throws me off.

Usually, he's all jokes and easy smiles, but when he's focused, he's . . . different. The way he moves, the way his green eyes flick between the piece and the screen, it's like watching someone step into a role they were born to play. It's effortless, deliberate, and oddly captivating.

And maybe that's why being around him feels so unsettling—because the more time we spend together, the more I find myself looking forward to it. Not just for his input or his ideas, but for him. For the way he makes everything feel lighter, even when it shouldn't. For the way he fills the quiet without taking over.

It's not just that he's helpful or insightful. It's that he's present. And there's a part of me—one I'd rather not examine too closely—that's starting to enjoy his presence a little too much. Too easily, too often, and I can't afford to think like that. Not now.

Chapter Nine

LIAM

WE'RE UP 2-1, and it's the seventy-fifth minute. My lungs are burning, legs heavy with that familiar ache that means we're in the thick of it. The ball's at my feet, and I'm sprinting down the sideline, eyes locked on the Louisville defender shadowing me.

I fake left, cut right, and then I'm free—just for a second. Long enough to whip in a cross toward Chase, who's already charging the box like a freight train.

It's a good ball. The kind I've practiced a thousand times, and Chase knows it. He meets it perfectly, sending a header rocketing toward the top corner of the net.

The crowd's breath catches. The keeper dives, fingers brushing the ball as it deflects—straight off the post.

"Shit," I mutter under my breath, already turning to hustle back on defense. No time to celebrate, no time to dwell. That's soccer—one second, you're on top of the world; the next, you're chasing someone down, hoping you don't get caught flat-footed.

Coach Harris is yelling something at us, but I block him out, too focused on the game. There's still fifteen minutes left. Plenty of time for things to change.

Plenty of time to screw it all up.

By the time the final whistle blows, we've held on for the win, 2-1. Chase's earlier goal was enough to secure the points, and the bench explodes in cheers, clapping each other on the back and pulling into quick embraces.

But I'm already thinking about the bus ride. And Birdie Collins. The field starts to empty as we shake hands with Louisville's players. Coach is giving his post-game speech in the background, talking about our grit, our persistence. But I'm not really listening. My head's somewhere else.

Somewhere back in the studio, two days ago.

I should be feeling amped right now, but I'm more focused on how Birdie's day went. She'd signed up for some off-campus studio critique at a neighboring university—one of those big deals with a reputation for being brutally honest.

She'd been wound tighter than a spring when I left her on Friday, anxious about what her peers and the professor would say. I tried to reassure her, tell her her work was killer, that she had something different, something people would notice. But I could still see that doubt in her eyes.

I shake my head, focusing on getting back to the bus. The last thing I need is to be distracted in the middle of a win. Chase catches up to me, clapping a hand on my back.

"Hell of a game, man. That cross was perfect. Just a damn shame about the post, huh?"

"Yeah," I mutter, "real shame."

Chase doesn't notice the sarcasm. He's too busy talking about the match, reliving every play like we didn't all just live through it together. I zone out, only half listening as I find a seat on the bus, pulling out my phone.

It's late, almost nine, and I'm sure Birdie's critique is long over. I want to text her, ask her how it went, but I hesitate. She'll probably text me when she's ready, right? I shove my phone back in my pocket, trying to shake off the restlessness creeping up my spine.

The ride back is mercifully short, though it feels longer with Chase still chatting beside me. I respond here and there, but my mind keeps drifting. I wonder if Birdie's stressing out. I can picture her now, probably holed up in her apartment, dissecting every bit of feedback she got today.

I want to tell her she's overthinking it, that her work speaks for itself, but I know she's too hard on herself to see it that way. She always gets in her own head. We're similar that way, though I manage to distract myself better—or maybe I'm just better at faking it.

When we finally pull up to the hotel, I grab my bag and head straight for the room. Chase follows me, still talking, though I'm barely paying attention. The team dinner's in an hour, and all I want to do is lie down and shut my brain off for a minute.

As soon as we step into the room, I toss my bag on the floor and flop onto the bed. Chase heads for the bathroom, leaving me alone with my thoughts. I pull out my phone, staring at the screen for a second before opening my messages.

LIAM

how'd the critique go? still in one piece?

I send the text and toss the phone aside, rubbing my hands over my face. There's this weird, restless energy in me tonight, like I can't settle down. Maybe it's the game, the adrenaline still pumping through me. Or maybe it's something else.

My phone buzzes almost immediately, and I grab it, my pulse kicking up.

BIRDIE

barely. it was brutal. but constructive. I think?

LIAM

an award-winning combo

BIRDIE

seriously, though. the prof tore into one of my pieces. said it felt "contrived"

I sit up, frowning at the screen. I know how much effort Birdie puts into her work. Contrived? No fucking way.

> **LIAM**
> contrived, my ass. what a pretentious dipshit

Chase comes out of the bathroom, towel-drying his hair, and shoots me a knowing look. "You texting your girlfriend?"

"She's not my girlfriend," I say automatically, though my mind lingers on the word a little longer than it should.

He smirks. "Not yet, huh?"

I ignore him, my focus back on my phone.

> **BIRDIE**
> you're just saying that because you're biased

> **LIAM**
> or maybe I just know talent when I see it

I can almost hear her laughing through the screen, and something warm settles in my chest. It's weird how easy it is with her, how much I look forward to these conversations. Small talk isn't my thing. Yet, I find myself wanting to keep going with her, like the conversation could stretch on forever and I wouldn't mind.

> **BIRDIE**
> what about you? how was the game?

> **LIAM**
> stellar. I was bored

> **BIRDIE**
> lol if not even winning a game can keep your interest, we need to find you a new sport. ever considered bog snorkeling

I'm about to reply when Chase chucks a sock at my head.

"Hey, we've got fifteen minutes," he says. "You better get moving."

"Yeah, yeah." I shove the sock off my bed, still glued to my phone.

LIAM

no, but I know I'd be excellent at it. I have to go out for our team dinner now. talk later

BIRDIE

have fun xo

Chase leans against the doorframe, arms crossed, smirking. "You coming or what?"

I glance at my phone, the screen still glowing with Birdie's last text, and for a second, the pull to stay in and keep talking to her is overwhelming. But I shove the thought—and my phone—into my pocket, forcing a nod. "Yeah, let's go."

Dinner's loud, as usual. The team's riding high on the win. We're all squeezed into this dimly lit, family-style Italian place near the hotel. Plates of pasta and pizza litter the table, and the noise level's almost unbearable—laughing, shouting, forks clattering, the whole deal.

I sit back, picking at my slice of pizza, letting the guys' voices buzz around me. Chase is beside me, talking a mile a minute about his header that should have gone in if the crossbar hadn't been out for blood today.

His energy is endless, a constant hum of excitement that makes it hard to tune him out, even when I'm not in the mood. Finally, he turns to me and says, "Man, you've got it bad."

"What's bad?"

He gestures at me with a piece of garlic bread. "You're staring off into space. You've barely touched your food. If that's not a guy hung up on a girl, I don't know what is."

"Yeah, actually, I can't stop thinking about Birdie. You think that's bad?"

His grin doesn't falter. The man is like a dog with a bone, and he's not about to let it go. "No, it's good. If you like her, you should go for it."

"Go for what?"

He laughs. "Ask her out. Kiss her. Fuck her, if that's all you're after."

I smack him. "Try that again."

"In the three years I've known you, I haven't seen you date *anyone*. I figured it's because you'd rather not bother. I mean, are you looking for a hookup, or do you have real feelings for her?"

It's not that I don't want to date—I do. But connecting with people outside of what's familiar doesn't come as easily to me. My brother, his best friend Hayes, Chase—those relationships were effortless, built into the fabric of my life. Being teammates, roommates, it all naturally fell into place.

Forming new bonds is harder. There aren't a lot of places that make space for someone like me—someone who doesn't glide effortlessly into conversations or feel at home in big, boisterous crowds. It's like trying to join a game that's already halfway through, where everyone else knows the rules and I'm still scrambling to catch up.

"It's new," I tell him. "But I do think about her a lot. I want her to be happy. The idea of her stressing out all alone makes my stomach a bit sick."

He raises his eyebrows. "That's called feelings, my guy."

"Hadden," Santi interrupts, tossing a balled-up paper napkin at Chase's head. "Care to weigh in?"

Chase whirls around to face the others. "What are we talking about here?"

"How you whiffed that free kick," Amir chimes in from the end of the table, shaking his head as he pours himself more water.

The rest of the guys snicker and join in, while Chase just grumbles, shoving a piece of pizza into his mouth. It's the same routine—everyone ripping into each other like always.

Santi gestures wildly, clutching his chest in an over-the-top reenactment of Amir's missed slide tackle that sent him sprawling face-first into the turf. Amir just rolls his eyes, smirking, knowing there's no point in defending himself. With Santi in full performance mode, the ribbing isn't stopping anytime soon.

I sit back, soaking it all in. I like being the observer in these moments, letting the chaos swirl around me. It's easy to tune out the noise and just appreciate the energy of the team—the laughter, the teasing.

Once the food dwindles and Coach makes his rounds, reminding everyone we have to be back in the hotel by midnight, Chase turns to me with his usual cheeky grin.

"Back to pottery girl," he says, voice low. "You should call her when you get back to the room."

I shrug. "Maybe. She had a big critique today. Probably busy."

He raises an eyebrow. "Perfect opportunity for you to swoop in and be her hero. Lick her wounds a little."

I give him a look, but he just laughs, throwing an arm around my shoulder as we head out. The guys shuffle into the night, some veering toward the bar across the street, others trailing back to the hotel. A few seniors manage to convince Coach to let them stay out for one more drink, promising they'll cap it at two.

Back in the hotel room, I toss my bag onto the floor and flop onto the bed, immediately pulling out my phone.

LIAM

back from dinner. what are you up to?

BIRDIE

sitting on the floor, staring aimlessly

LIAM

sounds thrilling

> **BIRDIE**
>
> oh, it is. and I'm out of coffee, so I'm extra grumpy

> **LIAM**
>
> if I was home, I'd bring you some

> **BIRDIE**
>
> alas, you're stuck in louisville

> **LIAM**
>
> minor detail
>
> i'll be back tomorrow. you'll survive until then

> **BIRDIE**
>
> we'll see

I hover over the screen, Chase's suggestion from earlier playing in the back of my mind. I probably should just let her get back to work. She's undoubtedly deep in her element, focused and determined, probably miffed at every minor distraction. But before I can talk myself out of it, I hit Call.

She picks up on the second ring. "Liam, it's midnight."

"What, too late for you?"

"Hardly," she says with a soft laugh. "I just figured you'd be beat after your game. And, honestly, I didn't think you were the late-night phone call type. Your distaste for small talk is well-documented."

I snicker. "I'm full of surprises."

"Prove it."

"For starters, I can picture exactly how your hair looks right now. All messy from your floor-induced panic."

Her short bob is likely sticking up in every direction, the way it does when she's been running her hands through it all day. It's chaotic but in that pretty, effortlessly sexy way that makes me want to see it in person.

She huffs. "You're annoying, and that's not exactly a surprising anecdote."

"Am I wrong?"

"No," she admits, still laughing. "It's a disaster. Like, bird's nest level."

"Hot."

She groans, and I can hear the faint rustling of her moving around, probably trying to smooth her hair down. It's nice, this ease between us. Like I don't have to try so hard to be any version of myself around her.

I suppose that's why I called her instead of crashing like I should. Because I like this—hearing her voice, knowing I can get under her skin as easily as she gets under mine. But I don't say any of that.

Instead, I settle back into the bed, letting her voice fill the space around me. It's soft and steady, with a certain warmth that sinks in slowly, easing the tension until all the other noise in my head fully fades away.

Chapter Ten
BIRDIE

MONDAYS ARE NEVER EASY, but this one? It's got me beat before I've even made it out of bed. My eyes feel glued shut, my limbs heavy and unwilling to move, and all I can think about is how I'm not ready to face another week of grinding effort.

I groan, stretching beneath the blankets, my body stiff from a restless night of tossing and turning. Maybe it's the weight of the critique still clinging to me, or maybe it's the fact that I stayed up too late talking to Liam.

I knew he had an early flight out this morning—he's probably just landing in Raleigh now—but neither of us seemed willing to hang up. Every time the conversation lulled, we'd pick up again, something easy, something light, like the kind of chatter that fills the quiet when you're sitting with someone you've known forever.

Except I haven't known him forever. It's only been a few weeks, but it feels . . . natural. Necessary, even. Like we've somehow skipped over all the usual barriers that make getting to know someone so exhausting.

I throw an arm over my eyes, replaying the weekend in my head. The critique at NCU, the professor's cutting words echoing like a broken record: *contrived*.

I had thrown that piece together Friday night, dragged it into the critique unfinished and raw, full of potential but far from complete. And he still called it contrived. How? How could it feel fake when it was the truest thing I'd made in weeks?

I told myself to take it in stride, to see it as constructive feedback, but it's hard to do that when it cuts so deep. Standing there in front of my peers, I felt gutted, and I wondered if he was right. If maybe I wasn't cut out for this after all.

But then Liam's voice was in my ear. Steady, unshakable. "It's just one person's opinion. You know what your work is. Don't let some loser tell you it's not good enough."

He made it sound so simple. Like I could just decide not to let it bother me and move on. And for some reason, coming from him, it almost felt true.

I roll onto my back, staring at the ceiling. His words are still there, faintly hovering in my mind, easing some of the tension in my chest. He didn't have to stay on the phone, not when he had a flight to catch at dawn. But he did.

And the weirdest part? I don't feel guilty for taking up his time. Usually, I'd be spiraling, worrying about whether I was a burden, but with Liam, it's different. I don't have to overthink everything. I can just be.

My phone buzzes on the nightstand, breaking the quiet, and I reach for it, fingers sluggish as I grab it. I squint at the screen—it's a message from him.

LIAM

just landed. hope you're still sleeping off that grumpy coffee deprivation from last night

BIRDIE

just woke up. barely functioning. how was the flight?

LIAM

short. missed out on sleep tho . . . wonder whose fault that is?

BIRDIE

definitely yours. you're a terrible influence

LIAM

glad to know I have such an effect on you

I shake my head, biting back a smile, but there's no stopping the warmth that blooms in my chest. It's too damn early to feel like this—like I'm walking around with some silly, giddy secret. But here we are.

I push myself out of bed and shuffle toward the kitchen. Sena's already left for her seven-thirty class, so there are no distractions this morning. It's just me, my coffee, and my thoughts about everything I still have to tackle.

I glance at the fridge, at the sticky note with my to-do list that's hanging crookedly next to a picture of me and Sena at a festival. A get-to-know-you day before we officially moved in together, filled with cheap sangria and half-hearted critiques of overpriced art.

That day feels like a lifetime ago. The stillness before the surge.

Now, it's everything at once—meet with Professor Tanaka, finish two more pieces for the proposal, somehow find time to polish my presentation, all while juggling work shifts and classes. And as if that weren't enough, there's the constant self-doubt creeping in every time I sit down at the wheel.

It's still my happy place, but lately, I've started second-guessing. Overthinking. Doubting. Thank the heavens for Liam and his ever-present reassurances, always showing up like a lifeline just when I need it most.

I couldn't lean on my old friends. After the accident, I didn't want to let them in—not fully, not at all. They weren't the kind of people who stick around when things get tough, and I think, deep down, I always knew that.

But with Liam, it's different. Trusting him feels easy, effortless. Almost like it's second nature, something I don't have to question or force. But I've got enough on my plate without constantly over-analyzing my feelings for him.

Right now, I need to focus. It's Monday, and I've got shit to do.

By the time I make it to Tanaka's advanced hand-building class, the caffeine has only done half its job. My body's here, but my mind? It's still stuck in that hazy space between sleep and everything else demanding my attention.

It doesn't help that hand building has never really been my thing. I've always been more at home with wheel throwing, carving, glazing—the techniques where the motions flow easily, where I can let my hands do the thinking.

Sculpting is a bit of a nightmare.

This class is a requirement for graduation, though, part of the practical application side. Some 3D4M majors seem to specialize in the wheel, along with sculpting, mold-making, and metalwork. It's impressive, really—their ability to switch between fluidity and precision.

But hand building, for me, has always felt like the outlier, the one form that refuses to click. There's something too deliberate about it, too meticulous. It's like every single motion has to be carefully planned. And right now, planning isn't exactly my strong suit.

Still, I sit down at my station, determined to will myself into some kind of productive mindset. In front of me sits a half-formed sculpture of a human hand, the fingers awkwardly splayed and misshapen.

It's supposed to be part of a study on gesture and tension. Right now, it looks more like a deformed claw—or maybe a blob that can't quite decide what it wants to be.

The frustration bubbles up again. I've been putting so much effort into mastering hand building—pushing myself to improve in this class, to step outside my comfort zone—but the progress has been agonizingly slow.

Professor Tanaka enters the room a few minutes later, moving with his usual air of quiet authority. He's not the type to demand attention through volume or theatrics; instead, he commands the space with a calm, steady presence.

Unlike Professor Hall, my wheel-throwing instructor who thrives on critique and fast-paced energy, Tanaka is methodical and introspective. He has a way of observing your work that feels almost unnerving, as if he can see past the surface—every misstep, every flash of creativity, every bit of uncertainty that went into making it.

But he doesn't criticize. He observes, reflects, and then offers something insightful, almost poetic.

As he moves through the room, I focus intently on my unsettling half-finished hand, trying not to fidget under the weight of the silence stretching between us. Finally, he stops at my table.

"Collins," he says, his tone thoughtful. "I can see you're pushing yourself here. There's good progress."

The praise makes me sit a little straighter, warmth flickering in my chest. It's gratifying to have my effort noticed—to know that all the late nights and moments of doubt are amounting to something.

"Yeah, well . . . it's been a slow crawl forward," I admit, a wry smile tugging at my lips. "A painful shuffle, if you will."

Tanaka frowns. "Progress is still progress. Don't undermine it just because it's not happening as fast as you'd like."

He's right—I'm always so quick to brush off my accomplishments, like they don't count unless they happen perfectly and all at once. But the doubt still lingers, gnawing at the edges. "I don't know . . . It's just—it looks a bit like a horror movie prop, doesn't it?"

Tanaka gives a knowing smile. "The tension you're trying to

capture is there. Look at the lines, the way the fingers curve inward. You're conveying something that's unresolved, like there's movement just beneath the surface."

I blink at the sculpture, squinting to find what he's talking about. All I've been seeing is a disaster, but his words make me pause. Maybe I was too close to it, too wrapped up in my frustrations to see the potential.

"I guess I was too busy focusing on what it wasn't to see what it actually is," I say quietly. "It's hard not to fixate on what I can't seem to get right."

"That's part of the process. But don't lose sight of what's working in your favor. You've got a strong foundation here, and if you keep at it, you'll find the resolution you're after."

In other words, he wants me to know that I'm allowed to take my time. That I'm not failing just because I'm not there yet. What a novel concept.

"Okay, thank you."

"So, how's the fellowship coming along?" he asks.

"It's . . . a lot." I swallow heavily. "But I'm getting there. I'm trying to balance everything: work, classes, and getting these pieces ready. Sometimes it feels like I'm drowning."

"That's expected. The pressure is part of the experience. But from what I've seen of your work, you're more than capable. You've got the skill. Now it's about showcasing it for the judges."

"I hope so," I murmur. "Thank you again for your letter of recommendation. That certainly takes some weight off."

"Of course," Tanaka says. "I meant what I wrote. And if you need anything else, don't hesitate to ask. Just trust your instincts, Collins."

As he moves on to the next student, I sit back in my chair, his words settling into the space left by my doubts. I've been so caught up in trying to make everything perfect—to prove something to myself, to everyone else—that I forgot to give myself room to breathe.

Tanaka is right. Art isn't about getting it right every time. It's about pushing through the messy, uncomfortable parts and trusting that, somewhere along the way, you'll stumble onto something real.

Something that's yours.

Chapter Eleven

> **BIRDIE**
>
> so, do I name the creepy hand sculpture I've been working on, or do I just let it speak for itself?

I CHUCKLE UNDER MY BREATH, glancing down at my phone, where Birdie's latest text is lighting up the screen. I'm sitting in the dining room at my parents' house, but my attention is half here, half on my phone under the table where no one can see it.

> **LIAM**
>
> "The Grab"

> **BIRDIE**
>
> maybe "Grasping at Straws"?

> **LIAM**
>
> my life in a nutshell

She sends a laughing emoji, followed by a picture of the sculpture she's been working on. It's exactly what she's been describing —creepy, severed, and kind of awesome in a weird way. I can tell she's put in a lot of hours on it.

> **BIRDIE**
>
> told you it's weird, right?

LIAM

weird, yes. but also badass

A grin creeps across my face as those three little dots appear. But before a reply comes through, my mom interrupts. "Liam, honey, are you paying attention?"

I snap my head up. Mom and Dad are sitting across the table, looking at me like they've just asked something important. I'm sure whatever it is, it's probably something I'm supposed to care about.

These biweekly dinners are always the same. Polished silverware, a spotless tablecloth, and conversations that feel more like check-ins than actual catching up. I've mastered the art of nodding along, but tonight, my focus is clearly slipping.

It used to be me and James, both of us sitting here pretending we weren't counting down the minutes until we could leave, but now I'm flying solo. James is off in the minor leagues, and I'm left with the full brunt of their attention.

I blink a few times, trying to piece together what I've missed. "Uh, yeah. Sorry," I say, stuffing my phone into my pocket. "What were you saying?"

Mom exchanges a glance with Dad, who's frowning slightly like he's already tired of this conversation. Tired of me. Great.

"We were talking about your internship for the summer," Mom says, her voice carefully neutral. "We spoke to Oliver, the head of development at Welch City Planning, the firm I mentioned a few weeks ago? He's agreed to take you on as an intern."

I sit up straighter. "Wait, what?"

"Liam, we told you about this. We've been working on setting it up for you." Dad says slowly, painfully, like he's explaining something to a five-year-old. "It's a great opportunity."

I blink again, trying to process. "Urban planning?"

"Yes," Mom says giddily. "Oliver's one of the best in the field. This will give you excellent experience—"

"But I'm not interested in doing that."

Sure, it's experience, but it's not the kind of experience I want. It's more theory, more meetings and planning sessions, and I'm all about execution. I like to actually see things come together in real time.

My parents both exchange a look, their expressions a mix of surprise and mild disapproval. Maybe they thought I'd just go along with it, smile and nod like I usually do.

I should probably dial it back, try to sound more grateful or something, but I can't help it. My brain's already buzzing with everything I'll be missing if I take this internship: the training camps, the tournaments, the chance to really focus on soccer this summer.

Mom frowns, brushing a strand of hair behind her ear in that precise, deliberate way she does when she's trying not to get upset. "What do you mean? This is a perfect fit for you. We've already pulled strings to make it happen."

"I'm more into construction management," I explain. "Overseeing projects, being on-site, making sure things actually happen. Urban planning is more . . . *planning*. I'm more hands-on."

Dad leans back in his chair, fork gripped tightly in one hand. The man is armed and ready to lecture me on responsibility or some shit. "Liam, you need to start thinking about your future. This is a real career path, something stable."

Bingo. They're starting to realize I may actually be leaning toward soccer instead. The tension between what they want for me and what I want for myself has been building for months, but I guess the idea of me steering away from their perfectly paved road is finally hitting home.

"I know it's stable, but I've been looking at other opportunities, too. There's this construction firm that specializes in large-scale projects, and—"

"*Liam,*" Dad interrupts, voice hardening like he's already

decided what's best for me. "You can't just chase after whatever catches your attention at the moment. You need an actual plan."

"I have a plan," I shoot back. "But it's not *urban* planning. And taking a summer internship would mean missing out on soccer training. Pre-draft stuff. Camps. That's what I actually care about."

My parents sigh in unison, that same exasperated sound they always make when I bring up soccer. My stomach sinks. They don't get it. They never have.

"Liam," Mom says calmly. "Soccer is great, and you've done so well with it. But it's not a guarantee. Civil engineering is a guarantee. This internship will set you up for a long-term career."

"I get that," I say, forcing down the irritation. "But if I take this internship, I'll be stuck behind a desk all summer. I'm not built for that."

Dad's jaw tightens. "And what happens if you don't get drafted? What's your fallback?"

"I'm not saying I'm ditching my degree," I argue sharply. "But I want to give soccer everything I've got while I still can."

They're silent, staring at me with that blank parental mix of concern and quiet judgment, so I push further.

"I've got one more year. One more year to prove myself on the field. If I can enter the draft after that, I need to be ready. I don't want to look back and wonder what would've been."

"The professional sports world is cutthroat," Dad says flatly. "It's not realistic for most athletes."

"Sorry?" I choke down the lump rising in my throat. "Isn't your precious arts degree the same thing? A long shot? Something you were passionate about that didn't come with your realistic guarantees?"

His face tightens, but I don't back down. I've kept this in for too long—the feeling of being cornered into one path because it's safe. Because it's what they expect.

"Don't compare the two," Dad snaps. "The arts are just as

valid, but they're different. You have a practical fallback. Soccer isn't—"

"I'm not giving up before I even try," I cut him off, my voice firm. "I'll have plenty of time to be an engineer, but if I don't take this shot, I'll regret it for the rest of my life."

The table falls silent again. My heart pounds erratically, frustration and anger bubbling up because they just don't see it the way I do.

"Liam," Mom says gently, her tone soft like she's trying to reason with a child. "We want what's best for you. We know soccer is important to you, but what if—"

"What if I actually make it?" I interrupt her, leaning forward. "What if all this work pays off and I do get drafted? And I'm successful? And you two will have to sit there, eating your words, wishing you'd supported me from the start?"

Dad sighs, rubbing his temples like this conversation is physically draining him. "And if it doesn't work out?"

I wave a hand in the air. "It did for James. Look what he's accomplished since graduation. His first rookie season, and he's already making a name for himself."

There's a long, uncomfortable pause. My mention of James hangs in the air like a challenge they're unwilling to take on.

Mom finally breaks the silence, her voice careful, measured. "Just think about it, Liam. You don't have to decide right now. The internship will be waiting if you change your mind. We can tell Welch to put a pin in it."

I nod, but the decision has already been made. Their doubt, their avoidance—it sealed it. Soccer is what I care about. Soccer is what I want.

And even if it wasn't, I'd probably pursue it anyway—just to prove them wrong.

. . .

WHEN I PULL into the driveway, the weight of the night hasn't let up. My parents' expectations, the internship talk—it all builds up inside me until it feels like I might burst from the pressure.

Chase is out for the night. He's probably crashing at someone's place or hitting up one of those parties he's always trying to drag me to. Usually, I'm fine being on my own. Hell, I prefer it.

But tonight? The thought of sitting in an empty house, alone with my thoughts circling back to the same tired conversation, feels unbearable. And worse, the idea of not having someone to talk to who actually gets it—who won't just dismiss it or try to fix it—makes me all sorts of itchy.

I reach for my phone, scrolling through my messages to find Birdie's last text about her speech. She's become that person for me, hasn't she? Just as trusted as Chase. Maybe even more.

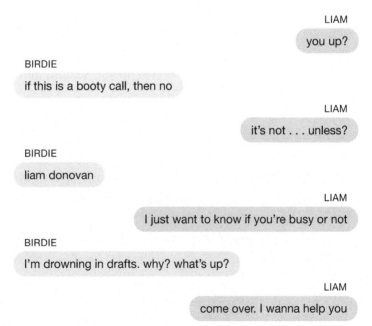

LIAM

you up?

BIRDIE

if this is a booty call, then no

LIAM

it's not . . . unless?

BIRDIE

liam donovan

LIAM

I just want to know if you're busy or not

BIRDIE

I'm drowning in drafts. why? what's up?

LIAM

come over. I wanna help you

That sounds casual enough, right? I mean, I *do* want to help. But I also just don't want to be alone right now, and I think Birdie would get that. She doesn't expect me to be anything other than what I am.

BIRDIE

I don't know. aren't you tired of helping me yet?

LIAM

trust me, I'd love nothing more than to whip your speech into shape

BIRDIE

okay then. text me your address, and I'll be over soon

I text back, then tuck my phone away before heading inside. The house is too quiet—the kind of silence that's more suffocating than peaceful. I toss my keys onto the counter and start pacing, trying to shake off the leftover frustration from dinner. But it clings to me, heavy and unrelenting, like wet clothes after a storm.

Twenty minutes later, there's a knock at the door. Birdie steps inside with her notebook and laptop tucked under her arm. She's in one of those oversized sweaters, her hair clipped back with those barrettes she always wears. She looks . . . content.

Beautiful as always, but also calm. Like she carries none of the tension I'm drowning in and might even be able to help me wade through the water.

"Hey." She gives me a sweet smile, and the coil of heat in my chest loosens, spreading into something softer. "You serious about helping me with my presentation, or was this just a ploy to get me to come over?"

"Both." She follows me into the living room and drops her stuff onto the coffee table. "But I do want to help. Make sure you're not being too . . . you know, flowery with your words."

She snorts as she settles onto the couch. "Great. You think I'm flowery?"

"You artists tend to be," I tease, sitting beside her. "Meanwhile,

I get straight to the point."

"Alright, Mr. Straight Shooter. Let's see what you've got." Her eyes narrow as she opens her laptop. "I'm supposed to explain my artistic process and how it relates to the themes—delicate versus raw, chaos versus order, all that good stuff. But every time I try to put it into words, it sounds . . . pretentious."

I lean over to glance at her screen. "Classic case of over-thinking."

"That's what I do," she mutters.

"Ah, really? You've been hiding it so well."

She elbows me, but a secret smile tugs at the corner of her mouth. For a moment, I watch her, taking in the way she bites her lip in concentration as she queues up another draft. When Birdie's around, I can let my guard down. She pulls me out of my own head, makes it easier to breathe.

"Alright, hit me with what you've got so far," I say, settling back into the couch.

She scrolls through her notes and clears her throat. "My work explores the delicate interaction between meticulously curated structure and the uninhibited essence of organic freedom—"

I hold up a hand, cutting her off mid-sentence. "Oh, God. Stop."

Her brow furrows. "What? Too much?"

"Way too much," I say, shaking my head. "It's like you're trying to win a game of Scrabble with your presentation."

She frowns down at her notes. "I thought I was supposed to sound . . . you know, professional."

"You're supposed to sound like you," I counter. "Not like a thesaurus exploded on your page. I know you're smart, Birdie. You don't need to prove it with ten-dollar words. The work is all about tension, right? Between the delicate and the raw. So, just say that."

She's quiet for a second, fingers hovering over the keyboard, before finally typing, retyping, cutting, and pasting. Then, she unclamps her barrettes, straightens her shoulders, and clears her throat.

"My work explores the tension between chaos and control. I'm fascinated by the spaces in between—the areas where we can't predict what's coming, but we still try to shape it, to create something that feels both fragile and powerful at the same time. With each piece, I'm challenging the idea that these two forces aren't opposites. Instead, I'm exploring how they coexist and inform one another."

"See? Way better. Now, tell me why it matters that you're the one creating this tension. Why should I care about *you* specifically?"

She furrows her brow, thinking for a moment. "I guess because . . . I've always been drawn to extremes, to things that seem contradictory but somehow make sense together. Like, I'm a perfectionist, but my favorite pieces are the ones where I let go of that need. I love working with delicate, intricate details, but I'm also obsessed with rough textures and imperfections. I think it's because I see myself in that contrast—trying to balance those two sides."

A slow grin spreads across my face. "That's your hook. It's not just about the art itself—it's about you and what you bring to it. You've got something to say, Birdie, so say it."

She looks at me, wide-eyed, like she's finally seeing something she hadn't before. Then she starts typing again, the keys clicking rapidly. "Okay, yeah. This feels . . . right."

"Good," I say, tapping her notebook. "No more hiding behind big words."

She laughs softly, the kind that starts in her chest and works its way up, and I can't help but feel a little proud. Not just of her work but also of the fact that she let me be a part of it.

I like this—spending time with her, helping her. It makes me feel useful, like I have a reason to stick around and just be here.

Present, grounded. Enough.

Chapter Twelve
BIRDIE

THE SOUNDS COMING from the kiln room aren't good. It's late, just past dusk, and Professor Hall's unloading last week's firing with a series of frustrated grunts and muttered curses that echo through the near-empty studio.

Hall is the opposite of Professor Tanaka in almost every way. Where Tanaka is composed and soft-spoken, Hall is blunt, big-voiced, and completely unfiltered. Tanaka teaches hand building like it's a meditation; Hall runs his wheel-throwing class like a workout session —loud, gritty, and peppered with an endless supply of commentary.

I hover just outside the doorway, my heart already sinking as Hall shoves his glasses higher up his nose and waves me over with a gloved hand. "Birdie, you're gonna wanna see this."

One glance inside the kiln tells me everything I need to know. Three of my newest pieces lie in ruins, fragments of shattered clay and dust scattered across the bottom rack.

It's a common kiln mishap. A piece must have exploded and hit the others—something that can easily happen during the bisque stage if there's an air bubble trapped in the clay or residual moisture in the walls. But knowing why doesn't make it any easier to look at.

"Looks like the kiln gods weren't feeling too generous this week," Hall says, shaking his head as he surveys the damage. "Little setback, but nothing you can't handle."

I swallow hard, fighting the tightness in my chest, the creeping sense of panic. It's not that I can't remake them—they were only in bisque, still unglazed—but the hours I already put in, the careful detailing, it's all gone up in smoke.

And with my fellowship deadline looming closer, these "little setbacks" feel monumental.

"Guess I'll just have to redo them," I mumble.

"Best you can do is roll with it," Hall says gruffly. "This won't be your last kiln catastrophe, I can promise you that."

He pulls out the remaining pieces that survived the firing and sets them on a nearby table. I try to focus on the positives. At least the vase I've been perfecting for weeks made it through unscathed. But it's hard not to fixate on what I've lost, especially with time running out.

Hall claps me on the shoulder—a quick, almost awkward gesture, but somehow, it reassures me. Then, with a final grumble to himself, he strides back to his wheel station at the far end of the studio.

Fingers itching for my phone, I consider texting Liam. He'd get it. He'd probably have some dry, sarcastic remark to make me laugh, to brush it off. And I would—reluctantly, but inevitably— feel better.

It's strange how quickly I've gotten used to that, to him being the first person I think of when I want to vent or when something goes wrong. And, if I were lucky enough for something to go right —really right—he'd probably be the first person I'd call to share that, too.

But he's in the middle of a home game against Pittsburgh right now, sprinting up and down the field, oblivious to my tiny pottery catastrophe. So, I can't text or call him to calm me down.

I sigh and try to focus on sweeping up the mess instead. But the frustration bubbles up again, and before I know it, I'm pulling out my phone anyway, scrolling past Liam's name and settling on Sena's.

> **BIRDIE**
>
> hi. I'm in crisis mode. three of my pieces broke in the kiln :(

SENA

omg. do you need sympathy, solutions, or sangria?

> **BIRDIE**
>
> probably all three. but mostly sangria

SENA

say no more. I'll get started

If anyone can turn a disaster into a half-decent night, it's my roommate. And I'm grateful for it now more than ever.

Once the broken shards are all swept up, I wipe down the table and take a deep breath, resolving to restart my work with fresh clay tomorrow. There's no point in wallowing tonight—especially not when Sena's already texting me about ordering pizza.

When I get home, the kitchen smells like fruit and cinnamon. Sena's there, slicing up oranges and apples, with bottles of red wine and rum set out on the counter. Music filters through the living room, something upbeat and warm, and she greets me with a grin as I walk inside.

"Well, look who survived the great kiln massacre." She winks, tossing the fruit into a big glass pitcher like she's done this a million times. "Feel like a little escape?"

"Definitely." I drop my bag by the door and lean against the counter, exhaustion melting into gratitude. "You're a lifesaver."

She waves me off. "So, what's the vibe? Just us drowning our sorrows, or should I call in reinforcements?"

I hesitate, weighing my options. Normally, I'd opt for a quiet night in, just me and Sena, but the thought of a lively apartment, full of laughter and distraction, feels like exactly what I need. "Just a few of your girls, maybe?"

Despite my distance from my old friends, I miss certain things about those carefree nights—the way the hours stretched endlessly, filled with laughter and easy conversation. It's been too long since I let myself enjoy something that simple and light.

Sena's face lights up. "That's what I like to hear." She pulls out her phone and starts texting. "Give me twenty minutes. We're about to have ourselves a proper girls' night."

Within half an hour, Sena's theater friends have all filtered in, their vibrant personalities filling every corner. Nessa, always the loudest in any room, is holding court by the kitchen counter, gesturing wildly with a glass of sangria in hand. Others mingle around her—Tazi, Leora, and Brynn.

The music gets louder, the sangria gets sweeter, and it's not long before the night slips into that comfortable blur. Everyone's cheeks are flushed from wine and laughter, and I'm feeling okay again.

By midnight, the four of us are sprawled across the couch together, tangled in a chaotic puzzle of limbs and wineglasses. Someone's foot rests on my lap—I don't even care to figure out whose—and my cheeks ache from smiling too hard.

"Alright, next question!" Nessa declares, holding up a half-empty wine bottle like a scepter. She slumps dramatically back into the armchair, squinting at a notecard through bleary eyes. "Who . . . in this room would you most want as a partner in a zombie apocalypse?"

Everyone groans, a mix of laughs and tipsy whines, and then we start debating. I barely register the answers, my head all heavy and warm. I'm on my fourth glass of the night, and the edges of the world have softened into a haze.

Sena's next to me, practically curled into my side, and I can't stop humming, this light, floating sensation buoying me up even though we're talking about something as ridiculous as zombies.

"Birdie," someone calls out, their voice cutting through the haze in my mind. "Would you bring Sena, or is she the first to get eaten?"

"Oh, she's definitely zombie bait," I reply, giggling as Sena elbows me, feigning offense. "But if she were a zombie, she'd be the type to incite riots."

Sena gasps in mock horror. "As if! I'd be the strong, silent type! Like a stealth zombie!"

Everyone bursts out laughing, and the last bits of stress from today slowly dissolve. The kiln disaster, the critique, even the looming fellowship deadline—they're all miles away.

Hardships that belong to someone else. Someone who isn't lounging on a couch with a glass of sangria in hand, wrapped in this moment of messy joy.

Sena nudges me. "Come on, Collins, you don't have to play hard to get. You know I'd be on your zombie team."

"That's because you're so lovely. So thoughtful and noble," I say with exaggerated sincerity.

She snorts. "You're damn right, I am."

That random foot presses into my bladder, and I wriggle out from under it, laughing as I push it away. "Alright, alright, I surrender. I'm tapping out for a second."

I stand and wobble down the short hallway to the bathroom. With the door behind me, I flip on the light and grip the edge of the sink for balance as the room spins in soft, blurry circles around me.

In the mirror, my face looks different, somehow. Flushed and alive. My hair's doing its usual wild thing, frizzing up around my face, and my mascara's smudged just slightly, but there's a hint of something in my eyes—something that feels good, if unsteady.

I can't remember the last time I had a girls' night like this, let alone drank enough to feel . . . well, drunk and out of control. I grin, swiping a stray curl out of my face, and dig my phone out of my pocket.

I should text Liam, shouldn't I?

The idea pops into my head like a spark catching dry wood, quick and insistent. I could tell Liam about the disaster in the kiln, about the ridiculous zombie debates, or I could just say. . . Something. Anything, really.

> **BIRDIE**
>
> hi *butterfly emoji* *fairy emoji* *zombie emoji*
>
> I'm having a mini breakdown bc my pieces blew up today but sena's making it better with sangria and zombies. would you survive an apocalypse?

LIAM

are you drunk?

> **BIRDIE**
>
> miiiiight be. why? would u judge me if i am?

LIAM

never

> **BIRDIE**
>
> good bc I would totally survive an apocalypse better than you

LIAM

wanna bet?

My heart gives this funny lurch, like a little somersault I don't entirely understand. It feels nice, though, whatever it is—light, unguarded, the kind of ease I've been needing.

> **BIRDIE**
>
> would you save me? If it came down to it, would you fight them off to rescue me???

LIAM

always

BIRDIE

thought so. you know I'm rly glad I met you, right? for more than just the pottery stuff, I mean

LIAM

yeah. I know. me too, birdie.

There's a knock on the door, and then Sena shouts, "Birdie, you okay in there?"

"Yeah!" I call back. "I'll be out in just a second!"

I stare at the screen for a long while, feeling that little flutter again, that mix of excitement and warmth that seems to bubble up every time we talk. It's silly, but I feel like I can hear his voice, steady and strong, cutting through the fog in my head.

"Birdie!" Sena's still knocking on the door, a bit more insistent now. "Stop flirting with yourself in the mirror and come out here!"

I lock my phone, tuck it back into my pocket, and take a steadying breath. I don't know why my chest feels so light, why the corners of my mouth keep trying to pull into a smile that I'm not sure I can suppress.

Maybe it's just a little crush, or maybe it's something else entirely—something I'm not quite ready to name.

When I finally open the door, Sena's standing there, one hand on her hip and the other holding a freshly poured glass of sangria. "Good God, woman! Thought we'd lost you to the depths of the toilet."

I laugh, stepping out into the hallway and playfully nudging her. "Sorry to disappoint, but I'm still alive and well."

"For now," she quips, holding the glass out to me like a peace offering. "Drink this and get back to the couch. Nessa's declared herself the queen of the apocalypse, and I'm about to stage a coup."

I take the glass, the warmth of the moment wrapping around

me like a blanket, and let her pull me back to the living room. Whatever's happening in my chest—the lightness, the fluttering—it can wait.

Right now, there's alcohol to drink, theater majors to debate, and a fleeting kind of happiness I'm not ready to let go of.

Chapter Thirteen

LIAM

THE FLOODLIGHTS GLARE over the field, cutting through the dark as a light rain drizzles. It's a Wednesday night game, late October, and the air's thick with that edge of chill that creeps in just before winter in Carolina, the kind that finally makes you pull your sleeves down and your collar up.

But I'm warm, my body humming from pre-game adrenaline and hours of training. It's everything that's been building to these last games before the season's end.

As I stretch on the sideline, shifting my weight from one foot to the other, I catch a glimpse of the bleachers filling up. Not exactly packed—midweek games rarely are—but the stands have a decent crowd already.

I scan the seats with a mix of nerves and anticipation. Birdie mentioned maybe coming. She texted me earlier, something about being swamped but wanting to try. And the thought of her sitting up there, watching me, makes my pulse kick up a notch.

It's Chase who snaps me back, clapping a hand on my shoulder. "Focus up, man. Let's show them what we've got." He's grinning, always keyed up before games, his usual smirk replaced with something sharper. The kind of focus I've been trying to channel all season.

Then the whistle blows, and we're on.

Twenty minutes in, we're already down 1-0, so tension's high.

I've barely managed to hold possession against their defense—they're quicker than I'd anticipated, cutting off every angle.

I glance up, and in the split second before I refocus on the game, I spot Birdie, a dot of familiar comfort on the bleachers. She has a hoodie pulled over her head, sitting alone. Watching. My stomach flips.

"Donovan! Push left!" Coach Harris' voice cuts through my thoughts, and I pull away, darting toward the open wing.

The ball comes over, a clean pass from Amir at midfield. I take it, sprinting down the left side, the defender on my heels. I fake right, then cut back left, just enough to throw him off, and now I'm free. There's just enough time to whip in a cross toward Chase, who's already charging into the box like a bull.

It's a good ball, sharp and angled. Chase connects, but the shot ricochets off the keeper's gloves, deflecting out. We groan in unison as the opposing team clears it. Our game's been like this all night—close but just out of reach.

We're still 1-0 at halftime, and Coach is ripping into us in the locker room, pacing like a caged animal. His voice is low, furious, controlled. "We've been too damn soft. Every time you hesitate, they're capitalizing. Donovan, keep pushing that left side. Their right back's weak; you've got the speed to beat him."

I nod, rolling my shoulders to shake off the tension. The guys are quiet, all of us soaking in the pressure. Chase mutters something to me as we're heading back out, something about getting a shot in the net this time. I nod, clenching my jaw. We're close. I can feel it.

The second half isn't much better. We're fighting tooth and nail, but it's like we're always a step too slow, an inch off. I manage a few crosses, some decent runs, but nothing's breaking through.

Each time I lose the ball or a pass falls short, the frustration mounts. I'm inside my own head, and I keep catching myself looking toward the bleachers, wondering if Birdie's still watching, if she's seeing every misstep, every missed chance.

Finally, with five minutes left on the clock, we get a break. Amir wins the ball at midfield and sends it wide to me. I take off, pushing everything I've got left into my legs, feeling the burn as I tear down the field. The defender's on me again, but I cut inside this time, faking him out with a quick flick to my right foot.

Chase is in the box, his eyes locked on mine. I send a low cross his way, hoping this one connects. He meets it, sending a sharp shot toward the far post. The ball spins, angling perfectly, and for a second, it looks like it's going to sneak in—just edge its way over the line.

But it doesn't. Instead, it glances off the post with a dull thud and ricochets out. I freeze, staring as the rebound clears the box. A collective groan echoes from the stands, and the defeat settles over us like a deflated balloon sagging in slow motion, heavy and inevitable.

The whistle blows a minute later, ending the game. Final score: 1-0.

I'm doubled over, hands on my knees, breath coming hard. As Syracuse celebrates their win, I glance up toward the bleachers, half expecting Birdie to be gone. But she's still there, watching, waiting. That steadies me, even if only a little.

Chase, though, is simmering. He walks past me, his jaw clenched, frustration etched across his face. I can practically see the thoughts spinning behind his eyes, the missed shot, the sponsor deal he's been gunning for—all slipping further out of reach. He shoves his hands through his hair, muttering a string of nonsensical curses under his breath.

We don't exchange a word as we head off the field. Chase's shoulders are rigid, his gaze fixed straight ahead as we enter the tunnel. I want to say something—crack a joke or offer one of those cheesy pep talks—but he's too far in his head. Chase always shoulders the loss like it's his personal failure, and tonight's no exception.

Coach gives us a short, tense talk in the locker room, telling us to shake it off and push harder for the next game. His words are aimed at the team, but his eyes linger on Chase a little too long.

It's one loss in a string of close matches. It sucks, yeah, but it doesn't gnaw at me the way it does him. I'm not the one with an Adidas contract dangling in the distance.

After a quick shower, I pull my bag over my shoulder and head out of the locker room, scanning the exit for Birdie. She could've bailed right after the game, but something tells me she didn't.

Sure enough, there she is, standing by the gate, hands shoved into her hoodie pocket, staring up at the sky like it's personally offended her. When I call her name, she jumps a little, then grins as she spots me.

"Hey," I say, rougher than I mean to. I rub the back of my neck, the sting of the loss still fresh. "Thanks for coming."

"Couldn't miss it. You played great. Really, Liam, that cross at the end? Beautiful."

I huff out a small, humorless laugh. How does she even know what a cross is? "Doesn't mean much if we don't win."

She tilts her head, her gaze softening in that way that makes me feel both seen and called out. "You gave it everything. I could see it."

"Yeah, well," I say, managing a smirk, "apparently my everything just isn't good enough."

She sighs, nudging me with her elbow. "Maybe you just need better teammates."

I laugh despite myself, the tension in my chest loosening just a little. "Careful. Chase might hear you and start crying."

She grins. "Wouldn't be the first time, I'm sure. Wanna grab something to eat? My treat."

I raise a brow, but a small smile breaks through. "You don't have to do that."

"I want to," she says, nudging my shoulder again. "Besides, you need consolation fries."

I let out a long breath, finally relenting. "Yeah, alright."

"Deal," she says, already turning toward the parking lot.

We walk away from the stadium, her shoulder brushing mine every few steps. The frustration of the game doesn't disappear, but with Birdie beside me, it fades to something quieter, something manageable. Something that feels like maybe tonight wasn't a total loss.

THE NOISE from Lucky's hums around us, a low, comfortable murmur of voices, the clinking of glasses, the occasional cheer from a nearby table. We're wedged into one of those small, sticky booths that makes it impossible not to bump knees, and Birdie's ordered us a basket of waffle fries and two dark lagers I can't pronounce.

I pick up the glass and take a sip, only to stop mid-swallow, fighting the urge to make a face. "Oh God," I mutter, setting it down a little too quickly. "Did you pick the most bitter beer they had on purpose?"

Birdie raises her eyebrows, clearly amused. "You said 'surprise me.' So, here you go. Welcome to the acquired taste club."

"Acquired, huh?" I say, giving the drink a wary look. "How long do I have to drink this before it doesn't taste like liquid regret?"

She laughs, nudging the glass closer. "You get used to it, I promise. Just think of it as building character."

I raise the glass again, eyes narrowing. "Building character through suffering. Got it."

She shakes her head, laughing, before lifting her glass for a sip, and we fall into easy conversation. Not a single mention of the fellowship, the game, or anything else with a shadow looming over it. It's nice. A rare moment where we're not trying to fix or unpack something, just existing in this small, happy place.

She grabs a fry, and her eyes light up like she's struck gold. "Oh, I almost forgot," she says, leaning forward with a conspiratorial smile. "I saw a sign advertising chocolate lava cake that's literally the size of my head. Do you want to try it?"

My face twists in mock disgust. "A Lucky's lava cake will probably take a decade off my life. Besides, the entire concept is disturbing. Why would you want chocolate soup inside a cake?"

She gasps, her mouth dropping open in exaggerated offense. "Excuse me? Lava cake is a work of art. It's gooey, chocolatey perfection."

I chuckle, pulling out my phone and typing quickly. "What if I told you I had a better option?"

She arches a brow. "Better than lava cake?"

I hold up a finger, pretending to be serious, then finish my search with a grin. "Pie. They give out birthday pie over at Sweet Seasons, and it just so happens . . ." I trail off, letting the suspense hang in the air as I flash my phone screen at her. "I have a birthday coupon."

Birdie stares at the screen, her eyes widening. "Wait—are you telling me today's your birthday?"

I scoff, shaking my head. "No. I just . . . know a little hack."

"Is that so?" she asks, leaning forward, intrigued.

"Birthday perks," I say, like it's the most obvious thing in the world. "Most places give you something free on your birthday. All you have to do is sign up with a different birthday for each account, and voilà—you get rewards all year."

She blinks, clearly taken aback. "You're kidding."

"Nope." I lean back, grinning. "I used to have a whole spreadsheet. The goal was to fill as many days as possible. I'm talking a free donut on January third, free tacos on March twelfth, then there's smoothie day, ice cream on August twenty-first." I shrug. "I'd gotten up to one hundred forty-three days of birthday rewards last year, but then it just got time-consuming. Decided it was too much work."

She's staring at me, torn between amusement and amazement. "Liam Donovan, I swear, you are a full-time job all by yourself."

I laugh, taking a sip of my disgusting beer. "A job with excellent benefits."

She laughs. "Let me guess—you're the kind of person who dives headfirst into something new and then, I don't know, drops it the second you get bored."

"Pretty much," I admit, grabbing another fry. "But only with my side quests. The real stuff—the things that matter—stick around."

"Like soccer," she says, her eyes studying me with that piercing look she gets sometimes, the one that makes me wonder if she can see right through all my deflections.

"Yeah, exactly," I reply, feeling the easy humor melt into something quieter. "Soccer's different."

She tilts her head, curiosity flickering in her eyes as she leans closer. "What makes it different?"

I pause, not quite sure how to explain it in a way that doesn't sound cliché. I'm not usually the type to dig deep into feelings, but there's something about Birdie that makes it easier. Maybe it's the way she's looking at me, like she's genuinely interested, not just waiting for a punchline.

"It's . . . just always been there," I say slowly, picking at the label on my beer glass. "When everything else gets complicated or changes, soccer's the one thing that stays steady. I get out there, and all the noise inside my head, all the pressure, it just . . . fades."

She watches me for a beat, a soft smile tugging at her lips. "I'm glad. It's good," she says, "to have something that grounds you like that."

I clear my throat, shifting under her gaze. "Yeah, keeps me from spinning off into a thousand different directions like usual."

She watches me, something softening in her eyes, her mouth curving into a gentle smile. "I hope you know you don't have to do that with me."

I look up. "Do what?"

"Self-deprecate," she says softly. "It's a bad habit of mine, too. Feels a bit like hiding."

"You don't want me to hide from you, Birdie?"

"I'd prefer it if you showed up, actually. Flaws and all."

"Okay." I give her a small grin, leaning back. "But don't say I didn't warn you."

Chapter Fourteen

BIRDIE

ON FRIDAY EVENING, I grit my teeth and tug at the kiln door, which creaks open with a slow, metallic groan. Professor Hall wanted me to do the honors after my last mishap. So, I steady my breath, already bracing myself as I pull out the first shelf, scanning for any sign of shards or cracks lurking beneath the surface.

My gaze lands on the three pieces I rushed through, remaking them after the disaster earlier this week. They sit there, pale and matte from the bisque firing, perfectly intact. Relief washes over me—they made it through.

Around me, other students are unloading a separate kiln, carefully setting their pieces on cooling racks. There's Aria, with her brightly colored home-mixed glazes; Jonah, muttering to himself as he examines a warped bowl; and Nicholas Riordan. He's also a finalist for the fellowship. I'd like to tell myself his work is overrated, but that would be a flat-out lie.

They're geometric and precise, like they've been engineered rather than sculpted.

I don't know him well—he's one of those quietly meticulous types whose reputation precedes him. But I know he has immaculate control, every detail measured and intentional, the kind of perfection that leaves no room for chance.

Even now, he's setting his tools back in their exact spots, wiping down his work area with a cloth. When he catches my stare out of his peripherals, he glances up, his expression neutral. "Need a hand?"

"No, I got it, thanks," I reply, shifting a heavier piece into place.

"Well, if you change your mind, just let me know. I know some of those can be a pain to handle solo."

"Thanks," I say, brushing off some stray bits of clay from my hands. "They're a bit awkward, but nothing I can't manage."

He chuckles lightly, an easy, practiced sound. "I used to wrestle with pieces like that all the time in my first year. Learned the hard way that balance is half the battle."

I give a tight smile, unsure if that comment was meant to help or subtly remind me of his expertise. Either way, I decide to let it slide. "So true."

Nick's eyes drift back to his own pieces, his gaze careful, almost reverent, as he inspects each line like he's performing a sacred ritual. "It's funny," he says after a moment of silence. "I think ceramics keeps you humble, you know? Just when you think you've nailed it, the kiln decides otherwise."

"Yeah, a few of my pieces were in the kiln that exploded last week."

"Happens to all of us," he says with an easy shrug. "Some of my best work started out like that. Adapt and overcome, right?"

I force a smile, nodding like I'm in on the same joke, but inside, there's a stubborn knot tightening in my chest. *Adapt and overcome*, my ass. He's just being friendly, trying to share a moment, and yet . . . why does every tidbit of advice feel like a reminder of the gap between us? Of how far ahead he is, how composed he seems, how effortless he makes this look.

"Right," I say, trying to sound breezy. "Something to aspire to."

He chuckles, oblivious to the spiral tightening in my chest, and moves off to his own workstation. I watch him for a moment before turning back to my table, my focus flicking between the bisqued pieces and the jars of glaze lined neatly along the edge.

My hands hover indecisively. Glazing feels like the final step, the commitment—no going back once the color sets. And right now, my confidence feels about as stable as wet clay.

Maybe tomorrow, a small voice whispers. But tomorrow feels like a delay, an excuse to avoid finishing what I've started. With a deep breath, I grab the first piece, deciding to press on despite the heaviness tugging at my chest. One brushstroke at a time.

The others finish up and head out, one by one. Nick is the last to leave, giving me a brief nod as he pulls his bag over his shoulder and disappears through the studio doors.

I dip into a deep green glaze first and try to push down the lingering knot of inadequacy that's grown roots over the last hour. Carefully, I smooth the glaze over the fractured curves of one piece. Steady, deliberate strokes with a fine-tipped brush.

"Honey, I'm home."

I glance up, startled, and there's Liam, a camera slung casually around his neck. He's wearing a fitted hoodie and joggers, his hair a little damp from a post-practice shower. Disarmingly handsome, as usual.

"Wasn't expecting you," I say, my brush pausing mid-stroke. "Or did you kick another ball through the window?"

"Nah, Coach let us out early," he replies. "Figured I'd swing by, grab some more photos like I promised. You know, being the diligent assistant I am."

"Well, if you were hoping to see the work of a guaranteed fellowship winner, Nick Riordan just left."

Liam raises an eyebrow. "Well, whoever that is, he sounds like a complete tool."

I snort as he starts snapping photos, adjusting angles, crouching down to capture each piece in the soft, diffused light. He doesn't press for details about Nick or try to dig into my insecurities. He just is—present, steady, letting his actions do the talking.

After a few clicks, he turns his attention to my newly bisqued pieces, studying them through the lens. "These yours?" he asks, nodding toward the trio I'd just salvaged from the kiln.

"Yeah. They're replacements for the ones that shattered last week. Bisque-fired, so they're ready for glazing."

He's silent as he inspects each piece, his brow furrowing slightly, like he's actually taking them in. "They're good, Birdie. They look like they're on the edge of something. It's cool."

His words settle into me, filling in some of the cracks that doubt's been carving out all week. He talks with this easy assurance, like he's so sure of what he's seeing.

Here I've been, stuck comparing my work to Nick's polished perfection, tearing myself down before anyone else can. Wondering if what I'm doing even measures up. But Liam? He's looking past all of that, right to the heart of it. Like he knows exactly what I'm trying to bring to life.

Still, there's this nagging voice in the back of my mind, whispering that my theme's overdone. Predictable. A relentless doubt that digs in every time I get close to thinking I might have something worthwhile. What if, no matter how many ways I try to explain it, the judges dismiss it as shallow? Lacking depth?

Or worse—what if they don't see anything at all?

"Thank you," I murmur, avoiding his gaze. "Cool is all I've ever wanted to be."

He laughs, lowering the camera. "Are you hiding from me now?"

I flush, keeping my eyes on the piece I'm glazing. "Maybe. Maybe your annoyingly spot-on compliments make it hard to stay level-headed."

He tilts his head, considering me for a second. "Well, what if I told you it's more than just cool? It's unpredictable—like it's about to crack but somehow holding it together. Like you're daring people to look twice, and they *can't not*."

I blink, stunned. "That wasn't in my proposal, was it?"

"Nah, I came up with it myself."

"Wow, original and insightful. What a catch."

He feigns offense, pressing a hand to his chest. "Oh, come on, Birdie. Don't I get a little credit for my artist's eye by now?"

I smirk, leaning against the table, letting the brush dangle loosely in my hand. "Daddy Donovan must've taught you a thing or two over the years."

He freezes, staring at me with mock horror. "Please don't ever say that again. Ever."

"You're saying he didn't lecture you on 'the finer points of art critique' growing up? Watch. Next, you'll be calling my pieces 'mystical and transcendent' or some other pretentious nonsense."

"If that's what gets you the fellowship, I'll play along. 'Birdie Collins: her hands are magic.' I'll mention it at our next family dinner."

I laugh, but it's a little tight, a little uneasy. I know I asked Liam for help, but now that we're here, I can't shake the feeling that just knowing him—just being connected to him—gives me an edge the other finalists don't have.

Not that I should care about that. This is my work, my effort, my vision. But the thought nags at me anyway. I don't want Liam to feel like he's just a stepping stone, some unspoken obligation wrapped up in this competition.

"I don't need you to play messenger," I say quickly. "And you don't have to bring me up at dinner or, you know, anywhere. That's not why I—"

"Relax," he cuts in, a small grin softening his expression. "I'm kidding, Birdie. You're not some charity project, okay? I'm here because I want to be."

"Oh." I glance down, fiddling with the corner of my sleeve, my fingers tracing a loose thread. "In that case, carry on."

"Gladly," he says, his grin widening, lopsided and entirely too charming. "Not that you need it, anyway. Your work can speak for itself."

I glance back up, my lips quirking. "You think everything's that simple?"

He shrugs, leaning against the table, casually spinning his camera by its strap. "Not everything. But sometimes, yeah. People overthink. They twist themselves into knots trying to be perfect when really, all they have to do is show up and be real."

I pause, letting his words settle. "And what about you? Do you always just show up and hope for the best?"

"Depends," he replies, his tone teasing but not quite light. "Not always. Some things matter enough to get it right, to get it perfect."

There's something in the way he says it, the way his gaze holds mine, that makes my chest tighten. I blink, shaking off the weight of it, and pick up my brush. "Well, aren't you just full of wisdom tonight."

He grins, undeterred. "Must be rubbing off on you. Actually, now that I mention it, I would very much like to—"

I smack him lightly on the arm. "You have a point," I cut in before he can finish whatever nonsense he's about to say. "It's just . . . hard to think that way sometimes."

"Then let me think that way for you," he says. "I'll be your resident hype man, and we'll get you that fellowship, easy."

I give him a skeptical look. "You're talking about months of work, constant rejection, fighting for every bit of validation—"

"Yeah, and you're still doing it." He shrugs, leaning against the table. "Because it's worth it to you. And because you're damn good at it."

"Thanks, Coach. Glad to know you're in my corner."

"Always," he says, all soft and genuine, the teasing slipping away. It's like a promise, steady and certain. Then, with a glint in his eye, he adds, "So, how much would it annoy you if I told you I could whip one of these bad boys up in about thirty minutes?"

I gape at him. "I knew it. You've been hiding the fact you're a prodigy."

"Nah, I've never even finished a piece," he says, chuckling.

I squint. "It's hard to believe your dad never got you on the wheel."

"Oh, he did. But I haven't touched clay since I was a kid. I was more into running around and kicking shit. Though, really, how hard can it be to spin the wheel?"

"Oh, I see. You think you can just waltz in here and show me up? Be my guest."

"Give me a crash course?" he asks, feigning innocence.

"Gladly." I lead him over to the wheel, gesturing like a tour guide. "This is the wheel. This is clay." I grab a ball of wedged clay and smack it onto the center of the wheel with a satisfying *thud*. "Put them together and prepare to be amazed—if you think you're up for it."

"Am I meant to summon Patrick Swayze now, or will you be caressing me from behind?"

"Keep dreaming."

I know he's messing with me. He's seen the effort this takes—he's said more than once how much he respects the skill—but right now? He's having fun pushing his luck, and I'm curious to see just how far he'll take it.

He sits down, positioning his hands with all the finesse of someone holding a live fish. The wheel starts and takes off spinning, the clay wobbling as his hands slip, sending flecks across his shirt.

"Whoa, whoa!"

I step behind him, leaning in over his shoulder to guide his hands. "First off, don't fight it. You need to press a little more gently on the sides, keep it centered—yeah, like that."

"See? Not so hard," he says proudly.

I snort. "Congratulations, you're officially mediocre."

"Oh, don't sell me short. This is a masterpiece."

"It . . . sure is something," I mutter as he tries to shape it into a vague bowl-like form. Within seconds, it leans dangerously to one side, threatening to collapse. His eyebrows knit as he tries to salvage it, but it's a losing battle.

"Okay, maybe I was a bit overconfident."

I tsk. "Understatement."

He laughs and tosses his hands up. "Alright, you win. This wheel-throwing business is all yours. Better I stick to what I'm good at."

"Kicking balls?" I scrunch my nose. "Not so good with your hands, are you?"

His eyes spark, and a slow grin spreads across his face. "Oh, I don't know. Haven't heard any complaints yet."

"Guess I'll reserve judgment until I see more evidence."

"Careful, Birdie." He licks his lips, his voice dropping just enough to make my pulse stutter. "Might have to give you a full demonstration."

I swallow, trying not to lose my cool, but it's impossible. Heat creeps up my neck. My mind's already running away with the idea, and judging by the look he's giving me, his isn't far behind.

But I know it's just Liam being Liam—always walking that line, keeping the banter alive, no harm intended. Probably.

"Hold still." I clear my throat, forcing a laugh to break the tension. Before he can fire off another comment, I swipe a bit of clay from the wheel and smear it unapologetically across his cheek. "There. Now you're a real potter."

He freezes for a moment, then bursts out laughing. "Oh, you're gonna regret that." He scoops a bit of clay onto his fingers and flicks it at me, but it veers wildly off course, splatting against the wall instead.

"Wow. Amazing aim. Definitely stick to soccer."

"Hey, it was a warning shot," he protests, still chuckling as he leans back on the stool. "But fine. Point taken."

The lopsided grin he gives me softens his features, and for a second, I forget where I am. His piece is a complete disaster—smooshed, shapeless, an absolute wreck by any technical standard—but it's a nonissue. There's something oddly endearing about how he doesn't seem to care.

Failure doesn't embarrass him. He allows himself to stumble, to fumble, to laugh at his own mistakes without a second thought—and he does it all right in front of me, like it comes naturally.

And maybe that's what I like most. Nothing feels ruined when he's around. Just messy, and real, and somehow so much better.

Chapter Fifteen

GOD, I hate parties. The noise, the chaos, the people packed in like commuters on a rush-hour train. Touching me when I don't want to be touched. Looking at me when I'd rather not be perceived. It's all just a mess of sounds and smells, everyone yelling over the music that's way too loud.

But I've been dragged to enough of these things at Dayton to know when it's worth putting up a fight—and when it's better to go along for the ride, which, admittedly, happens more often than I'd like.

There was that neon rager during Welcome Week. The infamous foam party freshman year. Last Halloween, James, Hayes, and his girlfriend made me dress up as one of Bo Peep's sheep, and yeah, I've still got photos of that one. Now, here I am, getting dragged along by Chase to yet another soccer party.

It makes him happy, and it's easier for me just to play along than to explain why I'd rather be anywhere else. Sometimes, I have to let Chase's enthusiasm carry me along instead of resisting the tide.

"Come on, man. Loosen up," Chase says, nudging my shoulder as we make our way up to the porch. "It's Halloween. You're dressed like a vampire, for God's sake. Embrace it."

I adjust the plastic fangs that are digging into my gums and wipe a bit of fake blood from my lip. "It's quite literally a Monday night in the middle of the semester. Pardon me for not feeling so festive."

Chase just grins, eager to head inside to find some unsuspecting girl. He's all in, a gladiator in a getup that's one size too small. "Look, just have a drink, relax. You might actually have fun tonight."

The noise is already bleeding out—someone's cranked up "Thriller," and there's a burst of laughter that sounds like it's coming from at least half a dozen people. I roll my eyes as Chase disappears inside. Instead of following, I hang back alone, posting up by the door.

I asked Birdie to meet me here on a whim. It was a last-minute invite that I honestly didn't think she'd accept. But she did, and with her by my side, this party might actually be bearable. Maybe even enjoyable.

She texted that she'd be here soon, so I'm waiting.

Five minutes later, she's walking up the lawn, her wings catching the porch light as she adjusts them. She's dressed as a woodland fairy, all soft greens and browns, with her hair braided.

She looks so pretty, delicate, perfect. A version of Birdie that makes it hard to remember why I ever thought I didn't want to be here.

"So, are you just going to stare, or are you going to say hi?" she asks.

"Did you walk here?" The house is a decent trek from her apartment, and the thought of her walking it alone in the dark tugs at me.

She shrugs, brushing it off. "The wings make me faster."

"Uh-huh," I reply, unimpressed. "So, are you here to sprinkle magic dust, or are you more of the mischievous type?"

She taps her chin thoughtfully. "Depends. Are you here to drink people's blood or just to look menacing?"

"Mostly the latter." I flash the plastic fangs in an exaggerated grin. "Though these fuckers are killing me. Couldn't find a set that didn't feel like they were made for toddlers."

She laughs. "Yeah, you've got a little blood just there." She swipes her thumb across my lip to clean off the fake splatters. The casual touch throws me, and for a second, I'm too focused on the warmth of her hand to come up with a witty response.

"Thanks," I manage, clearing my throat. "You look . . . really good, by the way. Like you could actually live in a forest somewhere and talk to squirrels or something."

Her eyes light up, amused. "Squirrels, huh? I was hoping for something cooler."

"Like . . . a wood nymph?" I suggest.

"Or Edward Cullen, maybe. You know, *hop on, Spider-Monkey.*"

I wink. "I can be him. I'm halfway there already."

"Not sparkly enough," she quips, grinning.

I chuckle, finally gesturing toward the door. "Ready to head in? My roommate's probably in there plotting his next conquest."

She laughs softly, shaking her head, and we step inside together. The moment we do, we're hit with the usual wall of noise. People dressed in mismatched costumes—cowboys, superheroes, random togas—are crammed into every corner. The faint smell of stale beer lingers in the air, mixed with sweat and way too much cheap cologne.

"Welcome to the circus," I mutter under my breath.

Birdie wrinkles her nose as she scans the crowd. "I should've guessed. You're not a big fan of parties, are you?"

I give her a sideways look. "Not really."

"So, why are we here, then?" she asks, all low and playful.

"Just felt like it, I guess."

Her eyes narrow. "Did you?"

"Yeah, I'm trying to be good."

"*Good?*" she repeats, tilting her head.

I sigh, running a hand over the back of my neck before diving in. "Before, if I wasn't up for something, I'd just say no straight-away. No question about it. But . . . the last couple of years, I figured I should make more of an effort. If it makes my friends happy, then why not, even if it's uncomfortable for me? It's not that hard to pretend for a little while."

She looks at me, head tilted, lips pursed in thought. Finally, she says, "That sounds exhausting. Actually, I know it's exhausting. I used to be such a people pleaser, too, but somewhere along the way, I realized I didn't have to say yes to everything. Learned the hard way what can happen when you're not taking care of yourself."

People pleaser. That's not something I'd generally call myself. In fact, I've always seen myself as someone who doesn't really care what others think. But she's right. Sometimes, even without meaning to, I compromise more than I realize. Little sacrifices here and there, just to avoid rocking the boat.

Once again, Birdie manages to put words to something I didn't know I was feeling. She understands what it's like to go against what feels natural—to mask, to bend yourself into what other people want. There's a flicker of curiosity in me, wondering what happened to shift things for her. What moment taught her to stop saying yes when she didn't mean it.

But I let it go, for now.

"If I'm really feeling burnt out," I say, "I won't force it."

She raises an eyebrow, like she's debating whether to press for more, but in the end, she decides against it. Instead, she grabs my hand, tugging me through the crowd toward the kitchen.

The room is packed, a chaotic mess of bodies and noise, but we manage to carve out a small space by the counter. She grabs a couple of plastic cups, filling them from the keg with the precision of someone who's clearly done this a few times.

"To learning our limits," she says, raising her cup with a wry smile.

I tap mine against hers. "And to ignoring them every now and then."

We drink, the sharp taste of cheap beer making me wince, but it's manageable. As she takes another sip, I glance over her shoulder and spot a familiar face near the back of the room. I do a double take, almost convinced I'm imagining it.

Leaning against the wall with a scowl that could melt stone is Warren—my uncle's stepson and the absolute last person I expected to see at a party like this.

Birdie catches my expression and follows my gaze. "Who's that?"

"My cousin," I say, shaking my head. "He's on the swim team. Don't know what he's doing here, though. He hates parties even more than I do."

She narrows her eyes at him, intrigued. "Looks like he's plotting someone's demise. Is he always that . . . intense?"

"Pretty much. Warren's got one of those resting 'don't mess with me' faces. But he actually does hate everyone, I think. It's not just an unlucky expression."

Her lips twitch like she's trying not to laugh. "You're telling me he's the antisocial one in your family?"

"Hey, I'm plenty social when I want to be," I say, nudging her arm.

Birdie glances back at Warren. "Should we go say hi? Or would that just make him bolt?"

"Definitely bolt," I mutter. "Let's spare him the pain. He's probably already counting the seconds until he can leave. Seeing me would only speed up his exit strategy."

She grins. "You're being dramatic."

"No, I'm not. But I don't take it personally. Warren just . . .

doesn't like people. Period. But if you don't believe me, I'll prove it to you."

Before she can argue, I steer her through the crowd, weaving past costumes and clusters of half-shouted conversations. When we reach him, Warren doesn't so much as blink in surprise. His expression is as stoic as ever, his arms crossed tightly over his chest.

"Hey, Warren. Why are you here?"

Birdie slaps me on the shoulder, and it's only then that I realize how blunt that sounded. I quickly revise my tone. "I mean, what brings you to this fine social gathering?"

"Didn't have much of a choice," Warren replies, his voice low and grumbly. "Coach said something about 'team bonding.' Thought I'd make an appearance and then head out."

Birdie smiles, her voice light. "Well, you're doing great so far. Super approachable vibes."

Warren's lips twitch, almost imperceptibly, like he's debating whether to smile or not. "I'll take that as a compliment."

"It is," Birdie says, clearly amused. "Anyway, don't let us keep you from your 'bonding.' Looks like you're having a blast."

Warren raises an eyebrow, giving me a pointed look. "Your friend's a little too chipper for this crowd."

I shrug. "She grows on you."

Birdie rolls her eyes. "Come on, let's get out of his hair before he starts plotting our demise."

Warren watches us leave, shaking his head faintly, and I swear there's the tiniest glimmer of amusement in his eyes. Or maybe I'm imagining it.

"He doesn't seem so bad," Birdie says once we're out of earshot. "He seems like he can take a joke, at least."

"That's because you haven't been around him long enough." I shake my head. "I've seen Warren sit through family events with the same deadpan expression he wears now. Doesn't matter if it's

Christmas dinner or someone's retirement party. The guy's a statue."

Birdie quirks an eyebrow. "A Claus denier—sounds like a good time."

"At my uncle's wedding, he ditched halfway through the toasts to hide out by the catering truck. Later, I found him by the loading dock, sneaking wedding cake and muttering about how the speeches were all boring and fake."

That earns a laugh, and she pulls me toward the dance floor. She moves without hesitation, her wings fluttering in time with the music, her whole body alive with this unrestrained energy that's impossible not to notice.

She turns to me, hips swaying, and I step closer without thinking. The bass thrums between us, and I catch the faint shimmer of sweat along her collarbone. My gaze lingers, tracking the bead as it slides down. My mind flickers to a thought I can't shake, a thought I shouldn't have—of leaning down, tasting the salt and warmth of her skin.

Instead, I lean in just enough that her hair brushes my cheek. "You seem happy tonight," I murmur. "Like you're really letting go. It's a good look on you."

The shift is immediate. Her shoulders stiffen, and the light in her eyes dims, like I've said something to ruin the moment. The realization hits me like a gut punch, and I curse myself.

"I'm sorry," I blurt out, trying to recover. "I didn't mean to make it weird. I just—should've kept my mouth shut."

She lets out a shaky laugh, waving me off. "No, it's not you. Really, it's me. I don't usually let myself . . . feel like this. Ever. Not anymore." Her gaze flickers up to meet mine, hesitant. "But with you, I don't know. It's like I forget how not to."

"And that's . . . bad?" I ask softly, searching her face for something to latch onto.

She presses her lips together, clearly wrestling with something, and finally shakes her head. "It's not bad. It's just . . . complicated."

I don't push. Instead, I watch her rub her temples like she's trying to fend off the weight of her own thoughts. "Do you want to go?" I ask. "We can leave if you want."

She's quiet for a beat, her fingers brushing mine absently. Then she shakes her head. "No," she says, more firmly this time. Her hand slides up to clasp mine, pulling it around her neck. "We should stay. Dance more. Laugh more. Just . . . let ourselves be happy. No overthinking. No second-guessing."

I don't question it. I just slide my hand down to the small of her back, settling it gently beneath her wings. Her body softens against mine, and we sway together, barely moving but somehow perfectly in sync.

She looks up, her hazel eyes catching the shifting lights, open and searching. I want to kiss her, to tell her how she makes everything feel right. But I hold back, afraid of breaking whatever fragile thing we've built in this moment.

We stay like that, lost in the music and each other, her fingers tracing a slow path along my shoulder. It's not the kind of dancing that fits the chaos around us—it's quieter, softer, like we've found our own little world amid the noise.

And if this is pretending, I think, I don't want it to end. Because for the first time in a long time, it doesn't feel like pretending at all.

Chapter Sixteen
BIRDIE

TUESDAY MORNING BRINGS with it a dull, throbbing headache and the lingering glow of last night's party. It's not a migraine, thank God. I haven't had one of those in months. Still, the ache is enough to make me wince as I stretch.

I didn't realize just how late we stayed, how deep we let ourselves sink into the night's chaos. There's a fine ring of glitter on my pillow to prove it—a shimmering reminder of fairy wings and Halloween magic.

As I rub my temples, a nagging sense of worry tugs at the back of my mind. The last time I felt like this, it started as just a headache, too.

I grab my phone, scrolling through the notifications until I see "Dad" flash on the screen. I pick up, and before I can even get a word in, his familiar voice fills the line.

"How's my little Bridgie doin'?" he asks, warm, gruff, and instantly comforting.

I lean against the headboard. "I'm doing okay. Keeping busy."

"And how's your head been? Not pushing yourself too hard, I hope? You getting enough sleep?"

Three questions. A trifecta that instantly drags me back to the accident—the brain injury, the recovery, all the caution afterward. The doctors told me symptoms can linger longer than you'd expect, especially the headaches and exhaustion.

Lately, they've been cropping up more and more.

I'm sure it's just the extra weight I'm carrying: school, lack of funds, and the pressure to always keep pushing forward, even when it feels like there's no room left to breathe.

"Yes, Dad. I promise I'm getting enough rest," I fib, knowing the alternative would only make him worry more. "And I'm trying not to let things get to me."

"Good. Your ol' noggin's been through enough."

I shift, pulling the blanket tighter around me. "I know, and I'm being careful, I promise. I have someone helping me out with the fellowship stuff, which has been a huge relief."

"I know you'll do great, kiddo. But listen, Bridgie . . . if for some reason it doesn't go the way we want—and I have faith it will," he adds quickly, "but if it doesn't, maybe I can pick up some more shifts at the warehouse. It'd be no trouble, just a few extra hours here and there, and—"

"Dad, seriously. Don't worry about it." I swallow, guilt pooling in my chest like a slow drip. "You're already doing so much. Besides, this is on me. I'll make it work, okay?"

He sighs, long and heavy. "You're somethin' else, Bridge. Just know we're all rooting for you."

I smile at that, wondering exactly who "all" is. The guys from work, maybe? I can picture them, a bunch of warehouse workers in grease-stained caps and steel-toed boots, asking him every now and then, "How's your girl doin' with that fancy art stuff?"

"Thanks, Dad." I smile, blinking back a sudden sting in my eyes. "I'll keep you updated, okay?"

"Deal. Now, get some rest. Love ya, kid."

"Love you, too."

After I hang up, I want nothing more than to roll over, bury myself in blankets, and fall back asleep for the rest of the day. But duty calls. Life doesn't slow down just because my head's aching and my bed's warm.

I groan softly, swinging my legs over the edge of the bed and taking a moment to steady myself. Then, I shoot off a quick text to Liam.

> **BIRDIE**
>
> how's the hangover?

LIAM

alcohol level's fine. social battery's depleted

> **BIRDIE**
>
> aw, poor little bloodsucker

LIAM

I have glitter in my hair, by the way

> **BIRDIE**
>
> lol I hope you know that's gonna be there forever

LIAM

good. now I can look nice for my parents on friday night. they're making me go to the Montrose opening instead of our usual dinner

Is he serious? The soft opening of the new gallery downtown. The one I've been counting down the days for. It's exclusive, invite-only. I should've known Liam would have an in.

> **BIRDIE**
>
> I'm so jealous

LIAM

you wanna come?

> **BIRDIE**
>
> REALLY?

LIAM

yup. plus one is all yours if you want it

BIRDIE

oh my god, YES. I'll wear my fanciest . . . sweater dress? what do people wear to a gallery opening?

LIAM

you'll look perfect, don't worry. just promise you won't leave me alone with my parents

BIRDIE

deal. I'll be your personal buffer

LIAM

you can schmooze my dad all you want

BIRDIE

still scared of him. but I'm excited to get inspiration for my portfolio

LIAM

don't go changing things on me now

BIRDIE

I know, I like what I have. just might get a lil extra spark. thanks for letting me tag along. seriously.

LIAM

don't mention it. gotta keep you cultured

This kind of playful back-and-forth has quickly become one of my favorite parts of the day. Liam has a way of making things feel lighter, like whatever's heavy in my life could just be tossed aside, at least for a little while.

When we first met, I didn't expect him to be this easy to talk to. To click with. But it feels like he actually sees me, in a way that so few people do.

BIRDIE

just don't let me embarrass you too much

LIAM
trust me, if anyone's guilty of that, it'll be me. but
if you're there, I might actually survive the night

I smile, tucking my phone against my chest. He really wants
me there beside him. He's not just doing me a favor, humoring me;
he actually *wants* me there. It's new and thrilling, this feeling that
I'm someone's anchor in the middle of the chaos. And that maybe
he's mine, too.

Excitement buzzes in my chest—real, unfiltered excitement.
Not the anxious kind or the sort that comes with a thousand doubts
trailing behind it. Just the pure, giddy kind that makes me want to
savor the moment. The fellowship, him, everything—it's all starting
to feel like it might just fall into place.

Friday night arrives quickly. I'm dressed in my Sunday best,
a deep green dress and little brown Mary Janes. I slip on my coat,
smoothing down my dress and adjusting the delicate silver bracelet
my dad gave me. A present for my eighteenth birthday.

It once belonged to my mom. She left when I was barely old
enough to remember, but Dad's always spoken of her with kindness, as if her memory deserves to be cherished, not resented. He
says I'm his greatest gift—but that she once was, too.

Tonight feels like the right time to wear it, to carry a piece of
her with me. A small reminder of where I come from, of the broken
pieces I've had to mend, and the person I've grown into despite
them.

I take the bus into the city. The steady rhythm of the engine,
the wide seats, and the blurred city lights outside the window give
me a sense of calm I can't find in smaller vehicles.

Since the accident, car rides twist my stomach into knots, my hands clamping down on anything solid as if that might keep me grounded. The sound of tires skidding or the sudden shift of gears send my heart racing, a reflex I've never been able to fully shake.

I can manage it when I have to, but with a headache still lingering from earlier in the week, I'd rather not test my limits tonight.

Instead, I lean my head against the cool glass of the window, letting the hum of the bus carry me toward downtown. Toward Liam. Toward a night I can only hope will be as meaningful as the small, cherished weight on my wrist.

When I arrive, the gallery is glowing. Large glass windows reveal elegant guests milling about inside, and the hum of voices and soft music spills out when the door opens.

I spot Liam near the entrance, looking uncharacteristically polished in a dark suit. His usual messy blond hair is tamed just enough to look intentional, and the sharp, tailored lines of his suit make him seem taller, more composed. Still, there's an easy, effortless confidence about him that grounds the whole look.

He's wildly handsome, as usual.

When he sees me, his face lights up with a wide, genuine smile, the kind that reaches his eyes. Not a cocky little smirk, just a steady warmth that makes my heart flip.

"You clean up well," I say, trying to keep my cool.

"You too." His gaze lingers, and then he brushes the crux of my elbow lightly. "Come on, I want to introduce you to my mom."

He leads me through the crowd, weaving us past clusters of people holding champagne flutes and gesturing animatedly toward the art. The space feels alive, buzzing with energy, but Liam moves through it with ease, his hand just grazing my arm to keep us from getting separated.

When we reach Mr. and Mrs. Donovan, they're deep in conversation with another couple. Liam clears his throat softly, catching their attention.

"This is Birdie Collins," he says, his voice steady but with a hint of pride. "My good friend. She's an artist, too."

David's sharp eyes flick to me, narrowing slightly as they sweep over me. He glances back at Liam with a subtle, questioning raise of his brow. It's quick, a silent exchange, but I catch it. Then he turns back to me, his expression shifting into a practiced, charming smile.

"Ah, Miss Collins," he says smoothly, his tone polished and even. "We spoke briefly at the showcase, didn't we?"

"Yes, and it was an honor," I reply, keeping my voice steady even as my stomach twists.

"It's always nice to see such young talent." His smile doesn't quite reach his eyes before he excuses himself, murmuring something about catching up with someone across the room.

Mrs. Donovan gives me a brief, apologetic smile before following after him, leaving Liam and me standing there in the awkward vacuum they've left behind.

I glance at Liam, whose jaw is clenched tight, his hand shifting awkwardly in his pocket as he watches them disappear into the crowd. His expression is a mix of embarrassment, frustration, and something deeper—something resigned, like this is a dance he knows too well.

"Sorry about him," Liam mutters, his voice low, almost bitter. "It's—" He stops, exhales sharply, and shakes his head. "He just . . . does that."

"It's fine," I say quickly, even though my chest feels tight. "Really, it's okay."

But it isn't. Not entirely. The way David's smile barely held and the tension radiating from Liam—it leaves me wondering. Does he not like that I'm here now, standing next to his son? I'm a fellowship finalist, but I'm not here to show off or prove something. I'm just here with Liam.

"It's not fine, though. He—" He stops again, his lips pressing into a thin line. "He has a way of making people feel like they don't belong. It's not you. It's him."

I force a small smile. "Well, good thing I'm used to being underestimated."

He runs a hand through his hair, frustration giving way to something softer. "You shouldn't have to be. You deserve more than two seconds of his time."

I try to brush it off, but there's a prickle of disappointment creeping up, settling like a splinter beneath my skin. I've seen Liam do the same thing—shutting people out when he's done with a conversation. But it's different with David. He isn't brushing me off out of habit; he just doesn't think I'm worth the effort.

And Liam sees that—feels it, too, on my behalf.

Rather than dwelling on it, we turn our attention to the exhibits, walking slowly through the rooms, studying the pieces in silence. The art around us is stunning, everything from sleek modern sculptures to intricate, gravity-defying installations.

It's humbling, and it fills me with a kind of quiet awe. A renewed drive to create.

We stop in front of a vivid, abstract painting, its sweeping lines and textures drawing me in, when Liam shifts closer, his voice low. "Hey, thanks for tagging along tonight."

I glance at him, surprised. "Of course."

It's like a gift for me to be here, soaking in the art and finding the tiniest spark of inspiration again. And he's thanking *me*?

"No, I mean it," he says, his gaze steady on the painting, like he's gathering his thoughts. "This is the first event like this I've gone to where I don't feel like I have to grit my teeth and fake my way through it. Even with my dad being his usual self, I actually feel like I can enjoy it. Like I'm just . . . here, at a gallery opening, with you."

His words are simple, but there's something about them that makes my chest ache.

"Good," I say softly. "Because I'm very glad I came."

He smiles, small and genuine, and we move on.

We're standing in front of a towering piece covered in platinum luster, the light catching every fold and ripple in its surface, when a deep voice calls out from behind us. I turn to find David again, this time with a woman beside him, elegant and striking. She has cropped auburn hair and sharp green eyes that I would recognize anywhere.

"Claire Mahler," David says. "This is my son and his friend Bridget Collins. She's in the running for the Dayton fellowship."

My heart skips a beat. *The* Claire Mahler. Fellow member of the selection committee. World-renowned ceramicist. A living legend.

"Hello," I say, nearly breathless. "It's such an incredible honor to meet you."

Claire smiles warmly, extending her hand. "Hi, Birdie. You're the one with the wildflower motif in your ceramics, right?"

"Yes, that's me. But I—I'm not here to try and impress anyone," I stammer. "I just wanted to see the new collection for myself."

"Don't worry," she says kindly. "I know the feeling. I was the same way at your age. Very wide-eyed and eager."

"Oh, thank you," I say, the words tumbling out. "I really have been a fan of yours for years, and I'm so inspired by your rise in the field. I'd never want to encroach where I'm unwelcome."

"You are very much welcome here." She gives me an easy, gracious smile. "Will you tell me a little about your own work? This isn't a test, so no pressure."

My nerves slowly settle. It takes me a few seconds to gather my thoughts, and then I launch into an explanation that's part ramble, part stammer, with a bit of awkward gesturing thrown in.

She listens attentively, her expression open and encouraging, and from there, we fall into an unexpectedly easy conversation. She's thoughtful, genuinely curious about my projects, even offering a few helpful suggestions. It's surreal—this moment of being noticed by someone whose work has always been a beacon for me.

I'm so absorbed that I barely register the faint pulsing at my temples. But as she tells me about her latest series, the feeling intensifies. The gallery lights seem sharper. The noise around us grows louder.

My vision blurs at the edges. A creeping sense of nausea builds in my gut, and I'm suddenly, desperately dizzy.

I try to keep my composure, but my body has other plans. A sharp, stabbing pain pierces through my head, and my knees buckle.

"Are you alright?" Claire asks, her voice gentle but alarmed.

"I . . . I'm sorry," I manage, forcing a tight smile despite the pounding in my skull. "I think I just need a moment."

Without waiting for a response, I turn away, barely registering the shared look of concern between Liam and his father. My sole focus is on escaping the suffocating crush of noise and light in the gallery. Each step sends another jolt of nausea through me, the pain in my head building like a relentless drumbeat.

I push open the heavy gallery door and step into the cool night air. The sharp contrast of quiet and chill feels like a relief, but it's fleeting. Leaning against the wall, I breathe deeply, trying to steady myself.

It's no use.

The migraine has me firmly in its grip now, dragging me under. My stomach twists violently, and I clutch at the wall for support. There's no stopping it—the rising wave, the inevitable conclusion.

The vomit comes suddenly, spilling out onto my shoes and splattering against the cold concrete. The humiliation hits almost as hard as the pain, and for a moment, I squeeze my eyes shut, willing the world to just slow down.

Behind me, I hear the faint creak of the door and a familiar voice cutting through the haze. "Birdie?"

Chapter Seventeen

LIAM

BIRDIE PUKED. There's vomit on her shoes, and she's doubled over, struggling to catch her breath, the remnants of whatever composure she had left splattered on the pavement.

Not exactly an elegant exit, but at least she made an impression.

Tears are streaming down her cheeks, her breaths coming in shallow gasps, and I wish I could wave a hand and take this moment away for her. Erase it, rewind it, do anything to spare her from this.

For a moment, I just stand there, trying to figure out the best approach. She's already embarrassed enough, and the last thing she probably wants is me charging in like a bull in a china shop.

But she needs me, needs something steady to hold on to, so I push forward.

"Birdie, baby," I murmur, keeping my voice low and gentle as I crouch down beside her. "Hey, you okay?"

Her watery eyes dart to mine, filled with both misery and mortification. She shakes her head faintly, and I can see the effort it's taking for her to stay upright.

"M—migraine," she stutters out.

"Okay," I say softly, inching closer without crowding her. "Let's get you sorted out, yeah? No rush, no judgment. Just me and you."

She wipes at her eyes with the back of her hand, smearing what's left of her makeup. "They think . . . I'm a mess?"

I shake my head, already reaching for her arm to help her up. "Nah, it's not like you planned to projectile vomit all over the sidewalk."

She lets out a wet, shaky laugh. "Un . . . helpful."

"Yeah, I'm not exactly great at this stuff," I admit, sliding my arm around her waist to steady her. "But I can be good at getting you out of here. Let's go."

Birdie leans into me, her body trembling. The migraine's clearly wrecking her, and I don't know how long these things usually last, but I know enough to get her anywhere other than here.

"Okay, okay," I mutter as I scan the street. "Let's just get you to my car."

"Your . . . dad."

"We don't need to explain anything to my dad or Claire right now," I say gently, shifting my grip to support more of her weight. "You just need to lie down."

She shakes her head weakly. "But they'll won—"

"Screw them," I cut in, keeping my tone firm but soft enough not to jar her. "They'll live. You're the priority right now, Birdie. You're about to collapse out here. Let's get you somewhere you can rest."

She hesitates, then nods, her eyes closing as if the simple act of agreeing takes too much energy. I guide her carefully toward my car, keeping my movements slow and steady, making sure she doesn't have to do more than shuffle along.

When we reach the car, I open the passenger door and ease her inside, tilting the seat back so she can lie down. She covers her eyes with her arm, trying to block out even the dim streetlights.

"Just breathe," I say, crouching beside her and brushing a stray strand of hair from her face. "We'll figure everything else out later. How's the pain?"

"Better," she mumbles, her voice thick with exhaustion. "I just need . . . dark. Quiet."

"Got it." I shut the door gently, then slide into the driver's seat. "We'll be at my place in ten. I've got blackout curtains and aspirin. And you can sleep it off there, okay?"

"Okay," she whispers, her breath hitching.

I reach over, squeezing her hand briefly before pulling away. I'm not good at physical or emotional comfort, but if I can get her through this, maybe that'll be enough. My chest tightens as I feel her pain, and it's like there's a weight pressing on me, freezing up my words.

Birdie's strong, but that doesn't mean she has to be invincible all the time. She's always trying to prove that she's got it together, but she deserves someone to lean on when things get hard. Even now, she's trying to apologize, trying to hold it together.

She doesn't have to do that, not with me.

I grip the wheel a little tighter, focusing on the road ahead, each turn bringing us closer to my place. The hum of the engine and the rhythm of the tires on the pavement steady my thoughts. Right now, that's what matters—getting her somewhere safe, quiet, where she can rest.

It hits me that I could've taken her back to her own place— probably should've. But for whatever reason, my mind jumped to this, to bringing her to my house. Maybe because I didn't want her to be alone, or maybe because I didn't want to leave her. Either way, this felt like the only option that made sense.

We pull up to my place, and I cut the engine. Chase is gone for the night—probably off at some party, making the most of his Friday. That's one less thing to worry about. I unbuckle my seat belt and turn to Birdie.

She's already trying to push herself up, but her body sags and trembles with exhaustion. "Hey, easy," I say as I rush to her side. "Let's take it slow."

I help her out of the car, and we pause on the porch together. She needs to catch her breath, to steady herself. So, for a moment, I just let her lean against me. It's quiet, grounding, and I hope it's enough to give her even a sliver of peace.

When her breathing evens out, I glance toward the bench tucked against the porch railing. "Come on, let's sit for a second," I murmur, easing her down onto it. She leans back, her shoulders slumping.

"I'm gonna take these off before we go in," I add softly, crouching down to unbuckle the strap on her shoe. She shifts forward, fumbling with the clasp herself, but I gently bat her hands away. "I got it, don't worry."

She lets out a tired huff. "So embarrassing."

"It's really not," I reply simply, sliding her puke-stained shoes off and setting them aside by the door. "It's life. Happens to the best of us."

Once she's free of them, I slip an arm around her shoulders and guide her carefully inside. The living room is dimly lit, and the quiet hum of the fridge from the kitchen fills the space. Chase is gone for the night—thankfully—so the house feels peaceful, still.

I steer her toward the bathroom, grabbing a little Dixie cup and filling it with mouthwash. "Here," I say, holding it out to her. "Swish this around. Might help with the taste."

She accepts it, her fingers brushing mine briefly, and takes a shaky sip. As she leans over the sink, rinsing her mouth, her short hair falls forward, strands slipping into her face. Instinctively, I reach out, brushing it back and holding it gently out of the way.

Her shoulders stiffen for a moment, but she doesn't pull away. When she straightens, dabbing her lips with a tissue, her eyes meet mine, wide and searching.

"Thanks," she says softly, her voice raw and small.

I drop my hand and step back, giving her space but staying close enough to steady her if she needs it. "Anytime," I say, and there's a tightness in my chest I can't quite shake. "Come on. Let's get you to bed."

I guide her toward my room, knowing it'll be more comfortable for her than the couch. The blackout curtains are already drawn, and I quickly cut the lights. The room is quiet and dim, the perfect retreat for someone who just wants the world to stop spinning.

"Just rest for a while," I say, helping her to the bed. She crawls under the blankets, pulling them tight around her shoulders, and I slip out to the kitchen. A moment later, I return with a glass of water and a couple of aspirin. Propping up a few pillows behind her, I hand her the glass and place the pills on the nightstand.

"It's not much," I murmur, "but it might help."

She takes the water with trembling hands, and I watch as she settles deeper into the blankets, almost disappearing beneath them, like she's trying to cocoon herself from the weight of the night.

"I'll be right outside if you need anything."

I step back, lingering in the doorway for a moment. There's something about seeing her there, curled up in my bed, that tugs at something deep inside of me. It's not just about wanting to take care of her—it's the quiet trust she's giving me, even at her lowest.

I pull the door mostly shut, leaving a small gap in case she needs me, and head back to the living room alone. I sink onto the couch, staring at the ceiling as the night stretches on, the sound of her steady breathing faintly reaching me through the walls.

Eventually, I grab my phone, the glow of the screen almost too harsh after the dim light of the room. A flurry of texts from the family group chat stares back at me.

MOM
Where did you disappear to?

DAD

Is it your personal mission to embarrass us?

Do you even understand the importance of
appearances at an event like this?

I don't have the energy for them right now. Not after everything tonight. With a sigh, I power down the phone, tossing it onto
the coffee table before grabbing a sudoku book and a pen.

There's something soothing about mind puzzles, about
numbers fitting together in a predictable way—logic with rules I
can actually rely on. Usually, they're enough to clear my head, to
give me a sense of control when everything else feels off-kilter.

But as I scan the grid, the house feels oppressively quiet. The
steady hum of the fan does little to fill the silence, and no matter
how hard I try to focus, my thoughts keep drifting. All I can hear is
Birdie's soft, pained breaths from earlier, echoing faintly in my
mind.

Hours pass. I've filled out a few pages, but the quiet continues
to press in, heavy and unrelenting. I try turning on the TV for
background noise, but it feels too loud, too intrusive, so I switch it
off again.

By the time I glance at the clock, it's well past midnight. My
eyes are heavy, and I'm half-asleep, sprawled across the couch with
the sudoku book still open on my chest, the pencil dangling from
my fingertips.

That's when I hear the soft shuffle of footsteps behind me.

I turn, blinking against the dim light, and there she is—my
Birdie, standing at the end of the hallway. Her short hair is mussed
from sleep, sticking up in every direction, and her cheek is marked
with faint pillow lines. She's wrapped in one of my oversized hood-
ies, the sleeves swallowing her hands.

"Hey," I say softly, sitting up and setting the book aside.
"Shouldn't you be resting?"

She shrugs, fingers tugging at the hem. "Couldn't stay asleep. Head's still pounding, but it's a little better."

I stand and cross the room to her. "You need anything? Water? More aspirin?"

"No, just . . ." She pauses, her voice dropping. "Didn't want to be alone."

The words hit me square in the gut, and for a moment, all I can do is stare. Not only is she embarrassed and sick, but she's also lonely. It's the last thing I want her to feel.

I reach out, resting a hand lightly on her shoulder. "You're not. Come sit with me."

I guide her to the couch, grabbing a blanket and draping it over her as she sinks into the cushions. She curls up against me, tucking her legs beneath her.

"You okay here?" I ask, my voice low.

She nods, her eyes already half-closed. "Yeah. Thanks, Liam."

I don't say anything else, just grab the sudoku book again and pretend to focus on the numbers. But out of the corner of my eye, I watch as she drifts back into a fitful sleep, her breathing evening out little by little.

In a weird way, this feels exactly like where we were supposed to end up tonight. Not at the gallery, not surrounded by strangers, but here—curled up on the couch together after a long, messy night. And though I'd rather she not be sick, there's something oddly comforting in being the one she leans on.

The one to make her feel safe.

Chapter Eighteen

WE HAVEN'T TALKED about it. The onset of the migraine, the ensuing vomit, and especially not the fact that I rode in the passenger seat of his car without totally panicking.

It probably helped that I was already incapacitated. Too distracted by the pain to focus on the usual fear, the white-knuckled grip I'd otherwise have had on the door. And I haven't told him that it was the first time, in nearly a year, that I made it through a car ride without feeling like I was going to crawl out of my own skin.

He doesn't need to know that.

It's been a week since that disaster of a night, and we haven't spoken much at all. Liam's in the final stretch of the season. His last home game was Wednesday night, and after that, the team is off to the conference playoffs.

If they win, they'll secure an automatic bid for the NCAA tournament, which means even more time on the road. Part of me wants to wish him luck, to say something, but I've been holding back.

I'm embarrassed—by the way my migraine made me unravel in front of his parents and Claire (to whom I wrote a personal apology email). But also by the fact that I've let myself rely on him so heavily in such a short amount of time.

Of course, it's nice having someone willing to show up, no questions asked. But it's terrifying, too, because I can't shake the feeling that I'm about to let him see too much. All the ugly cracks in the carefully constructed version of myself I've been trying to maintain.

He doesn't seem to mind, takes it all in stride, but I . . . I think I *like* him. No, I know I like him. I'm crushing, hard. And maybe, despite my hang-ups, I want more.

I can't let myself spiral, not now. With a sigh, I push all thoughts of Liam to the back of my mind and focus on what I can control: the fellowship presentation. It's less than two weeks away, and I need it to be perfect.

Winning this would mean financial stability—no more juggling extra shifts to pay for supplies or stressing over how I'll make next semester's tuition. It would mean validation, proof that the risks I've taken, the sacrifices I've made, have been worth it. Most importantly, it would be a step toward building the career I've dreamed about since I first stepped into a studio.

It has to go right. Because if it doesn't, I don't know what plan B looks like. And that scares me more than anything else.

I boot up my laptop and pull up my presentation slides. The PowerPoint is already half-finished, but there are still tweaks to be made, details to perfect. I set my phone on silent and plug it into the charger, determined not to let any distractions pull me away.

The slides flip past: bold text, high-resolution photos of my work, a few quotes from past professors and critiques. I've laid it all out meticulously, but I still don't feel confident. There's one last piece I need to finish. A piece that will tie the whole portfolio together.

It's sitting in the studio now, waiting for its turn in the kiln next week. A ceramic vase inspired by Grecian amphorae but with my own twist—a cluster of sculpted wildflowers blooming from the rim, each petal delicately carved to symbolize growth and rebirth.

It's the most intricate work I've ever attempted, blending everything I've learned over the past three years into one cohesive form.

I poured myself into it, hoping it will reflect the transformation I've gone through, both as an artist and as a person.

For now, all I can do is wait and hope that when I open the glaze kiln next week, it'll be exactly as I envisioned.

Taking a deep breath, I try to refocus. I flip through the rest of the photos Liam took for me. There's one where I'm smiling up at the camera, my hands covered in clay, a streak of it on my cheek.

The way he captured me—laughing, carefree, in the middle of sculpting—it's like he saw a version of me I'd forgotten how to be. The me before the accident, before the stress and pressure of the fellowship.

It's strange seeing myself like that again. So happy and lively.

Usually, when I catch my reflection, all I notice are the tense lines in my face or the shadows under my eyes. But in this photo, I look so much lighter. It makes me hopeful that I can be that person again. Not my old self, but a healthier, happier version of my new self.

I turn back to my laptop, reviewing the next slide, trying to memorize my key points and transitions.

"Good afternoon, esteemed members of the fellowship committee," I mutter under my breath, pacing the room.

Liam told me not to force it, to let it flow. To speak from the heart instead of trying to impress anyone. Why is that so easy to do when he's around but nearly impossible when it's just me, alone with my doubts?

I close my eyes, centering myself, before moving on to the final slides. My phone buzzes from the counter, interrupting my focus. I glance over, expecting a calendar reminder or an email notification, but it's a text from Liam.

LIAM

can you let me up?

BIRDIE

I thought you left already!

LIAM

bus in an hour. wanted to see you first x

I press the button to buzz him in, my heart tripping over itself. The door downstairs clicks open, and I scramble to tidy up the papers and photos scattered across my living room. My stomach is doing full somersaults now, the nervous kind that come with anticipation.

A moment later, there's a light knock at my door. I swing it open to find Liam standing there, slightly winded, still in his Dayton Soccer hoodie and sweats. His cheeks are flushed from the cold, and there's something in his eyes—an intensity, a kind of vulnerability—that makes my pulse stutter.

"Hey," he says, his lopsided grin tugging at the corners of his mouth, sending a ripple of warmth through me.

"Hey yourself," I reply, leaning against the doorframe. "Shouldn't you be halfway to the tournament by now?"

"Yeah, well . . ." He rubs the back of his neck, his gaze flicking away for a second before locking back onto mine. "I wanted to see you before I left. Thought maybe . . . you'd wanna see me, too."

I grin, feeling the heat crawl up my neck. "I've never seen you act like this. So sheepish."

It's a good look on him—disarming, endearing, completely unraveling me. My crush is no longer just a quiet undercurrent; it's a full-blown tidal wave, and there's no pretending otherwise.

He lets out a huff of laughter, but then it's like a dam breaks inside him. "Look, I know I usually just say whatever's on my mind, and yeah, it gets me into trouble. But with you . . . it's different.

"You never look at me like you wish I'd shut up. But at the same time, I—I don't know, Birdie. I just want to get it right, you know? Saying the right thing, the best thing. Because making you smile feels like—God, it feels like I've finally done something right, and I just want to keep—"

I don't let him finish. The words are perfect, too perfect, and they're undoing me faster than I can manage. In one quick move, I step forward, bridge the gap between us, and thread my fingers through his hair, pulling him down into a kiss.

It's bold and reckless and everything I've wanted to do since the moment he walked through my door. And judging by the way he melts into me, his hands finding my waist like they belong there, it's everything he's wanted, too.

He groans deep in his throat, and suddenly, his arms are around me, lifting me up as if I weigh nothing. I'm pressed flush against him, my feet dangling. It's all soft lips and tentative brushes of his tongue against mine.

An overwhelming kind of need—his warmth, his touch, the way his fingers thread through my hair and grip tight, like he's afraid I might slip away.

We stumble back, and before I know it, I'm on the couch, his weight fully pressing into me. I can feel the solid length of him through the thin fabric of his sweatpants, and oh God, he's so hard already.

Heat pools low in my belly, spreading like wildfire, and I can't stop the soft gasp that escapes me.

He pauses, eyes darkening as he takes me in, like he's trying to memorize every detail. "Birdie," he murmurs, voice rough, lips brushing against my ear. "You feel so goddamn good."

I don't even recognize the sound that slips out of me in response—half whimper, half squeal. My hands slide under his hoodie, desperate to feel the heat of his skin. His breath hitches as my fingers graze his abs, and then, we're kissing again, deeper, hungrier.

His hips rock into mine, and I swear my mouth waters at the

sensation of him, hard and ready, pressing against me. My mouth. Literally. Waters. What the fresh hell is happening to me?

I've never felt like this before. Never wanted someone this much.

But then—his phone dings in his pocket. At first, we ignore it, lost in the heat of each other, but it dings again. And again. And then it's buzzing, vibrating insistently against my thigh where it's pressed between us.

"Fuck," Liam mutters, breaking the kiss, his breaths coming hard and fast. He pulls back just enough to fish the phone out of his pocket, and there's a flicker of panic in his eyes as he glances at the screen. "Shit. I have to go."

I'm still breathless, dazed, my lips swollen and tingling. "You're gonna be late, aren't you?" I ask in a whisper, even though the last thing I want is for him to leave.

He looks at me, eyes blazing with something that sends a shiver down my spine. Slowly, almost reverently, he swipes his thumb over my bottom lip, his touch lingering. "Yes, but we're not done here," he says, voice low and rough. "I promise. And—I want you to know I'll miss you this week. Okay?"

I swallow heavily. "You too."

It's a few frantic beats before he's gone, and the door clicks shut behind him. The room falls into a heavy silence, the echo of his touch still sizzling on my skin, and all I can think about is how much I want him back. How much I already miss him.

How much I *need* him, screw my defenses.

Chapter Nineteen
LIAM

THE SUN'S BARELY UP, and we're out on the practice field in Cary, prepping for the conference championships. This is it—the final stretch. Everything we've been grinding for since August comes down to these next few days.

I tap the ball lightly between my feet. Chase is across from me, stretching his quads, while a few of the guys are passing around to warm up. The grass is dewy, slick under our cleats, and all I can think about is how sticky and damp the air feels against my skin, like it's clinging to me in all the wrong ways.

It's the kind of sensation that sets my teeth on edge, makes me hyperaware of every shift in my jersey, every bead of sweat. Sensations that draw me out of the game and into my own head. Not a good place to be right now.

Chase catches my eye and smirks. "Donovan, you gonna feed me some decent service, or is that too much to ask?"

"You can fuck right off," I shoot back, flicking the ball toward him. He traps it effortlessly, laughing, and passes it back with a spin that sends it skimming just past my shin. "Keep talking, and I'll purposely shank every cross your way."

Chase rolls his eyes. "Coach wouldn't like that. I'm his golden boy."

He's all swagger, oozing confidence like he's untouchable. But underneath that cocky grin, I can sense the pressure simmering. For both of us. For all of us.

It's not just another game. This is the conference championship, and there's more at stake here than bragging rights. There are scouts in the stands—MLS reps and agents, eyes dissecting every move, every pass, every miss.

I still have next year to prove myself, but Chase doesn't. If he doesn't secure the Adidas contract this year, then he'll have to enter the draft as a senior, just like I plan to. It would be a gamble, I think, for him to take that route and risk not getting picked up.

I have a backup; Chase has staked his whole future on this.

I spin the ball with the side of my foot, letting my mind focus on its movement, on the rhythm that usually drowns out the noise. But today, it's failing.

Not just because of the sensory hell that clings to me but because I'm caught up thinking about Birdie, too. About our kiss last Friday night. The way she fit against me, the softness of her lips, the quiet sound she made in the back of her throat when I—

"Hey, earth to Liam." I blink, snapping out of it. Chase is staring at me, eyebrows raised. "You good, man? You've been kicking that ball around like it owes you money."

I grin. "I'm thinking about Birdie, actually. We kissed just before I left, and her lips were soft as hell, like—"

Chase snorts a laugh. "Jesus, man. Did you know you can keep some things to yourself? A gentleman never kisses and tells."

"You asked," I say with a shrug. I'm not embarrassed that I'm thinking about her, missing her. So, why would I bother coming up with some bullshit response instead of just telling him the truth?

Coach's whistle cuts through the air. "Bring it in, boys!"

We jog over, forming a loose huddle around him. Coach Harris has that no-nonsense look in his eye today—the one that says he expects nothing short of a dominant performance. One of our assistants, Coach Reilly, steps in with a clipboard, gesturing emphatically as Harris speaks.

"We're up against UNC," Coach says, his voice cutting

through the chilly morning air. "They're going to come at you hard, especially on the wings. Their midfield's solid, so we've got to keep it tight and make them work for every inch."

"They'll be looking to isolate our defenders," Reilly chimes in. "Don't let them pick you apart. Stay compact, stay sharp."

They're right—UNC's no joke. They've got some of the best talent in the conference, and they're hungry for a win. But so are we. And right now, all that matters is what happens on this field today, not what they've done before or what anyone expects.

The coaches keep talking, laying out our strategy in precise, clipped tones, but my mind drifts. Not to Birdie this time but to everything riding on this game. There's a scout from Orlando City up in the stands, and if I can show him what I'm made of, maybe this could be my shot at the MLS, too.

Chase elbows me, snapping me out of it. "You hear that? They're going to try and cut through your side."

"Yeah," I mutter, "no shit."

The whistle blows again, signaling the start of our pre-game drills. I fall into line, weaving through the cones, my feet moving on autopilot. Focus. Zone in. Tune out. It's a mantra I repeat in my head, over and over, willing everything else—the noise, the pressure, the sticky jersey—into silence. Just the ball. Just the game.

As we transition into a scrimmage, I finally let myself get lost in it. The solid thud of the ball as it connects with my foot, the slap of cleats against the turf, the grunt of effort as I shoulder past a defender. It's like music—the only kind I've ever really understood.

The rhythm of play takes over, washing out the static in my head and replacing it with something clear, something simple. But scrimmages don't last forever.

When the game kicks off thirty minutes later, it's at a breakneck pace. UNC isn't messing around. They press hard, their midfielders controlling the tempo, trying to box us in. I'm sprinting up the wing, lungs burning, heart pounding.

Santi and Amir are holding the line in the back, and they're a damn wall. Amir's as solid as ever, shutting down any attackers who try to break through, while Santi is chirping nonstop, getting into the heads of their strikers.

I spot an opening and call for the ball. Chase nods, threading it through two defenders with a slick pass. I take off down the sideline, cutting in just as a defender lunges at me. I sidestep him, glance up, and Chase makes a run toward the far post.

"Hadden!" I yell, swinging my leg back. The cross flies off my foot, arcing over the heads of two UNC defenders, curving just enough to drop right in front of Chase. He traps it like it's glued to his boot, takes one touch to steady himself, and then slams it past the keeper.

"One-nil, baby!" Chase yells, pumping his fist in the air. I sprint over, adrenaline coursing through me as I slap him on the back. The team swarms us, and for a second, I let myself get lost in it. But I know better than to relax now.

UNC comes back at us hard, like a wounded animal. Their midfielders are relentless, pinning us deep in our half, trying to claw their way back into the game. For a solid fifteen minutes, it's all defense.

Finally, UNC breaks through. Their forward manages to squeeze past, latching onto a through ball, and slams it into the bottom corner. 1-1. The stadium roars to life, and it's a whole new game.

The equalizer shakes us, but it's like a jolt of electricity running through my veins. I steal the ball from one of their wingers, cutting him off before he can send it into the box, and sprint down the sideline. My legs are burning, but I push harder, faster.

I cut inside, dodging a defender, and suddenly, there's open space ahead of me. Coach is barking orders at me, but I don't need them. I know what to do. I drive forward, the goal coming into focus.

I cut past another defender, and the box opens up. I've got one chance. I take a deep breath, focus on the ball, and swing my leg back. The shot is clean, the kind you dream about. It rockets past the keeper's outstretched hands and slams into the back of the net.

The stadium explodes. I barely have time to register what's happening before Chase tackles me, nearly knocking me over. "Top bins, baby!" he shouts in my ear, laughing like a wild man.

But it's not over yet. There's still time on the clock, and UNC isn't going down without a fight. They push back with everything they've got. Their forwards are throwing themselves at our defense, desperate to equalize again.

Amir blocks a shot with his chest, grunting as he absorbs the impact, while Marco, our left-back, clears the rebound with a powerful kick.

The pressure is relentless. I'm gasping for breath, every muscle in my body screaming for a break, but I can't stop now. I won't. Not when we're this close.

There's a corner kick for UNC in the final minute. The ball flies into the box, and it's chaos—legs and elbows everywhere. But Amir rises above everyone, clearing it with a monster header. The ref's whistle blows, and that's it.

We've done it. 2-1. We've secured our bid for the NCAA tournament.

The guys are hugging, shouting, piling on top of each other. Coach is actually smiling—hell, I didn't even know he could do that. I just stand there for a second, hands on my knees, letting it all sink in.

"Donovan!" Chase yells, dragging me into a bear hug. "We did it."

"Fuck yeah, we did."

"We shouldn't have let that soft goal in."

I huff, pulling away from him. "Can you just celebrate in peace for once?"

"No, no I cannot," he says, grinning wide.

We make our way back to the locker room, and it's pure chaos —guys spraying water bottles like they're champagne, shouting victory chants, and slapping each other on the back. And I'm caught somewhere between exhilaration and exhaustion.

It would be nice to have a moment to just come down from it all, to breathe, to let the high ebb away on my own terms. Instead, it's an overwhelming sort of frenzy, the noise and movement bouncing off the walls and hammering against my already worn-out senses.

The coaches finally corral us for a quick debrief, where Harris tries to look stern, but the gleam in his eyes gives him away. "We came here to get the job done, and you did just that. We've secured our spot in the tournament, boys."

The locker room erupts again, guys pounding their lockers and shouting at the top of their lungs. I hang back, my body starting to feel the strain—aching legs, burning lungs. Part of me just wants to slip away to a quiet corner, close my eyes, and let the exhaustion hit me full force.

But there's no escape yet. Once the debrief wraps, we pile back onto the bus to head to the hotel. The second we board, I make a beeline for the one and only lone seat at the back. I sink into it, hoping I'll finally get a bit of peace.

But Chase has other plans.

"Hey, buddy!" His head pops over the back of my seat like an overexcited puppy. He rests his chin on my shoulder, grinning ear to ear. "You coming out with us tonight, or do I have to drag you along kicking and screaming?"

I lean my head back against the seat, groaning. "You realize I'm running on fumes, right? We've got a bus ride back to Dayton at the crack of dawn."

He rolls his eyes. "Yeah, yeah, you can be a grumpy old man

tomorrow. Tonight, we celebrate. You owe us at least one round for that beauty of a goal."

I sigh, rubbing my hands over my face. In truth, what I really want is to go back to the room, crawl into bed, maybe call Birdie. Hear her voice, tell her about the game, ask how she's been. But the guys . . . they deserve this. They've worked just as hard as I have. And if celebrating with them means a few hours of pretending, then so be it.

"Fine," I say, giving in. "I'll go. But if I decide to rot in a corner, that's on you."

He slaps me on the shoulder. "That's the spirit. We'll get you some shots to wake you up."

Once we're back at the hotel, we drop our stuff and start to deflate. Coach gives us the usual speech about curfew. "Midnight, gentlemen. I don't care where you are or what state you're in—your asses better be on this bus tomorrow at 7:00 a.m. sharp."

We're dismissed, and the guys are already plotting which bar to hit up. I take a quick shower, change into a clean shirt, and before I know it, we're piling into Ubers to hit up some local dive.

The bar is packed with a mix of locals and college kids. It's not our territory, so the vibe is cautious at first. But there's no confrontation, no territorial chest-thumping. This is soccer, not a Southern favorite like football, so we're mostly ignored by the regulars.

It's awkward at first, just the team clustered at the bar, but then, "To the conference champs!" someone yells, and the tension breaks.

Soon, we're clinking glasses and laughing like we're on top of the world.

It all becomes a blur pretty quickly. Every time I turn around, there's another drink waiting for me—vodka, rum, something blue that Chase assures me is "the good stuff." I'm trying to pace myself, but every time I manage to put my glass down, another one appears in my hand like magic.

"Donovan, you lightweight, catch up!" Santi yells, thrusting a beer toward me. I'm pretty sure he's already slurring his words, but I grab it anyway, taking a long swig. The world's starting to spin a little, but in a good way.

Everything's warm and fuzzy, like I'm floating just above reality.

At some point, Chase pulls me onto the makeshift dance floor. I've got no rhythm left, my limbs flailing more than anything resembling dancing, but I'm laughing so hard my sides hurt. Someone starts a chant—"Don-o-van! Don-o-van!"—and it just makes me double over, nearly spilling my drink.

The lights are flashing, the music's pounding, and everything's moving in slow motion. By this point, I've lost track of time. I don't even know if it's before or after midnight, and I don't care. Coach's rules be damned.

"Chase!" I shout over the noise. "I think I'm about to lose all motor function if—" The rest of my sentence gets lost in a loud hiccup, and Chase doubles over, cackling like it's the funniest thing he's ever heard.

Eventually, I find myself slumped in a corner booth, my head resting against the back of the seat. The team's still going strong, their laughter and shouts blending into a chaotic background hum, but I'm teetering on the edge of sleep. My body feels heavy, my thoughts slow and syrupy.

My phone buzzes in my pocket, and I fumble for it, squinting at the screen through bleary eyes.

BIRDIE

congrats on the win, soccer star. miss ya over here

A dopey smile spreads across my face, and I try to type back a response, but the letters keep dancing around the screen, refusing to cooperate. Giving up, I snap a selfie—eyes half-closed, a lazy grin on my face—and hit Send.

"Don-o-van!" Chase's voice booms as he materializes out of nowhere, slinging an arm around my shoulders. "You're not done yet, are you?"

I blink up at him, the effort it takes to form words feeling monumental. "I think . . . I might actually be . . . done."

He laughs, slapping my back. "Alright, Grandpa. Let's get you back before you *really* embarrass yourself."

The next thing I know, I'm being half dragged, half carried out of the bar, Chase's laughter ringing in my ears. The cool night air hits me like a wall, sharp and sobering, and I stumble, almost face-planting on the sidewalk.

"Easy, tiger," Amir says, appearing on my other side to grab my arm and steady me.

"Yeah, yeah," I mumble, leaning heavily on both of them as they haul me back toward the hotel. The world spins around me in a dizzying blur, but I don't mind it so much.

Somewhere in the back of my mind, I know I'm going to regret this in the morning—the pounding headache, the dry mouth, the vague embarrassment of a night half remembered. But right now? Right now, everything feels good.

The win, the team, the drinks, and Birdie's text still buzzing in my pocket.

For tonight, I've got everything I need.

Chapter Twenty

BIRDIE

IT'S PAST MIDNIGHT, and sleep is nowhere in sight. I've been tossing and turning for hours because my mind refuses to settle. I know I need rest, more time to recover. That migraine from nearly two weeks ago still lingers in the back of my mind, a warning I can't ignore.

It proves I've been pushing myself too hard—that I'm not invincible, no matter how much I pretend otherwise. Yet I can't force myself to slow down, can't quiet the thoughts swirling through my head.

Right now, it's not even the fellowship presentation that's keeping me up. It's him. Liam Donovan.

I stare at the ceiling, replaying that kiss over and over. Liam taking that small, unsure step into my apartment. The way his lips felt against mine, soft but urgent, like he'd been holding on to those feelings for far too long. The warmth of his hands on my waist . . .

And the way his touch still lingers—a quiet hum of desire that flares up every time I think about it.

It's driving me up the wall, how one kiss has unraveled me so completely, leaving me restless, yearning for more. So, when my phone lights up on the nightstand again, dragging me out of the loop inside my head, I lunge for it.

For the past hour, Liam's been sending me a flurry of messages. Texts that range from sweet to completely nonsensical. Half of them I can't even decipher, like they're written in some code only for the drunk to understand.

LIAM

birdie birdie birdie. guess what

ur lips r a gift

i think i lost my shoe

birdie i think i left my head in the bathroom??? or maybe it was the bar???

I bite back a smile, turning onto my stomach and propping myself up on my elbows. It's entertaining, sure, but it's hard to know if it's drunk honesty or just noise. Sometimes intoxicated ramblings are just that—nonsensical and fleeting, gone by morning.

My phone buzzes again.

LIAM

miss u. ur so pretty

gonna kiss u forever

I laugh quietly into my pillow. God, he's such a dork. A part of me is tempted to let him continue his tirade without responding, but then another message pops up that makes me pause.

LIAM

birdie. need 2 talk 2 u

My heart stutters. I'm supposed to be sleeping, trying to get my head on straight before tomorrow, but who am I kidding? My eyes are wide open, and curiosity's got me hooked.

I swipe to call him. The phone rings. And rings. And rings. Each second stretches out longer than the last, worry creeping up the back of my neck. Just when I'm about to hang up, there's a click, and his voice filters through, all soft and sleepy.

"Birdieee, you there?"

Relief floods through me. "Yes. How drunk are you right now?"

He chuckles, a low, lazy sound that makes my stomach flip. "Why? Are you judging me?"

I smile. "Never."

"Good," he breathes out, a bit of a sigh mixed with a chuckle. "Because now that I know how good your lips feel on mine, you're never getting away from me."

I flush, my cheeks burning hot. "Oh, my God."

"That was a good kiss, wasn't it?" he asks, sounding almost boyish, like he needs to hear me say it.

I bite my lip, and a wave of butterflies swarms in my stomach. "Yeah, it was. Really good."

"The best," he says, like it's the most obvious thing in the world. "We should do it again."

I can hear the smile in his voice, and my heart skips a beat. God, he's such a flirt, even when he's halfway conscious. "Oh yeah?" I tease. "When were you thinking?"

"I'll come find you when I get back tomorrow. And I'm gonna kiss the hell out of you."

I bite my lip to keep from squealing like a teenager. "It sounds like you've had quite the night."

"You have no idea." There's a rustling on his end, like he's shifting in bed. "But none of it matters because . . ." He trails off, and for a second, I think he's fallen asleep. Then he speaks again, quieter this time. "Because I wanted to talk to you."

"Well, here I am," I say, my voice softening.

"Good." There's a beat of silence, and then, "Do you ever think I'm, like, too much sometimes?"

"Too much?"

"Yeah," he says, sounding small. Vulnerable in a way I've never heard before. "I talk too much. Say the wrong things. I don't know when to shut up. I mean . . . I dunno."

My chest tightens. "No, you're not too much. Not for me."

"Really?" His voice lifts, like he doesn't quite believe me.

"Really," I say firmly. "You're . . . exactly right, actually."

There's another long pause, and I wonder if he's processing my words or just too drunk to reply. Then, finally, he says, "Birdie?"

"Yeah?"

"You're my favorite."

My breath hitches. "Liam—"

"God, I'm so tired. I think I might actually be floating."

"Oh, okay," I say, biting back a laugh. "You should get some rest, then."

I can almost picture him now, sprawled out on his hotel bed, eyes half-lidded with that goofy grin on his face. The thought makes my stomach flutter, warm and light.

"Sleep tight, Liam," I murmur.

"Mmhmm," he mumbles, his voice slurring with exhaustion. "Night."

I wait for the line to disconnect, but it doesn't. Instead, I hear the soft sound of his breathing—slow, steady, and unmistakably on its way to a snore. My heart melts.

"Liam?" I whisper, smiling even though he can't see me. "You're supposed to hang up, you know."

No response, just the faint, rhythmic sound of his breathing. He's out. Completely.

With a quiet laugh, I take my phone away from my ear and press the red button to end the call. Then I'm left lying there with a head full of him—his voice, his laugh, the promise of his lips on mine. He called me his favorite.

It's intoxicating, this feeling that's wrapping itself around me, warm and insistent. I didn't know I could feel like this again—so excited to wake up tomorrow. So hopeful, like the world's suddenly a little brighter just because he's in it.

. . .

It's not even seven, and I've already been up for hours, flipping through my presentation slides—tweaking, rearranging, and trying not to let my nerves completely devour me.

By the time Friday rolls around, I know I'll be a wreck. They've given me the last presentation slot, the so-called "grand finale" of the week. That means I'll be facing the fellowship panel with every other finalist's brilliance still fresh in their minds. It's like the universe decided my stress level wasn't quite high enough.

And then there's Liam. Because why not add another layer of chaos to my already spiraling thoughts?

He said he'd find me yesterday when he got back, and I waited. I sat there like a lovesick fool, jumping every time my phone buzzed, checking the door every time I heard footsteps in the hall. But nothing. Radio silence.

Sena tried to reassure me last night, saying he was probably just wiped out from the away game. But that didn't stop the over-thinking. What if he forgot? What if he was just drunk talking that night, and now he doesn't mean what he said?

I'm brushing my teeth, staring blankly at the bathroom mirror, replaying every overanalyzed second of our last conversation. There's still an hour until my first class, and I've been half-heart-edly running through my presentation notes to keep my mind occupied.

But all that goes out the window when there's an unexpected knock at the door.

My heart leaps into my throat.

I spit, rinse, and nearly trip over myself as I rush to answer it. I probably look like a half-drowned raccoon, but I can't bring myself to care. I yank the door open, and there he is.

Liam Donovan, in all his glory.

He's standing there in his Dayton Soccer hoodie, hair still damp from a shower, looking way too awake for this hour. That lazy, crooked grin of his—the one that makes my knees feel like jelly—is firmly in place.

"Hey, Birdie," he says like he's done this a thousand times before.

"Hey," I squeak and then clear my throat. "I didn't, um, expect to see you this early. Or, you know, here at all."

"You said you were picking up your pieces from the kiln this morning, right?" He rubs the back of his neck, looking almost sheepish. "Figured I'd walk with you."

I blink. "You . . . remembered?"

"Of course." He steps past me, casually slipping inside the apartment without waiting for an invitation. "I also remembered that I promised to help you with any last-minute fellowship stuff this week."

"Oh, right." I tug awkwardly at the frayed hem of my sweat-shirt, unsure if I should be flattered or mortified by how much I was spiraling yesterday. "I thought maybe . . . I'd see you yesterday."

He winces, guilt flashing across his face. "Yeah, sorry about that. I slept most of the day. And then I realized I had a midterm this week that I'd totally forgotten about. Spent all day cramming so I could be free to help you now."

"Oh." My heart does a weird flip. Relief floods through me, and I feel a little ridiculous for how worked up I got over nothing.

"Yeah, so," he says, rocking on his heels, hands tucked into his hoodie pocket. "You ready to head out? Or do you need a few more hours of staring at those slides you've definitely memorized by now?"

I let out a laugh, my nerves loosening. "Okay, okay. Let's go."

We leave my apartment together, my bag slung over my shoulder and Liam's hands shoved deep into his pockets. It's a short walk to campus, and everything feels deceptively normal. Just a regular morning with my buddy ol' pal.

But as we near the arts building, my mind drifts back to that night. To the way he sounded on the phone, all sleepy and sweet, telling me he'd kiss the hell out of me when he saw me again.

Now he's here, walking beside me, but he hasn't brought it up. Hasn't even tried to hold my hand.

I glance at him out of the corner of my eye, trying to gauge his mood. He looks focused, like he's lost in thought, his brow furrowed ever so slightly. But then, without warning, he stops in his tracks, turning to face me.

"You're acting weird. Very . . . un-Birdie-like."

I snort, crossing my arms over my chest. Of course he would notice. "Yeah, well, it's probably because . . . the other night, you said some things."

"What kinds of things?"

My cheeks flush. "You know . . . about me."

His lips twitch into a teasing smile, his eyes sparkling with amusement. "I'm listening."

My stomach flips. "Like . . . you said you'd kiss me when you saw me again. But you haven't—"

He steps closer, leaning in just enough to make my heart skip a beat. "Birdie, baby," he murmurs, his voice dropping low, "if you want me to kiss you again, you should just come right out and say it."

The nerve. My mouth opens, but no sound comes out, and the smug glint in his eyes tells me he's fully enjoying this. "So, you weren't just drunk when you said that? You didn't forget?"

"Course not. How could I forget something like that?"

I'm standing there, rooted to the spot, my mind racing. And then he's cupping my cheek, his thumb brushing over my bottom lip. His touch is so gentle, reverent and lovely.

"You gonna ask me, or do I have to make the first move?"

"Kiss me," I murmur, barely able to get the words out. "Please."

That's all it takes. He's on me in a flash, his mouth crashing into mine, his hands sliding around my waist to pull me close. I gasp, but then I'm melting into him, my fingers tangling in his hair.

God, this is what I wanted, what I needed.

It's all heat and urgency, like he's been waiting days for this moment. And maybe he has. There's a certain tension in his grip, the way he's holding me like I might slip away if he loosens his hold.

His hand slides to the back of my neck, holding me in place as he deepens the kiss. I'm dizzy, my head spinning, but it's all him—his touch, his taste, the sizzling heat between us. His teeth graze against my lip, a sharp pull, and I moan, instinctively leaning into him.

When he pulls back, his forehead rests against mine. "I've been thinking about that for days," he mutters, low and raspy. "About you. About this."

I laugh softly, my hands still fisted in his hoodie. "You're such a sap."

"Yeah, well," he says, grinning. "You make me one."

The sound of distant laughter reminds me where we are, and I pull back slightly. But Liam doesn't seem to care. He just grabs my hand and starts walking again, like we've been doing this since the start. Like nothing else has changed between us.

We reach the arts building, and my heart is pounding for a whole new reason now. I'm about to see my final piece—the one I've poured my heart into over the last few weeks. The one that could make or break my chances at the fellowship.

Liam squeezes my hand, his eyes softening. "You ready?"

I nod, but my stomach flips as we step into the studio. It's quiet and empty at this hour, the silence almost too much. My footsteps echo as we head toward my workspace.

There's a note propped up on my table, written in Professor Hall's unmistakable scrawl:

Pulled it out early this A.M. Didn't want to risk anyone's grubby hands getting on the masterpiece. Good job, Birdie.

I read it once, then again, my heart beating a little faster. A compliment from Hall is rare. But I don't want to read too much into it. Not yet.

Liam stands beside me, our shoulders brushing as I reach for the cloth covering my piece. My fingers tremble slightly, betraying the calm I'm trying to project. I pull the sheet back slowly, hesitation curling in my chest.

And holy shit, it's absolutely perfect. Better than I even imagined.

The glaze caught every detail, the wildflowers blooming from the rim as if they grew there naturally. The soft, muted colors are exactly as I'd hoped, blending into each other seamlessly. It's breathtaking—like it has a life of its own.

Liam exhales beside me, his voice low with awe. "Birdie . . . it's incredible."

I can't believe it—everything I envisioned, brought to life. A masterpiece, if I've ever seen one.

My chest tightens, and I blink quickly, trying to ward off the tears threatening to fall. "I—I didn't think it'd turn out like this," I whisper.

Liam chuckles softly, bumping his shoulder against mine. "Why not? You're the best there is."

I laugh, a shaky, breathless sound. "That's a bold statement, Donovan."

"Bold," he says, wrapping an arm around my shoulders. "And truthful."

I stare at the piece in front of me, flushed with both relief and pride, and think that maybe he's right. Maybe I can win this.

Chapter Twenty-One

LIAM

COCKTAILS ARE ALREADY FLOWING by the time I arrive at the Donovan family estate. The scent of roasted meat and garlic fills the air, and the weight of my mother's perfectionism hangs in every corner of the house.

I step inside, and the pressure of the evening settles on my shoulders like a heavy coat. My brows furrow as I make my way through the foyer. The polished floors gleam under the chandelier, and the air hums with quiet, practiced conversation. A house that feels more like a showroom than a home.

But then again, I guess it was never really *my* home to begin with.

I move past the open door to the dining room, where a long wooden table is meticulously set with gleaming silverware and fresh floral arrangements. I have no clue what's happening here, but everything about the evening seems so perfectly orchestrated, so on brand for my parents.

I glance into the living room, where people are gathered, drinks in hand, chatting casually. A few familiar faces linger among the crowd—alumni from their university days, some of my dad's associates—but none I want to talk to. I'm not here for small talk, anyway.

Stepping back toward the foyer, I veer into the hallway, out of sight but still within earshot. From this vantage point, I can see the whole scene play out. My father is holding court at the center of the living room—surrounded by a few of his business associates, a couple of college friends, and a handful of faces I don't recognize. Fellow students, I assume.

Pulling out my phone, I quickly scan for context, confused and irritated. A couple of clicks later, I find an event on our shared Google calendar: *Fellowship Finalists Dinner*. A last-minute addition that no one bothered to mention to me.

Not even Birdie, who I just spent the night with—finalizing her presentation, calming her nerves. She should be here, shouldn't she?

I glance over the crowd once more, scanning for her familiar face, but she's nowhere to be found. Instead, I clash eyes with my dad. He looks calm—too calm. It's the kind of calm that hides something else entirely, something calculated. It only serves to confuse me more.

Taking a couple of steps toward the bar, I find my mom deep in conversation with an older man. I offer the obligatory smile as I greet her. "Liam," she says warmly, reaching out to hug me. "So good to see you. Have you had a chance to make the rounds?"

"No, not really. I just got here."

She frowns, tilting her head in that subtle way that always feels like a reprimand. "Well, I do hope you make an effort. Just . . . please don't give your father another reason to lecture you tonight. He's already in one of his moods."

"I'm not gonna step out of line," I mutter, disheartened. "Don't worry."

She pats my shoulder gently, but her attention is already drifting back to her previous conversation. It's a familiar dance of forced politeness and quiet judgment.

Sighing, I pull out my phone again—still nothing from Birdie. Maybe she declined the invitation. I guess it's better that she's focused on the actual presentation tomorrow. She doesn't need to waste her energy on this stuff. One extra night of anxious schmoozing isn't going to help her, anyway.

The chatter dies down a bit as people start wandering toward the dining room. I follow, still scanning the room, and send one last message:

LIAM

hey, where are you? dinner's starting

My father's already ushering people to the table, arranging everyone in their "proper" spots like it's some kind of power play. The whole room feels suffocating, like a show he's making me sit through for his own amusement. I glance at my phone again, and my pulse kicks up. Still nothing.

I check the door. No sign of her. I glance around the dining room, scanning the faces more carefully now, my chest tightening with each second. My eyes catch my dad's again, and something about the way he looks at me—calm, strangely satisfied—makes the feeling in my gut worse.

Something is most definitely off. I don't know what it is yet, but I know this feeling well. It's the one I get when I'm not in control of a situation—when things aren't going the way I expect. The same feeling I had when James first left for the minors. The same feeling I get when the game plan shifts mid-match and I don't know where to position myself.

And tonight, for reasons I can't yet put into words, it feels like I'm about to lose.

I push back from the doorway and cross the room. "Dad," I say, pulling him to the side, away from the rest of the group. "Can we wait a minute? I think Birdie must be running late."

"I didn't invite Miss Collins here tonight."

I freeze, my pulse skipping. "What do you mean?"

"What I've just told you," he says flatly, straightening his tie as if this is a perfectly normal thing to drop on someone. "Miss Collins was not invited to this dinner."

"Why the hell not?" Heat creeps up my neck. *This isn't happening. This can't be happening.*

He gives me that look—the one that's half disappointment, half condescension. "She's had enough of a leg up, don't you think?"

I stare at him, the words barely registering. "What are you talking about?"

"She was already invited to the gallery opening," he says in that clipped, dismissive tone that always grates on me. "And I know you've been helping her with the presentation. That's an unfair advantage."

The words hit like a punch to the gut, knocking the air out of me. My chest tightens, and for a moment, I can't even breathe. "You're telling me you excluded her because of me?"

His gaze doesn't waver. "It's not personal, Liam. It's about fairness."

"That's ridiculous," I spit, low and furious. "Birdie deserves to be here. She's worked harder than anyone."

"Enough," he snaps. "I'm not discussing this with you."

But the damage is already done. My blood is boiling, and all I can see is Birdie's face—the way she would have walked in here, steady and determined, ready to hold her own. And now? She doesn't even get the chance. All because of some petty, manufactured nonsense my father's conjured up to suit his narrative.

I realize then that he's already written her off. No matter how brilliant her presentation tomorrow, no matter how hard she's worked, he's decided she's not the "right fit" for this fellowship. But he's not the only judge, and if there's any way to level the playing field, I'll find it.

"She's gonna be devastated," I mutter, the anger simmering just beneath the surface. "You have no idea what this is going to do to her."

"She'll recover," he says with that maddening calm. "This isn't the end of the world."

It feels like the end of something. The tension coils tighter in my chest, suffocating. "You don't know her at all," I say through gritted teeth. "You don't know what this means to her."

He doesn't respond, just gives me that same detached look he always does when he thinks he's won. And maybe he has. There's no undoing what he's already decided. He's never going to see Birdie the way I do.

"Forget it," I mutter, spinning on my heel and heading back toward the dining room.

My gut screams at me to walk out, to leave him to host this pretentious circus on his own. But I force myself to stay. If there's even the slimmest chance I can learn something useful tonight, something that might help Birdie tomorrow, then I'll suffer through it. For her.

The chatter at the table settles as my dad gestures for everyone to take their seats. I glance at the place cards lining the table, my name neatly written in calligraphy near the end of the table. I sit down, trying to ignore the tightness in my chest as conversation starts up around me.

It doesn't take long for someone to catch my attention. A guy a few seats away leans in when my dad speaks, hanging on his every word. He's polished—too polished—with a blazer that probably costs more than my car and a grin that screams smarmy over-achiever.

"Nick," my dad says, his tone dripping with approval. "I was just telling Margaret here about how your approach to marrying design with narrative is exactly the kind of forward-thinking perspective we need more of in the contemporary art world."

Nick. The name clicks. Birdie mentioned him once before, in passing, when she was being self-deprecating about her chances. *If you were hoping to see the work of a guaranteed fellowship winner, Nick just left.*

I sit back, my jaw tightening as I watch the guy lap up my dad's praise. He's smooth, poised, and clearly used to being the center of attention. Everything Birdie isn't—and it's pissing me off.

As dinner is served, I wait for my moment. Nick's talking about his artistic process now, something about how his work "challenges societal expectations" by merging industrial materials with organic forms. I can't help myself.

"Form and function?" I cut in, raising an eyebrow. "So, like . . . IKEA?"

Nick glances at me. "It's about more than that. It's about redefining how we engage with functionality. When we consider traditional boundaries, we—"

"Or is it more like art you can sit on but not actually use?" I add, tilting my head innocently.

A few guests chuckle outright this time, and Nick's composure slips for a fraction of a second. My dad clears his throat, his eyes narrowing at me from across the table. "Liam."

"What?" I shrug, leaning back in my chair. "I'm just trying to understand the *genius* of it all."

Nick tries to redirect the conversation, but the tone's already shifted. A few of the other guests are smiling, and even my mom looks like she's fighting not to smirk. My dad, on the other hand, looks like he's about to explode.

"Liam," my mom says suddenly, her voice tight. "Would you mind helping me with something in the kitchen?"

I know what this is, but I stand anyway, following her into the other room. As soon as we're out of earshot, she spins on me. "Are you being a bug on purpose, or are you just that thoughtless?"

A bug. She used to call me that when I was a kid. When I said, or did, or looked at something the wrong way. It made sense to me then. I'm a bug—small, annoying, easy to swat away. But now, it stings in a different way.

I lean against the counter. "What do you mean? I'm just having a conversation."

"You're embarrassing your father in front of his colleagues!"

I laugh under my breath, shaking my head. "This whole dinner is a charade. It's not about the fellowship—it's about him showing off. And we both know he's just going to pick the most hoity-toity loser with a piss-poor artistic vision anyway."

"Liam!" she snaps.

I push off the counter, my jaw tight. "You know what? I'm done. If I have to hold my tongue at my own dinner table, then I might as well not be here at all."

Her eyes narrow. "Don't walk out of here. You always do this, Liam. Leave when you don't like what's happening. It's not what adults do."

But I'm already heading back toward the dining room. I stop just long enough to step into the doorway, catching my dad's eye. Then I salute him, a sharp, sarcastic motion that makes a few heads turn.

"David Donovan, everyone. Dayton's own patron saint of posturing. Long may he reign."

And with that, I'm gone.

Chapter Twenty-Two

BIRDIE

I leave the Ellsworth feeling strangely light and cautiously hopeful. Sure, I fumbled a little during my presentation—who doesn't when they're nervous?—but overall, I know I did well.

My pieces looked exactly the way I'd envisioned, shining under the gallery lights, every fine detail pulling its weight. From where I stood, the judges seemed engaged, leaning forward as if they wanted to hear more.

Liam's dad asked thoughtful questions about my choice of materials and process—curious, reverent, and not the least bit pretentious. And Claire Mahler? She didn't seem at all fazed that I'd bolted the last time we met. She even smiled when she called my work "brave," which, coming from her, might as well be a standing ovation.

The thought of them deliberating tonight, weighing my presentation against the others, makes my chest flutter with something I haven't felt in a while: faith. I gave it everything I had, poured my heart into this, and for once, it feels like it just might be enough.

As I walk across campus, my phone buzzes with messages from Dad and Sena congratulating me. I promised them I'd call later, but right now, there's only one person I want to talk to. Liam.

He promised to cook dinner tonight—something just for the two of us at his place. A quiet celebration of his conference championship win and my finishing the application process.

Thanksgiving is right around the corner, and after that, Liam will be taking early finals before heading off to the NCAA tournament. We won't have much time together for a while, so tonight feels even more important.

Still, I can't shake the weird feeling from our texts last night. He was hounding me about something.

It seemed odd. Not just odd—pointed. Like he wanted to ask me something but thought better of it. When I pressed for context, he backpedaled: *just wanted to wish you luck tomorrow. you're gonna kill it.*

Flattery will get you everywhere, I'd replied.

The whole strange exchange has been rattling around in my head ever since.

By the time I get to Liam's off-campus apartment, though, my mood has lifted again. None of that matters right now—not when there's so much to celebrate. Not when I'm about to see him.

I knock, and the door swings open almost immediately. Chase is standing there, grinning wide. "If it isn't the artist herself," he says, stepping aside to let me in. "Liam's favorite potter."

Before I can respond, the man of the hour appears, barreling toward me like an overexcited golden retriever. His grin is so wide and unrestrained it makes my heart flip. He wraps me in a hug, lifting me clean off the ground and spinning me in a circle.

"You did it!" he exclaims, his voice brimming with pride.

I laugh, holding on tightly. "I don't even know if I won yet."

"Doesn't matter," he says, setting me down but keeping his arms around me. "You're amazing, and we're celebrating. Champagne's already popped."

Chase saunters over with three glasses in hand, handing one to me. "To Birdie and her masterpieces," he declares, raising his glass. "Something something, let them eat cake."

"And to you two, the conference champs," I add, intertwining my wrist with Liam's as we drink.

Chase clinks his glass against ours, then takes a long sip.

"Alright, lovebirds, I'm heading out to do some celebrating of my own." He waggles his eyebrows suggestively, and I laugh. From what little I know about Chase, he's nothing if not predictable when it comes to women.

"Have fun," Liam calls after him as Chase grabs his coat and heads out the door, leaving us alone.

The apartment goes quiet, save for the soft hum of music playing from Liam's speaker. It's unexpectedly tidy—dishes put away, surfaces wiped clean, like he put extra effort into getting it ready for tonight. I set my glass down on the counter and turn to him, my smile softening.

"So, you're really proud of me, huh?"

His grin doesn't falter as he steps closer, wrapping an arm around my waist. "Ridiculously proud."

My heart feels so full I can't hold back anymore. I lean up and press my lips to his in a long kiss. It's sweet and unhurried, filled with the kind of happiness I haven't felt in a long time.

Liam responds immediately, his hand slipping to the back of my neck to deepen it. His lips are warm, gentle but insistent, as if he's trying to pour everything he feels into this moment.

But when I pull back, his smile falters. Just for a moment—just enough to make my stomach twist.

"What?" I ask softly, suddenly unsure. "What's wrong?"

He shakes his head quickly, his grin snapping back into place, but it doesn't quite reach his eyes. "Nothing," he says, his voice a little too casual. "You're perfect."

Perfect. The word lands softly, but something about it doesn't sit right. Maybe it's the way his voice dipped, like he didn't quite believe it. Or maybe it's just my own overthinking getting the better of me.

"You know what I really like about you?" I ask, forcing my tone to stay light.

He checks his nonexistent watch. "Don't think we have enough time to run through the list by the end of the night."

I roll my eyes. "One thing of many—it's that you don't sugar-coat things. Meaning, you would tell me if something weird was going on, right?"

"Right. But the thing is, you're very happy right now. Confident, even. Accomplished." He steps away and gestures toward the kitchen. "And I cooked us this dinner. I'm not great at cooking. In fact, some would say I'm terrible. But I put my best effort in, and I think it's at least edible."

I frown, confused. "Where are you going with this?"

"I'm just saying, maybe we should enjoy tonight. Eat." He raises his champagne glass in a faux toast. "Drink. Be merry. I can tell you the bad thing tomorrow."

Bad thing. My stomach trips over itself. What bad thing?

I wish I could be the kind of person who ignores the warning signs, who can compartmentalize well enough to just enjoy myself for a while. But I'm not, and I never will be.

"Yeah, that's not happening," I mutter.

Liam runs a hand through his hair, exhaling a long, heavy sigh. Finally, he places a gentle hand on my shoulder and guides us over to the couch. We sit together in stilted silence.

"I'm going to tell you something now," he says carefully. "Something about my dad and the fellowship finalists. And I don't want you to freak out."

Naturally, I freak out.

This is it. I didn't get it. Oh God, I didn't get it.

He already knows. Of course he already knows—it's his dad's committee. And he probably told Liam to break it to me gently, like that would somehow soften the blow. But it doesn't. It just makes it worse because now the guy I'm crushing on has a front-row seat to my failure.

How am I supposed to look him in the eye after this? How am I supposed to act normal, knowing the thing I've poured every ounce of myself into isn't enough?

He's watching me carefully, waiting for some kind of response, but I can't get my breathing under control. My chest tightens, and I press my palms into my knees, trying to steady myself.

"Birdie," he says softly. "It's not—it's not that."

That? I force myself to glance up at him. His expression is tight, his jaw clenched like he's bracing for impact. Whatever it is, it's bad.

"Then what is it?" I whisper, my throat tight. "What did your dad do?"

"Last night, the dinner with my parents . . . it was a fellowship dinner."

I tilt my head, confused. "A fellowship dinner?"

"For the finalists," he says slowly. "Except you weren't invited."

It takes a second for his words to sink in, and when they do, it feels like the air's been sucked out of the room.

"What?"

"My dad didn't invite you. He said it was to keep things fair because I've been helping you. That you already had enough of an advantage. He wanted to 'level the playing field.'"

"Enough of an advantage," I repeat, the words foreign and jagged in my mouth. "He didn't think I deserved to be there."

"That's not true," Liam says quickly, urgently. "He's just—he's like that. He thinks he knows what's best, and he's obsessed with appearances. It doesn't mean anything about you, Birdie."

But it does. It absolutely does.

I stare at the floor, my thoughts spinning. All I can see is the gallery earlier today—my pieces under the lights, the judges' questions, Claire Mahler's smile. For once, I let myself believe I belonged in a room like that. That maybe I'd finally done something right.

And now? Now, it just feels like a cruel joke.

"I should've told you last night," Liam says, his voice breaking through the fog in my head. "I know I should've. I just didn't want to mess you up before today. I didn't want you to feel psyched out or like you had to prove anything to him. You've already done enough."

He's right about one thing: if he'd told me last night, I probably wouldn't have made it through today. I would've fallen apart before I even set foot in that gallery.

"I get it," I say quietly. "You were right not to tell me. I just . . ." My voice cracks, and I force a swallow. "It sucks. It really, really sucks. I worked so hard, Liam. I thought maybe for once, it would be enough."

"It is enough. *You* are enough," he says fiercely, leaning forward. "What he did has nothing to do with you or your work. It's about him. You're incredible, Birdie. You blew them away today, and you can still win this thing. He's not the only one making the decisions."

The conviction in his voice almost makes me believe him. Almost.

But if I wasn't invited to a dinner the night before the application cycle ends, that means I'm probably already out of the running. David Donovan might not make the sole decision, but he's the largest donor. His voice carries the most weight.

And even if by some slim chance I did win . . . how could I work alongside him, knowing what he really thinks of me? That I took advantage of his son? It would be awful. Wrong.

I nod stiffly. "Yeah. Thanks."

He studies me for a long moment, then stands, holding out his hand. "Come on."

"What?" I blink up at him, quiet and uncertain.

"Let's get out of here. We can't sit around and let my dad's bullshit ruin your night. We'll go somewhere—anywhere you want."

"What about your 'at least edible' dinner?" I ask, my words falling out in a flat, hollow tone.

He grins softly, his hand still extended. "There's this new invention called a microwave. We can heat it up when we get back."

I hesitate, staring at his outstretched hand like it holds the answer to all the conflicting thoughts swirling in my head. A big part of me wants to stay right here on the couch and let the disappointment settle—feel every ounce of it, let it wash over me until it passes.

Because that's what I usually do. I dwell. I overthink. I replay every decision, every word, every moment, searching for where I went wrong.

But another part of me—the softer, squishier part—wants something else. Wants to be distracted, even just for a little while. Wants to be anywhere but here, with Liam's hand in mine, pretending for a night that things don't hurt as much as they do.

Tomorrow, I'll let myself wallow. Tomorrow, I'll replay every second of this and let the weight of it crush me if it wants to.

But tonight, I'll let myself be with Liam.

I slide my hand into his, and his fingers close gently around mine. He pulls me to my feet, his grin widening just a fraction as he tugs me toward his room.

"Wait here," he says, disappearing for a moment. When he comes back, he's holding a big, baggy Dayton Soccer sweatshirt. "Here. It's cold out."

He helps me pull it over my head, and it smells like him—clean and faintly woodsy, with a hint of detergent. The sleeves swallow my hands, the hem hanging well past my hips, but it's comforting in a way I can't explain.

"Better?" he asks, his voice low, his smile softer now.

I nod, letting him lace his fingers through mine again. Together, we walk to the door, hand in hand, and I let myself believe—just for tonight—that things might still be okay.

Chapter Twenty-Three
BIRDIE

LIAM CONFIDENTLY LEADS me across campus. We weave between darkened buildings and quiet walkways, steady but unhurried. The chilly air nips at my cheeks. It's nearly winter, and though we're in the south, the cold still finds its way in, curling around us like a quiet reminder of the season's end.

"Where are we going?" I finally ask, breaking the silence.

"You'll see."

We turn a corner, passing the glow of the main fountain, where students are gathered. A few late-night dwellers, who laugh as we walk by. But Liam doesn't stop us there. Instead, he veers toward a cluster of older buildings, the kind with faded plaques and ivy creeping up the sides.

When we round the last corner, he slows, gesturing ahead. "Here we are."

At first, I don't see it. Then, the faint trickle of water catches my attention, and my eyes adjust to the dim light. It's a small fountain, tucked between two engineering buildings, almost forgotten by the rest of campus. The basin is shallow, and the stone is worn with age.

And there's something living in there, too.

A small turtle, lazily swimming in circles, its small head breaking the surface every so often.

"There's a little turtle in there," I whisper, crouching closer to get a better look.

"Yeah," Liam says, settling beside me. "Found this place my freshman year. I come back every now and then. Figured you'd like it."

I watch as the turtle pauses, floating near the edge before paddling off again. "Do you think he's always been here? Like, is this his only home?"

Liam tilts his head, considering. "Maybe. Or maybe he wandered in when he was older. Got lost and decided to stick around. I've been calling him Otis. Seems like an Otis, doesn't he?"

"Yeah, I suppose. Do you think he got separated from his mom when he was little?" I ask softly, my voice catching in a way I don't expect. "And now he's here. In this fountain. Just . . . living."

He leans in, his shoulder brushing mine. "You okay?"

I wipe at my eyes quickly, but it's no use. A tear slips down my cheek, followed by another. "I don't know."

"Is this about the turtle or something else?" he asks, warm, teasing, gentle.

"It's everything," I say, laughing weakly through the tears. "It's nothing. It's you and me and this damned turtle. And I just . . . I wish I could keep staring at this fountain. That I didn't have to wake up tomorrow and face the music."

He shifts closer, his hand brushing against mine. "We can face it together."

I glance up at him, his face lit faintly by the nearby lamppost. His expression is steady, unwavering.

"Okay," I whisper.

For a long moment, we sit in silence, the faint gurgle of the fountain and the soft splashes from the turtle filling the quiet. Liam's hand slips into mine, his thumb brushing lightly over my knuckles.

When he finally speaks again, it's barely above a murmur. "You know, I think this turtle's got it all figured out. He doesn't care about where he's supposed to be or what anyone thinks. He's just here, doing his thing."

I let out a soft laugh, leaning my head against his shoulder. "Very profound."

"Extremely," he agrees, chuckling.

And we stay like that, watching the turtle glide through the water, until the cold starts to creep in too deeply. Liam stands, tugging me gently to my feet, and we head back the way we came, hand in hand, the little fountain and its solitary resident fading behind us.

Monday comes, and it's all cold and gray, the kind of morning where even the sun can't be bothered to show up. My stomach's in knots as I sip my too-strong coffee, scrolling through my inbox and waiting for the email I already know is coming.

It lands at 10:07 a.m. The subject line might as well be in neon: *Dayton Fellowship Results*. I hover over the trackpad for a moment before I click it open, dread twisting low in my stomach. This is it. The moment I've been bracing for.

The words blur together at first, but I force myself to focus.

Dear Miss Bridget Collins,

Thank you for your application to the Dayton Fellowship in the Arts. The selection committee was impressed by the exceptional quality of your work and the passion evident in your presentation. Choosing a recipient from such a talented pool of finalists was not an easy task.

After much deliberation, we have selected Nicholas Riordan as this year's fellowship recipient.

We encourage you to continue pursuing your artistic vision and to consider reapplying for future opportunities. Your talent and dedi-

cation are evident, and we have no doubt you will go on to achieve
great success.

Sincerely,
Margaret Ellis
Director, Dayton Fellowship in the Arts
Dayton University

Nick Riordan won, and I lost.

I read the letter over again until it loses all meaning. Just letters on a blurry screen. My throat tightens, and a hot ache settles deep in my chest. It's not a surprise—not really. But that doesn't make it hurt any less.

I worked so hard. I poured everything I had into this. And now, what do I have to show for it?

On autopilot, I pull up my bank account next. My stomach drops when I see the numbers. Between medical bills, the money I donated to Emily's family, and the rising cost of living, there's almost nothing left.

Next term is covered, but after that? I'm tapped out. My dad makes just enough that financial aid doesn't cover my full tuition, and I've been supplementing the rest on my own. But I can't stretch it any further.

Without the fellowship, I can't afford to stay at Dayton. It's over.

I press the heels of my hands into my eyes, willing the tears away. I knew this was coming. After not being invited to that dinner, the writing was on the wall. Still, hope's a stubborn thing. It clung to me like a second skin, refusing to let go, whispering that maybe I could still pull it off.

But now, it's official. I'm out.

Sena's already left for the break, and I'm alone in the apartment, surrounded by the echoes of my failure. I tuck my knees up into my chest on the couch, letting the weight of it all crash into me.

The tears come in waves, each one heavier than the last, until my chest aches from the effort. I don't know how long I stay there, but it's long enough that day becomes night.

When Liam shows up later, he knocks softly, so hesitant and careful, like he already knows something's wrong. I think about ignoring him—letting him stand out there until he gives up—but it's Liam. He won't give up.

When I open the door, his eyes go straight to mine, narrowing with concern. "Birdie." He closes the door gently, like he's trying not to spook me. "I heard the emails went out."

"From your dad?"

"No, from stalking the fellowship forum online."

"I was going to tell you," I mumble.

"Why didn't you call me?" he asks, his voice soft, careful.

"What was I supposed to say?" I snap, immediately regretting it. "I'm sorry. I just—I didn't want to talk about it."

He comes near and brushes a hand over my hair. "It's okay to be upset. You worked so hard—"

"It doesn't matter," I cut him off, my voice breaking. "I didn't win. And now I can't even afford to stay in school next year. What was all that hard work for?"

He opens his mouth like a fish out of water, but no words come out. Whatever he wants to say, it's stuck somewhere between us, tangled up in the tension.

"I feel so foolish. I went to you for help, thinking it might actually make a difference, but all it did was make me look desperate. Your dad obviously thought I was just using you. God, what was I even thinking?"

"Stop," he says sharply. "You're not desperate, and you didn't do anything wrong. My dad is—" He pauses, exhaling heavily. "My dad's an asshole, babe. But that doesn't mean your work wasn't incredible. It was. It is."

I shake my head, ignoring him. "What did I expect? That I could just waltz into your world and somehow belong there? That I'd get this life-changing opportunity because of talent or hard work or whatever nonsense I convinced myself mattered? It doesn't matter. None of it matters."

"You don't actually believe that."

"Don't I?" I snap, my arms wrapping around myself like I can hold everything together if I just squeeze tight enough. "Because right now, it feels like no matter how hard I try, I'll never be enough. Not for your dad, not for the judges, not for—"

"For me?" he interrupts.

I blink, faltering. "I didn't mean—"

"Good," he says firmly. "Because I never asked you to be anything but yourself. And if you think for one second that you let me down, that I'd ever see you as anything less than incredible, then you don't know me at all."

He reaches for me again, but I take another step back, wrapping my arms around myself. "Please, don't. I can't—I just can't handle anyone being sad with me."

His face falls. "Okay," he says softly. "Then what do you need?"

"Time to process, maybe," I whisper, swallowing hard. "I'm going home for Thanksgiving. I'll talk to you after the break before you leave for the tournament. I just . . . I need to figure things out first."

"Birdie, baby, I—"

"I'm sorry, but I just need a little time alone to wallow."

"Okay," he says quietly. "If that's what you need, you got it."

I bite my lip to keep it from trembling. "Thank you."

He watches me for a moment longer, his expression heavy and

unreadable, like he wants to argue more but knows better. Then, with a soft exhale, he finally turns and leaves.

I sink back onto the couch, pull my knees to my chest, and sob. Violent, gut-wrenching sobs that leave me gasping for air. It's useless for me to try to hold it together now. I can't anymore, even if I wanted to.

Because I failed.

I failed. I failed. I lost the fellowship, and I failed.

The words loop over and over in my mind, relentless, each repetition cutting a little deeper, like a knife twisting in an already open wound. I failed, and now, I have no idea what comes next.

Chapter Twenty-Four
LIAM

I DON'T GO to my parents' house for Thanksgiving. Not this year. Not after everything with Birdie and the fellowship. Just the thought of sitting across the table from my dad, watching him carve the turkey like nothing's happened, makes me want to punch a hole in the wall.

I was a rowdy kid, but I've never been the violent sort. Better not start breaking character now.

They weren't thrilled when I told them. My mom sniffled a little, saying it wouldn't feel the same without me. A phony guilt trip if I've ever heard one. My dad just grumbled something about priorities.

I sold them on a made-up story about James being lonely. Something about a minor league community outreach project he was "obligated" to stick around for—not entirely true, but close enough to be convincing.

Baseball season's over, and he could've driven home if he really wanted to. But he'd mentioned wanting to lie low, avoid the usual family chaos, and I figured we were on the same page about that.

James doesn't need the family drama, and neither do I. I'll confront my dad eventually. When I have the energy for it. When I know what to say. But not today. Today, I just want to see my brother.

I drive to his place out in Stonewater.

It's not much—just a small apartment near the minor league

complex—but it feels a hell of a lot better than being at home. James doesn't cook, though, so we head out to the Cracker Barrel and settle in for a low-key Thanksgiving.

We sit in a corner booth, plates piled high with turkey, stuffing, and those little biscuits they keep bringing out in baskets. It's so far removed from our family's usual Thanksgiving—formal dining room, silver platters, wine pairings—that I can't help but like it more. It's weirdly perfect.

"So," James says, leaning back in his seat as he spears a piece of meat. "What's been going on with you? And don't mumble or dodge the question with a half-assed joke."

He's right—I'm usually a straight shooter—but talking about this stuff makes me antsy. It's like trying to talk around the real thing, dancing when all I want to do is stand still. But I know James. If I don't give him something real, he'll just keep pushing.

I shrug, swirling a forkful of mashed potatoes. "You remember that girl I mentioned before? The artist?"

James narrows his eyes slightly, already suspicious. "Yeah, what about her?"

"Well . . . I like her. Like, really like her. And we've been kissing."

He raises an eyebrow, smirking. "Kissing? Is that code for—"

"No," I cut him off, scowling. "Quite literally just kissing. That's all."

"Uh-huh, and?"

"And she's feeling really shitty right now," I add, ignoring his pointed tone. "She lost the fellowship, and she's super anxious. Like, shut-down-anxious. We said we'd handle shit together, but she's pulling away. And I don't really know how to help her other than to give her the space she's asking for."

James' smirk fades. "Yeah, that's tough." He sets his fork down, leaning forward slightly. "You, uh, you remember Declan? My buddy who moved away senior year?"

"Obviously."

Declan was practically a third Donovan brother for half of high school. While I had trouble making friends, my brother collected them like trophies.

"Well, he used to get anxiety attacks. Before a game, he'd be in the stands sniffing lemons. Said it helped calm him down. I guess it's a thing."

I stare at him, deadpan. "So . . . I should give her some lemons to sniff?"

"No, you dipshit." He rolls his eyes. "I'm saying you should think of things that calm her down. Things she likes, stuff that makes her happy. And try them with her. If you like her, show her."

I nod, chewing it over. "Like what, though?"

"How the hell should I know?" he says, grinning. "You're the one who likes her. Figure it out. Or if you can't, at least just . . . sit in the shittiness with her for a while."

We shovel the rest of the food into our mouths, the conversation trailing off into comfortable silence. The biscuits are good—like, I ate twelve of them good—and when the check comes, James insists on covering it, and I don't bother to argue.

"Consider it my contribution to your sniffing lemons fund," he says, smirking as we head for the door.

Despite everything, I laugh. It's a bad joke, but it feels good. Wholesome, even. And maybe James is right—maybe all I need to do is figure out what makes Birdie happy and lean into it.

When we get back from break, and she stops icing me out, I'll be ready with something better than just space. Something that shows her I'm here for the long haul.

I was wrong. Break's over, and Birdie's still keeping her distance. I showed up to her apartment a couple of times, knocked, waited, even texted to let her know I was outside. But nothing. It's obvious she doesn't want to see me.

She said we'd talk before I left for the tournament, and we didn't. Now I'm here, at the College Cup, trying to focus on the biggest week of my soccer career. A futile effort when I know she's back in Dayton, wallowing and shutting me out.

The team arrived in Ashworth three days ago, and it's been nonstop since. Practices, strategy sessions, media briefings—it's a whirlwind of activity that leaves little room for anything else. Which, I guess, is a blessing in disguise. If I wasn't this busy, I'd be losing my mind thinking about her.

The first game is relentless. We're playing Stanford, and it's brutal—physical from the first whistle, the kind of match that leaves you bruised and gasping for air. Chase scores early in the first half, a perfectly placed header off Amir's corner kick that electrifies the crowd.

By the time the second half rolls around, we're up 1–0, but Stanford's pressing hard. Their forwards are quick, incessant, and I'm stuck tracking one of them who feels like he's running on rocket fuel. My lungs are burning, my legs are screaming, but there's no time to slow down. Every tackle feels like a battle, every pass like a lifeline.

The final whistle blows, and we barely hold on for the win. Relief floods the field, but it's muted—we know we've still got more to fight for.

In the lockers afterward, the atmosphere is electric. Guys are cheering, clapping each other on the back, already buzzing with anticipation for the next game. But we know it's only going to get tougher.

And it does. The next game is a war. We're up against NCSU, the defending champs, and they're as sharp as everyone said they'd be. The match is a chess game from the start, every move calculated, every pass contested like it's the last. By halftime, it's tied at zero, and we're all running on fumes.

Coach gives us one of his fiery speeches during the break, the kind that's supposed to light a fire under you. But even that can't change the fact that they're just better. They score early in the second half—a quick counterattack that cuts through our defense like a knife—and no matter how hard we push, we can't find an answer.

We throw everything we have at them in the final minutes—long balls, desperate shots, every ounce of energy left in our bodies—but it's not enough.

The game ends 1–0, and just like that, our season is over.

The locker room is silent. No sharp speeches this time, no celebratory shouting. Just the sound of cleats being pulled off, of guys packing up their gear, of dreams ending in the span of ninety minutes.

And then Chase breaks the silence.

"I know this fucking sucks. We blew it, obviously. But I—I signed my contract," he blurts out, standing in the middle of the room with a grin so wide it practically splits his face. "Isn't that wild?"

We're still reeling from the loss, but a win like this, a moment this big—it cuts through the disappointment like a burst of sunlight after a storm. It's perfect timing, really. We needed something to remind us that the game doesn't end here, that there's more waiting for us beyond the final whistle.

Chase is beaming, soaking up the cheers and backslaps from the team. When he gets the chance, he tells me, "I report in January. Sorry I have to leave you, buddy."

I grab him by the shoulders, shaking him lightly. "Don't be sorry. This is huge, man. They're lucky to have you."

And it's true. A Generation Adidas contract—it's one of the

biggest deals a college player can get, a fast track to the MLS. It's everything Chase has been working toward, and he earned it.

"Hell yeah, they are."

By the time we get back to the hotel, everyone's wiped out. The mood is a strange blend of relief and finality, a quiet realization that this chapter is closing for some of us faster than others. Chase and I quickly retreat to our room, and once we're alone, he corners me.

"Hey," he says, his tone a little quieter now. "You're gonna be okay, you know? When I'm gone."

I shake my head. "Don't get all sentimental on me now."

"I'm serious," he says. "You're one of the best players on this team, Liam. You've got a bright future ahead of you. Don't let anything—not my leaving, not *anyone*—make you think otherwise."

The lump in my throat comes out of nowhere, and I nod, swallowing hard. "Thanks, buddy. That means a lot coming from you."

And it does. He's not the sentimental type. More of a jokes-first, feelings-later guy. If he's saying this now, it's because he means it.

He claps me on the shoulder, grinning again. "Now, get some sleep. You've got to hold down the fort for the rest of the year."

Chase has always had this larger-than-life energy, like he's built for more than just the everyday grind. Seeing him so certain, so ready for what's next, should feel bittersweet. But right now, it's just bitter.

He showers, climbs into the bed across from mine, and falls into an easy sleep. For me, the silence is loud, pressing in on all sides. The adrenaline from the game is long gone, replaced by this strange, heavy emptiness.

I scroll through my phone, reading the same notifications I've already cleared, hoping for something—anything—to distract me. A text from my mom asking about the game. An email from a professor reminding us about the final project. A random spam email about discounted protein powder.

Instead, I lie in bed staring at the ceiling, a bit hopeless. Chase is leaving. Birdie's still not talking to me. The season's over.

I feel untethered. It's like everything I've been holding on to is slipping through my fingers, one piece at a time. The team, my roommate, her. All of it disappearing at once.

I felt like this after James and Hayes left, too. Like the world was shifting under my feet, and I couldn't find solid ground. But things eventually got better. I found my rhythm again, settled into a new routine, and it didn't feel so uncertain anymore.

But Birdie isn't a roommate I can replace or a teammate I can adjust to losing. She's something else entirely.

I think about the way she smiles when she teases me, the way she kisses me like I'm the only person in the world. The way she makes me feel like I belong, like there isn't something wrong with me. Around her, I don't have to try so hard—I can just be.

And that's the thing. This doesn't feel like something I can bounce back from, not after a loss like that. Not when it's her.

I can't make it permanent. I won't. Not if I have any chance of fixing this. Birdie means too much to let her slip away without a fight.

Chapter Twenty-Five
BIRDIE

WE'VE BEEN on break for a week, and I'm still spiraling into self-doubt, into this pit of uncertainty I can't seem to climb out of. I haven't worked on any new pieces, haven't touched the wheel, haven't even sketched anything. The idea of starting something new, of trying and failing again—it's debilitating.

I haven't spoken to Liam, either.

He texted, right after Thanksgiving, asking if I'd made it home okay. I stared at the screen for twenty minutes before turning my phone off. When he showed up at my apartment, I pretended I wasn't there, even though I knew he could probably hear the TV through the door.

I know I'm being unfair to him, shutting him out when he's done nothing wrong. But facing him feels impossible right now.

Sena's home in Chicago, and I took the bus to stay at my dad's place for the entirety of winter break. It's been years since I've stayed over this long. I love my dad, but my independence is important to me.

Usually, I make excuses—work, classes, anything to keep the visits short and sweet. This time, I couldn't stand the thought of sticking around Dayton. Not with everything that's happened, where the reminders of my failures would be all around me.

I can't pick up any extra shifts at work, either. The bookstore is closed for the next month. There's no budget for seasonal help, and my usual hours are frozen until spring semester starts.

So, I've been filling the days with meaningless tasks. Cleaning my dad's house, binge-watching shows I've already seen, scrolling endlessly on my phone. I even reorganized the junk drawer in the kitchen yesterday, sorting every paperclip and rubber band into neat little piles like it was some kind of art project.

I'll do anything to keep my mind occupied, away from the glaring reminder of everything I've lost. And today, I have something real to occupy me—a one-year checkup for the accident.

The ride to the doctor's office is quiet, almost suffocating in its silence. My dad drives, his hands steady on the wheel, but I can feel his eyes flick to me every so often. He doesn't ask if I'm okay, doesn't try to fill the silence with empty words. He doesn't need to.

When we get to the office, I check in at the front desk and sit in the same stiff chair I sat in a year ago, waiting to hear if I'd ever fully recover. Back then, everything was blurry—pain, guilt, and grief tangled together into one endless knot.

Now, it's just . . . dull. The physical wounds have healed, but the weight of it all hasn't lifted.

A nurse calls my name, and I follow her into an exam room. She takes my vitals. She asks me the usual questions—any headaches, dizziness, or changes in vision?

"I had a migraine a few weeks ago, but none since. Just minor headaches here and there."

The nurse jots that down, offering a quick, reassuring smile before leaving the room.

The doctor arrives a few minutes later, flipping through my chart as he sits on the rolling stool. "Well, Bridget," he says gently. "How's everything feeling? Any lingering pain or discomfort?"

"No, everything feels fine."

He tip-taps away on his laptop, then, "That's good to hear. Your scans look clear—no residual issues from the fractures, and your head injury seems to have healed well. I'd say you're in excellent shape."

I nod, but the words don't bring the relief they should. Instead, there's a strange hollowness, like I've been expecting him to say something else, something that would explain why I still feel so stuck. So tragically unmoored.

"You're doing really well," he adds, his tone encouraging. "I know it can take time to feel like yourself again after something like this. But physically, you're all set."

The nurse hands me a printout of the visit summary as I leave the office, my dad trailing behind me. I'm nodding along, going through the motions, but the word sticks in my head like a splinter. Physically, I'm set. But emotionally? Mentally?

I don't know if I'll ever feel whole again.

In the car, Dad gives me a sideways look. "Want to grab lunch?"

I shake my head, staring out the window. "Not hungry."

He doesn't push, just nods and keeps driving.

When we get home, I retreat to my room, flopping onto the bed and staring at the ceiling. The silence feels too loud, pressing in on me, and the weight of everything I've been holding back settles on my chest. The doctor's words replay in my head, over and over. *Physically, you're all set.*

But what does that even mean? Set for what? For normal? For pretending like nothing happened? Like the cracks don't run so deep they might never close?

I pull out my sketchbook, flipping to an empty page. My pencil hovers over the paper, but no lines come. No ideas, no inspiration.

I think about Emily. About her family, spending another Christmas without her. About the check I wrote to them with money I barely had, as if it could somehow make up for what happened.

But nothing could. No amount of money or good intentions would ever bring her back. It's a truth I carry every day, like a stone stitched to my heart.

I think about Liam, the way he looked at me like I was the brightest thing in the room. The way his voice softened when he called me "Birdie, baby," like it was a name made just for me. I want to call him, to tell him about the appointment, to hear him say something that makes me believe I'm more than just the sum of my mistakes.

But I don't.

Instead, I close the sketchbook and roll onto my side, pulling the blankets up over my head. I let the darkness settle around me, warm and stifling, and tell myself that maybe tomorrow will be better. Maybe I'll feel stronger, braver, ready to face the world again.

Just not today.

Chapter Twenty-Six
LIAM

THE BOWLING ALLEY NEAR MY PARENTS' place doesn't smell like old shoes and popcorn. It's not nostalgic or charming. A piss-poor excuse for atmosphere and exactly the kind of place I wouldn't have chosen for a night out.

Yet, here I am, crammed into a lane with my brother and his friends.

What was supposed to be a triple date—Hayes and Emmy, West and Jade, plus some other couple they know—turned into a sibling outing when the latter bailed. James and I were the last-minute replacements, though I'm pretty sure neither of us fits the vibe they were going for.

A little less "cute couple energy" and a lot more beer and trash talk.

"Liam, you're up!" Jade calls, waving me toward the lane. Jade used to be a student at Dayton, too, in the same class as James and the others. She's dating West, a running back for the Carolina Bobcats in his first season.

I grab a ball that's too heavy, ignoring the sparkly purple one she insists is "lucky," and step up to the lane. My first roll veers into the gutter almost immediately, and the second isn't much better.

"Solid work," James says dryly.

"I'm pacing myself," I shoot back, shrugging.

Hayes snorts. "If that's pacing, I'd hate to see you try."

He may be my brother's best friend, but he was also my roommate for all of last year. We're close, and he loves to needle me whenever he gets the chance.

His girlfriend, Emmy, sits beside him. She has bleach-white hair and an effortless, edgy style. I like her. She's sharp and quick-witted, with a kindness that sneaks up on you. Right now, though, she's half watching the game and half answering emails on her phone. She's been juggling work with a startup company—a big digital marketing campaign she's spearheading.

"Don't listen to him," Emmy says without looking up, her fingers flying over the screen. "He's just cranky because I beat him at mini-golf last week."

Hayes grumbles, but there's a grin tugging at the corner of his mouth. He's been settling into his new job as the assistant coach for Dayton's baseball team, and from what James tells me, he's doing well. Coaching seems to suit him.

Unlike James, who always had his sights set on going pro, Hayes didn't have the same drive to chase the big leagues. It wasn't in the cards for him, and I think he's made peace with that long ago.

We used to be closer when we all lived together last year. Hayes was my go-to for advice, though he had a knack for deliv-ering it with enough sarcasm to make you question if he was being serious. But since he and Emmy moved in together, we've drifted.

It's not a big deal, I guess. That's just what happens when you grow up and start building your life with someone. Still, it stings a little.

Beside me, West is sprawled out in his seat, scrolling through his phone with the kind of calm that seems at odds with the rest of us. His season just ended, but you wouldn't know it—he carries that same effortless confidence, like nothing in the world could rattle him.

"Theo, it's your turn, baby," Jade says, waving him toward the lane, her sparkly purple ball already in hand for her next turn.

West—Theo to Jade and Jade only—stretches lazily, his movements slow and deliberate. Then he stands, grabbing one of the heavier balls. "Watch and learn, people."

He steps to the lane and rolls like he's testing his running back aim, the ball slamming into the pins with a satisfying crash. A strike.

"Show-off," Jade mutters, but she's smiling.

"Just lucky," West says, deadpan. "Because I got my girl here."

Jade shakes her head, grabbing her purple ball and stepping up for her turn. She's just finishing her first semester of grad school for journalism and keeps talking about some big investigative piece she's working on—something about corruption in collegiate football recruitment.

I thought about asking for more details, but sports outside of soccer don't really hold my interest. It's not that I don't care—well, actually, maybe it is.

Her roll knocks down seven pins, and she does a little victory dance. "See? Told you it's lucky!"

The next few rounds are more of the same. Emmy, surprisingly competitive, gets two strikes in a row and trash-talks Hayes the whole time. West tries to teach Jade how to roll with more power, but she just laughs and claims she's going for "artistic flair." James spends half his turns arguing about whether spin counts as a "real" bowling technique.

By the time we're halfway through, I'm leaning back in my seat, sipping my beer and letting the noise wash over me. It feels good to be here, surrounded by everyone's energy, even if I'm still half in my head about Birdie.

"You're up again," James says, nudging me.

I grab a ball and roll another gutter. No one even teases me this time. They must know I'm not in the mood to try.

When I sit, James gives me a look. "You good?"

"Missing Birdie," I tell him. "Wondering what she's up to. Hoping she's not just crying all alone in bed or something."

He sighs. "She's still giving you the runaround?"

"It's not the *runaround*," I say, shaking my head. "It's more like she needs space. And I get it. She's been through a lot, and I don't want to push her. But with Dad being on the committee, it's like there's this shadow over everything that's connected to me. And because of it, I'm worried she's never going to let me all the way in. She'll keep shutting me out because it's easier."

"So, what are you doing about it?"

I blink. "What can I do? She said she needed time."

"Time's great," he says, nodding slowly. "But have you thought about what you're gonna do after she's had that time? Did you come up with things that would make her happy like we talked about? Or are you just sitting here, hoping the perfect answer is gonna fall out of the sky?"

I glance at him, then at the others. West is lounging in his chair, clearly eavesdropping despite pretending to scroll his phone, and Hayes leans in a little, curious. Jade, who's just finished her turn, plops down across from me, her expression somewhere between amused and intrigued.

"Fine," James says, slapping his hands on the table. "Here's what we're gonna do. We're making a list."

I frown. "A list?"

"Yeah," Jade chimes in, her eyes lighting up. "A glad/bad list. Stuff that makes her happy on one side, stuff that stresses her out on the other."

"Because nothing says romance like a pros and cons list," I deadpan.

"Not a pros and cons list," Emmy cuts in, finally looking up from her phone. "This is actionable intel. Stuff you can actually use to help her feel better."

I roll my eyes but grab a napkin from the table. "Fine. Let's hear it."

"Bad things first," James says, stealing a pen from Hayes and clicking it dramatically. "What makes her upset?"

"Loneliness," I say immediately.

"Failure," James adds, knowing exactly why we're in this predicament in the first place.

"David fucking Donovan," I mutter, earning a collective groan of agreement from the table.

"Okay, solid start," James says, scribbling furiously. "Now for the glad things. What makes her happy?"

"Pottery," I say, a small smile tugging at my lips. "She's incredible at it. It's her whole world. And even though it's been tainted by losing the fellowship, I know she'll find her way back."

"What about family?" Jade asks. "Does she get along with them?"

"Yeah, she loves her dad," I say, thinking back to how she lights up whenever she talks about him. "That's where she is now."

"What else?" James asks, tapping the pen against the table.

"Sour candy." When I brought it to her in the studio, she practically salivated before ripping the bag open and devouring half of it in one sitting. It was kind of adorable.

"And Liam," Emmy says with a smirk, nudging Hayes.

"Liam," James repeats, adding it to the list with an exaggerated flourish. "Glad column, top of the list."

I shake my head, but there's a warmth in my chest I can't ignore. It's true—her smile changes when she's with me. It's freer, like she doesn't have to keep her guard up. I make her happy, and somehow, she makes me feel like I'm not so hard to figure out.

When James finishes, he slides the napkin across the table. "There you go. Your game plan. When she's ready to talk, hit her with the glad things. All the glad things."

I stare at the napkin, at the messy scrawl of words, and let out a slow breath. It's silly, maybe even a little juvenile, but it feels like a step in the right direction.

"Thanks," I say, pocketing the napkin.

"Don't mention it," James says, clapping me on the shoulder. "Seriously, don't. I have a reputation to uphold."

We all laugh, the tension breaking, and Jade grabs her ball for another turn. The game winds down not long after that, but the energy lingers as we pile into the cars and head back.

It feels good to have a plan. Like maybe I can help Birdie find her way back to herself. And when she does, I'll be there, waiting to catch her the next time she falls.

CHRISTMAS DINNER IS JUST as unbearable as I expected. The table looks like it belongs in a magazine—polished silver, crystal glasses, and garlands running the length of it, all meticulously curated by my mom, who thrives on making sure every holiday appears perfect.

But sitting here, everything feels off.

James is across from me, throwing out the occasional sarcastic comment to lighten the mood. My mom keeps glancing at my dad like she's bracing for impact, and my dad? He's carving the turkey with the same precision he uses to sculpt clay, like even this is some kind of art piece he's obligated to perfect.

"So," I say, breaking the stifling silence. "Thought you might like to know that Chase got his Adidas contract. He's leaving in January for whatever team picks him up."

James perks up, clearly impressed. "That's huge. Good for him."

My dad doesn't even look up from his plate as he mutters, "What about you, Liam? Any plans to get serious about what's next?"

And just like that, something snaps. I've been holding my tongue since the fellowship dinner fiasco, but I'm done pretending everything is fine.

"What's next?" I say, leaning back in my chair. "Maybe sabotaging more of my relationships. Seems like that's the family tradition, right?"

My mom freezes mid-cut, her knife hovering over her plate.

"Excuse me?" my dad says, his voice sharp and measured.

"You heard me," I snap. "Birdie worked her ass off for that fellowship, and you made sure she didn't even stand a chance. All because what—she asked me for help? I thought that's what you're supposed to do for the people you care about."

"This again?" His jaw tightens, his voice clipped. "That fellowship wasn't the right fit for her, and I wasn't the only one who thought so. Don't be naive, Liam."

"Oh, right," I say, my tone dripping with sarcasm. "Because you're such an excellent judge of character."

"Enough," my mom says, her voice shaking slightly. She's always the referee, swooping in to stop things before they spiral too far. "This is Christmas. Can't we just have one peaceful meal?"

I glance at her, then at James, who's giving me a subtle shake of his head. I wish I could be the kind of person who lets it go, who can bite his tongue and play along for the sake of peace. By now, that's the only thing that keeps the tension from boiling over.

My dad will believe whatever he wants, and nothing I say is going to change that. He's immovable, untouchable. God forbid I act the same.

I sigh and drag a hand through my hair. "Fine. Forget it. If you want to move on and pretend it never happened, then let's talk about something neutral, something that won't ruffle *David's* feathers." I cough to clear my throat. "Chase is leaving, which means I'm going to be roommate-less for the rest of the year."

"You should ask your cousin," my mom says, perking up like she's just solved world hunger. "Your uncle mentioned Warren needs a place. Wouldn't it be nice to be with family?"

I snort. "He's hardly family."

It's not a fair argument. Warren's mom married my uncle years ago, and by all accounts, they're part of the Donovan dynasty. But Warren? He was already a full-grown adult by then, and it shows. He's distant, like life handed him a bad deal, and he's still mad about it. Not exactly my idea of an ideal roommate.

My dad sighs. "If you're so particular, find someone else. But don't expect us to cover the difference if you're living alone."

I stab a piece of ham and chew it like it personally offended me. Warren's not ideal, but the thought starts to settle. He's grumpy, sure, but maybe that'll work. I'm not looking for a best friend—just someone to split costs with, someone who won't care if I come and go without small talk or forced bonding over video games.

"Fine," I say finally, my voice low. "I'll think about it."

My mom smiles like I've just saved Christmas, and James gives me a small, sympathetic smirk. I tune out the rest of dinner, retreating into my own thoughts about the tournament, about Birdie, and the looming reality of another semester filled with more questions than answers.

All I know is peace might be what my mom wants, but it's the last thing I'm feeling right now.

Chapter Twenty-Seven
LIAM

Winter break is nearly over, and my place feels twice as empty now that Chase is packing up to leave. Even with his shoes scattered near the door and the faint smell of whatever protein-heavy monstrosity he cooked this morning still lingering in the air, the space is hollow.

Maybe it's because I know he's leaving for good this time. Or maybe it's because I've been left on read by Birdie for what feels like an eternity, and my brain won't shut up about it.

I shake my head and shove another stack of red plastic cups onto the counter. It's New Year's Eve, and Chase's goodbye party slash New Year's bash is happening here. My contribution? Cleaning up the mess that Chase didn't bother with and preparing to host a hundred soccer players and their assorted hangers-on without losing my sanity.

"Liam!" Chase's voice booms from somewhere down the hall. "Where's the tape?"

I glance at the rolls of duct tape and masking tape sitting on the counter, then yell back, "Which one?"

"Any! Both! Doesn't matter!"

I grab the masking tape and walk to his room, where he's half-buried in a pile of boxes, a roll of bubble wrap dangling off his desk like some kind of sad streamer. He looks up, grinning from ear to ear.

"You're supposed to be helping," he says.

"I am helping," I say, tossing him the tape. "This is me helping you not look like a total slob when your guests show up tonight." He laughs and rips a piece off with his teeth. "Fair. But let's be real—you're only doing this so you don't have to think about Birdie."

"First of all, you don't need to point it out. Second of all, shut up."

"Uh-huh." He smirks, taping a box closed with the kind of enthusiasm only Chase can muster. "You're quite testy tonight." Before I can come up with a response, someone pounds on the front door, and Chase grins. "Better get that. Party's starting early."

As I head over to answer, I remind myself to breathe. Tonight is supposed to be easy—no overthinking, no spiraling, just a bunch of teammates and friends celebrating the start of a new year. I open the door to a crowd of familiar faces, and within minutes, the apartment is packed.

The music's blasting, people are laughing, and the smell of pizza mixes with beer and cologne in the air. Chase is in his element, moving through the crowd like a politician at a rally, shaking hands and clapping people on the back.

I stick to the kitchen, where it's quieter. Slightly.

Santi wanders in next, his hair somehow looking perfect despite the humidity of the packed apartment. He grabs a drink from the counter and leans back, surveying the scene for his own strange reasons.

"This is a fire hazard," he says dryly.

"It's Chase's fire hazard," I point out, taking a sip of my beer.

"You hiding in here?"

"Strategically positioning myself near the drinks," I tell him.

"Fair." He nods, his gaze drifting back toward the living room, where someone just cranked the music even louder. "So," he says after a beat, turning his attention fully to me. "You talk to Birdie yet?"

I nearly choke on my drink. "Why is everyone so obsessed with my love life?"

"Because it's like watching someone try to parallel park in front of an audience," Santi says, smirking. "Painful, but you kind of root for them anyway."

"Thanks for the vote of confidence."

I shake my head, but the teasing works. I'm more relaxed now than I have been all week. The conversation shifts to something else—who's going to puke first tonight, probably—and for a while, it's easy to pretend everything's fine.

Once Santi leaves, Chase barrels into the kitchen to drag me back out into the living room. "You're not gonna spend this whole party sulking," he says, practically shoving me into the crowd like I'm some antisocial recluse.

I end up near the couch, drink in hand, watching people dance and shout over the music. Someone hands me another drink I didn't ask for, and I take it because what the hell. It's easy to get lost in the chaos, to let the noise and the lights and the people blur together until nothing else matters.

But then Chase climbs onto the coffee table, and I'm both curious and bracing myself. He waves his arms, commanding everyone's attention.

"Hey! Listen up!" he shouts, grinning like a madman. "I've got something to say!" The crowd hushes, all eyes turning to him. "Here's to the Chicago Fire for drafting me, Adidas for the free cleats, and me for being the greatest thing to ever happen to soccer. Drink up!"

The room explodes into cheers. People are clapping, whistling, raising their drinks in a toast to Chase's boundless ego. He soaks it all in, throwing in a mock bow that makes the coffee table creak under his weight.

I laugh and clap for him, too, even as a pang of something sharp settles in my chest. It's pride, mostly. Envy, a little bit. But there's something else there, too—a quiet sense of loss. Chase is leaving, and everything's about to change.

As the night winds down and the crowd starts to thin out, Chase finds me sitting on the couch. He flops down next to me, still riding the high.

"You okay?" he asks, nudging me with his elbow.

"Sorta," I say quietly.

He studies me for a moment, then smirks. "Thinking about me?"

"Yeah, actually. I'll miss having you around. You're the only person I know who can burn a hole in a pan making scrambled eggs and somehow blame me for it."

His eyes go wide. "That was one time. And you did distract me by asking where the cinnamon was!"

"Cinnamon's not even supposed to go in eggs."

"Live a little."

We sit there for a minute together, quiet and thoughtful. I let my head fall back against the couch, my eyes drifting to the ceiling.

Chase was my constant after James and Hayes left. My buffer. My teammate in more ways than just soccer. If he hadn't been here, I probably would've retreated into myself, slipping back into the quiet space I tend to occupy when things shift too much.

And now, with him gone, it's going to be weird again.

I texted Warren earlier about the space being available, and all I got back was, *I'll let you know when I'm moving in.* No questions. No explanation. Just a statement of fact.

"You're gonna figure your shit out," Chase says finally. "Whatever's next—soccer, school, Birdie—you've got this."

I glance at him, swallowing the lump in my throat. "Yeah. You too."

He clinks his bottle against mine. "Damn right." Then he stands and grabs my arm, yanking me to my feet. "Come on. You're not sitting out the last party of the year like some kind of hermit. Flip cup. Let's go."

"I don't like drinking games," I argue, but it's half-hearted at best.

"You don't have to like them," he shoots back, dragging me through the throng of people toward the kitchen. "You just have to play them. And you're going to play them well because we're not losing to Amir's team again."

The back room is packed. Red Solo cups line the counters, and people are shouting over the music, arguing about whose turn it is.

Amir stands at one end of the table, arms crossed, a smug grin plastered across his face. "Finally decided to join your own party, Donovan?"

"It's not my party," I mutter.

He snorts. "We're literally at your house."

"Everyone calm down," Chase cuts in, throwing an arm around my shoulders. "Liam's finally quit his brooding to come play with us. And we're wiping that grin off your face, Alvarez."

"Big talk for someone who still hasn't mastered the wrist flick," Santi fires back, earning a round of laughter from his side of the table.

"I hate all of you," I groan.

But I step up to the table anyway. Chase shoves a cup into my hand, and before I know it, we're off. The first round is a blur of laughter, spilled beer, and increasingly questionable aim. Despite Chase's insistence that I play like a pro, I manage to miss my flip three times in a row, earning groans and jeers from everyone around me.

"Come on, buddy!" Chase yells, clapping me on the back. "You can do better than that!"

"Maybe if you stopped breathing down my neck, I'd actually make it!" I shoot back, flipping the cup with a little more force than necessary. It lands sideways.

We lose the first round but come back strong in the second. By the third, Chase is fully dialed in, shouting instructions like we're in the middle of a championship game. I can't stop laughing, and for the first time all night, I'm not thinking about Birdie or Warren or anything other than this ridiculous moment—this messy, chaotic kind of fun.

Midway through the fourth round, my phone buzzes in my pocket. I ignore it at first, focused on flipping my cup, but when the game ends and Chase drags me into another toast, I glance at the screen.

BIRDIE

Happy New Year.

That's it. Three simple words. But my heart stutters like she's just told me she's outside the house waiting for me. God, I wish she were. I wish I could pull her into the middle of all this and give her the kind of midnight kiss people write songs about.

"Who's got you smiling like that?" Santi shouts from across the table.

"None of your business," I say, locking my phone before anyone can peek.

He snorts. "Must be Birdie."

"Yeah, she makes me smile. You should try it sometime, Santi—having a personality that doesn't scare people off."

The guys around us howl with laughter, and Santi clutches his chest like I've just mortally wounded him. Then they set up for another game—quarters because Chase insists he's unbeatable. I'm usually decent at it, but tonight, I miss every shot. Every. Single. One.

I was having fun earlier, laughing, trash-talking, letting myself get swept up in the noise. But now? Now all I want is to talk to her.

Finally, I sneak away from the crowd, leaning against the wall in the hallway to catch my breath. My fingers hover over my phone screen, debating what to say.

LIAM

you too. want to meet up later this week?

The wait for her reply is torture. Every passing second feels like a countdown, the buzz of the party fading into the background. I glance at the time—seven minutes. I've been out here for seven minutes, staring at a blank screen like a lovesick loser.

"Earth to Liam," Chase says, suddenly appearing beside me. "What are you doing hiding out here? We're about to start another round of kings."

I pocket my phone quickly. "Just texting Birdie back."

He gives me a knowing look, his grin widening. "Oh, yeah? What'd she say?"

"She didn't yet."

He pats my shoulder. "Don't worry. Women love guys who are terrible at drinking games and sulk in hallways. Really endearing."

"Go away," I say, pushing him lightly.

My phone buzzes. I fumble with it, nearly dropping it in my haste.

BIRDIE

sounds good. maybe thursday?

LIAM

thursday works. let's meet at the Vault. you can tell me all about how you spent break avoiding me ;)

I immediately regret it. For a whole sixty seconds, I worry it was too soon to tease. A normal guy wouldn't overthink this. Wouldn't risk scaring her off before things felt steady again.

BIRDIE

lol. sounds fair. see you then x

The tight knot in my stomach loosens just enough for me to breathe.

"Come on," Chase nags. "We've got a legacy to defend."

"Legacy of what?" I ask, giving him a flat look.

"Being . . . legends," he mumbles. "Oh, whatever. I don't know. Just get your ass back in here."

I sigh but follow him anyway. It is Chase's goodbye party, after all. The least I can do is let myself get pulled back into the chaos. Let myself exist in the moment, even if it's fleeting.

And maybe a text back isn't as good as a midnight kiss, but Thursday is close enough. This time, I'm not going down without a fight.

Chapter Twenty-Eight
BIRDIE

BREAK'S COMING TO AN END, and campus is alive again. It's that jittery mix of dread and excitement that always comes with the start of a new semester. But I've only been back for two hours, and already the apartment feels warmer, more familiar, just because Sena's here.

Her laugh echoes from the kitchen as she unpacks a stash of overpriced snacks her mom insisted she bring back. "Do you know how many Trader Joe's bags I had to carry through the airport?" she calls, waving a box of maple leaf cookies in my direction.

I catch them midair, tuck my knees to my chest on the couch, and dig in. "The sacrifices you make for us common folk."

"You joke, but my mom is convinced you can't survive without these. 'What does Birdie eat?' she kept asking. Like I haven't seen you live off plain bagels and instant ramen for weeks at a time."

"Hey, don't knock the classics," I say lightly, though my throat tightens at her words. Sena's only just arrived, and already I feel a little more like myself. Break was long. Too long.

She catches the shift in my expression—of course she does. Sena always notices. She sets down the last of her bags and plops cross-legged onto the other end of the couch, her bright, knowing eyes locking on mine.

"Okay, spill," she says, waving a cookie at me like it's a pointer. "How was break? And don't even try to feed me some vague 'fine' bullshit."

I shrug and pop another cookie into my mouth, stalling. "But it *was* fine."

"Birdie."

I sigh and pick at the frayed edges of my sweater. "Okay, it was boring and sad. I stayed inside the whole time. Cleaned. Watched some terrible TV. Ignored my dad's subtle attempts to get me to socialize."

She raises an eyebrow. "And Liam?"

I gnaw at my lower lip. "We didn't talk much."

"Birdie," she groans. "He texted you, right?"

"A couple of times," I admit. "But I didn't text back until New Year's Eve. When he came by before break, I just . . . didn't answer the door."

She drags a pillow over her face with a dramatic groan. "No! Why? He likes you!"

"I know," I say quickly, guilt bubbling to the surface. "I know. He didn't do anything wrong. I just—I couldn't face him. Not after everything that happened. I felt so . . ."

"Defeated?" she offers gently.

"Exactly. And I didn't want him to see me like that. I didn't want anyone to see me like that."

She sets the pillow aside, leaning forward, her expression soft but firm. "You can't keep shutting people out, Birdie. You did that after the accident, remember? And you hated it."

I swallow hard, the memories rushing in. After the accident, I cut everyone off—friends, classmates, even my dad to a degree. I told myself I needed time, space, but the truth was I was scared. Scared of pity. Scared of being seen as fragile. Scared that no one would understand how heavy it all felt—like I wasn't just grieving the accident but the person I was before it.

And I was right. Most of them didn't understand. The friends I used to laugh with on weekends, complain about professors with—

they vanished. No texts, no visits, not even flowers. They just . . . stopped showing up.

And while I don't miss those shallow friendships, the thought of doing that to someone I do care about—someone like Liam— that's terrifying.

"I don't want to do that again," I whisper.

"Then don't," Sena says simply. "And it's not too late. If you ever want to reach out to anyone, I'll be there. Moral support and all that."

I blink at her, surprised. "You'd do that?"

"Of course," she says like it's the easiest thing in the world. "You've got me whether you like it or not. And if those old friends aren't worth it, screw them. But the people who matter? They'll still be there if you let them."

Her words sink in, loosening the knot in my chest just a little. Rebuilding trust feels impossible, but the idea of someone standing beside me makes it feel less so.

"Thanks," I say quietly. "For being here. For putting up with me."

She grins and nudges my shoulder. "You make it sound like it's a chore. Trust me, you're stuck with me." Leaning back on the couch, she adds, "So, tell me, what terrible TV did you watch over break?"

"Oh, you're not ready for this," I say, grateful for the change of subject. "First, there was the *Love Boat* reboot—yes, it's a dating show on a cruise ship. Then I fell back into the *Too Hot to Handle* abyss. But the worst? *MILF Manor*. It's like someone dared them to create the most chaotic, uncomfortable show ever, and they said, 'Bet.'"

She gasps, clutching a pillow. "You're lying. That can't be real."

"It is. And it's worse than you're imagining."

She groans, mock horrified, but she's smiling. "You need better coping mechanisms."

"Don't act like you're above it," I tease. "You'll be watching *MILF Manor* by the end of the week."

"Absolutely not."

For a little while, we keep talking and laughing like nothing's wrong. Like the world hasn't been crumbling around me. Like I didn't lose the fellowship or what little confidence I had left along with it.

It's nice, the ease of it. The way she makes everything feel easier, even when I'm carrying so much. And for now, I let that be enough.

It's Thursday, and my chest feels tight the entire walk to the pizza place Liam suggested, like someone's wrapped a rope around me and pulled it. Every step feels heavier than the last, and by the time I spot him waiting by the door, I'm ready to turn around and run.

But then he sees me. His face lights up with that effortless, crooked grin of his, and I unravel—just a little.

"Hey," he says, pulling the door open and gesturing me inside. "You're early. You nervous about seeing me or something?"

I let out an awkward laugh. "Don't flatter yourself."

He laughs too, a warm, quiet sound, and follows me inside. We grab a corner booth, tucked away from the rest of the world. I'm trying not to fidget, but I can't help it—my fingers pick at the sleeve of my sweater, my leg bounces under the table. Liam notices, of course.

He leans forward, resting his elbows on the table. "Birdie," he says gently. "It's just me."

And like that, the rope around my chest snaps. I shake my head, my throat tight as tears well up.

"Hey, hey," he says, sliding out of his seat and onto the bench beside me. "You're okay. I've got you."

"I—" My voice cracks, and I press my palms into my eyes. "I don't even know how to explain what I'm feeling. It's just—it's everything. It's too much."

He doesn't say a word. He just shifts closer, wrapping his arm around my shoulders. The weight of it steadies me, and when I finally drop my hands, his expression is patient and open, like he's ready to hold whatever I'm about to give him.

"You can start anywhere," he says softly. "Wherever it feels right."

So, I do. I tell him about the fellowship—how much I wanted it, how much I needed it. How losing it felt like the final nail in the coffin of a dream I've been holding on to since I was a kid.

I think he already knows how much it meant to me, how much I was relying on it, but saying it out loud makes it feel more manageable. Like I'm naming the loss, giving it shape, and letting it breathe.

Then I tell him about Emily, and that's the hardest part. I describe the accident, the guilt that's clung to me ever since. How I can still hear the crunch of metal, the blaring horn, the silence that followed. How I've spent the last year trying to make sense of it, trying to figure out how to move forward without letting it swallow me whole.

Liam doesn't interrupt, doesn't offer empty platitudes, or try to fix it. He just listens, his thumb brushing soothing circles over my shoulder.

By the time I'm finished, I feel raw, like I've just ripped myself open and laid everything bare.

"I'm sorry, Birdie." His voice is quiet, almost reverent. "You've been carrying all of that on your own?"

I nod, my throat too tight to speak.

"That's a lot," he says, and there's no judgment in his tone. Just understanding. "But you don't have to do that anymore. Okay?"

The tears spill over again, but this time, they're different. Lighter. Freer.

"I'm sorry," I whisper, wiping at my cheeks. "I wasn't there for you after you . . . lost the championship. I should've reached out. Should've put aside my own heartbreak to comfort you when you needed it."

He shakes his head, a small smile tugging at his lips. "Don't be sorry. It's not a big deal. I played well enough for the scouts, and I still have next year. Besides, I wasn't exactly expecting you to show up with pom-poms and a megaphone."

I laugh shakily. "You sure about that? I'd make a great cheerleader."

"Oh, I have no doubt," he teases, his grin widening.

We fall into an easy silence, the kind that feels like a balm after everything that's been said. I lean into him, his arm still draped around me, and I feel like I can breathe again.

After a while, he shifts, reaching into his jacket pocket. "I've got something for you," he says, pulling out a folded piece of paper.

"What is this?" I ask, taking it from him.

"Glad/Bad list," he says, like it's the most obvious thing in the world.

I unfold the paper, and sure enough, it's split down the middle with two columns labeled in his messy handwriting.

On the Glad side:

- Birdie texted me back.
- Birdie agreed to meet me.

On the Bad side:

- Birdie's been sad for too long.
- Birdie thought she had to go through all this alone.

I laugh, the sound bubbling up before I can stop it. "You're so . . . silly," I say, my voice thick with emotion.

"And yet, here we are," he says, his grin soft and steady. "I made one for you, too. Thought it might help."

My eyebrows lift. "Let's see it, then."

Liam pulls a second folded napkin from his other pocket, offering it with the same flair someone might use to present an Oscar. I take it, already bracing myself for whatever ridiculousness he's scrawled this time.

Unfolding the napkin, I find another Glad/Bad list, this one tailored just for me.

On the Glad side:

- Liam Donovan.
- Pottery.
- Birdie's dad.
- Sour candy.

On the Bad side:

- Loneliness.
- Failure.
- David fuckin' Donovan.
- Fellowship committee making bad decisions.

A rush of warmth and something sharper prickles under my ribs as I skim over the lists two more times. I blink hard, trying to make sense of the sudden swell of sweetness that lodges itself in my throat, leaving me unsteady. It's so quintessentially Liam—equal parts earnest and absurd.

"I can't believe you actually wrote this," I say, shaking my head. "And you put yourself at the top of the Glad side?"

"Of course. I take my research seriously."

"So, what's your plan, Dr. Donovan?" I ask, holding up the napkin. "To cure me with . . . sour candy?"

"Exactly," he says without missing a beat. "Which brings me to exhibit A."

He reaches into his pocket again and pulls out a bag of sour gummy worms, holding it up like it's the answer to all of life's problems.

I laugh. "Of course you have those."

"I'm a man of action," he says as he rips the bag open. "And I'm gonna work on this side." He points to the Glad column with a grin, then pops a gummy into his mouth.

For a moment, I just look at him, overwhelmed. By his humor, his thoughtfulness, the way he seems to know exactly how to take the weight off my chest. He doesn't just show up; he makes showing up feel like an art form.

"You really think this works?" I ask, holding up another neon worm. "Just a bag of sugar and all my problems magically disappear?"

His grin softens. "No. But I think it helps. And if it doesn't, we'll figure out what does. Together."

That word—*together*—wraps around me like a safety net. I didn't want to lean in on trusting it before, but now I think I could. I pluck another gummy worm from the bag and chew it slowly, letting the sweetness spread across my tongue.

"Fine," I say, sitting back in the booth. "You win. The gummy worms stay."

"Victory is mine."

I glance at the crumpled napkin on the table, the scrawled lists. I don't know how he does it—makes me laugh when I feel like crying, makes me feel less alone when I've spent weeks convincing myself I had to be.

"Liam," I say, quieter this time. "Thank you. For this. For being . . . so perfectly you."

His grin falters for just a second, his throat working through a heavy swallow. "Thank you for letting me be."

Chapter Twenty-Nine
BIRDIE

THE SMELL of wet clay and sulfurous glaze hits me as soon as I step into the studio. I used to love this smell—earthy, honest, full of potential. Now, it just feels heavy.

I take a seat in the back row. The stools are arranged in a semi-circle around the demonstration wheel, and I'm hoping to stay unnoticed. The semester might be brand-new, but everything else feels worn-out, like I've lived through this scene a hundred times already.

Dr. Hall stands at the center of the room, that perpetual scowl firmly in place. He's already got the wheel going, his hands deftly working a massive lump of clay into some unrecognizable form.

"Eight pounds," he announces in a gruff monotone. "We're starting large this semester, so if you've been coasting, it's time to stop. Mastery Wheel Throwing isn't for dabblers. If you're not up to it, drop the class now and spare me the trouble."

His words send a ripple of nervous laughter through the room, but I don't join in. I just stare at the spinning clay, mesmerized by how easily he coaxes it upward.

Dr. Hall's hands move with a confidence I used to dream of having. Now, I'm not sure if I ever will. The fellowship was the sole reason I even came back this year, and now that it's gone, it's like trying to relearn how to breathe.

I glance around the room, half listening as Dr. Hall critiques the imaginary mistakes we'll make when we try this ourselves next week. The other students are all nodding along or scribbling notes.

Nick is up front, sitting way too straight, his blazer hanging off the back of his stool like he thinks this is a board meeting and not an art class. The golden boy. The fellowship winner. The man who beat me.

He's nodding enthusiastically, like Dr. Hall is dropping life-changing wisdom and not just muttering about the importance of consistent pressure. It's infuriating. But the worst part is that he looks relaxed. Comfortable. Like he doesn't even realize what he's taken from me.

I'm not mad at Nick for winning. Not really.

His work is good—I'll give him that—and I'm sure he deserved it. But it doesn't help that I have to see his face after the fact. The sting doesn't care about fairness or merit. You'd think I've had the last month to stew in my own misery and get the fuck over it already, but I haven't.

Even with all the Glad stuff, the Bad stuff still wins out some-times. That's the thing about balance: it's fleeting. The scales tip, no matter how hard you try to keep them even. Today, the Bad is just louder.

I tighten my grip on my pen, staring hard at the notebook in my lap. I'm not writing anything, just doodling uneven lines along the edge of the page. Lines that wobble and overlap, just like the way I feel right now—messy and unbalanced.

Dr. Hall finishes the cylinder and begins shaping it into some-thing vaguely resembling a vase. "This is what happens if you don't center properly," he says, letting the walls of the piece wobble deliberately before they collapse. Then, with a practiced hand, he smashes the clay back into a lump.

By the time class ends, I'm drained. We didn't even touch the wheels today—just watched our professor throw around eight pounds of clay—but my shoulders ache like I've been holding up the weight of the room. Sitting so stiffly, pretending to absorb it all, takes more effort than I expected.

Next week, we're supposed to put everything into practice, and I'm already dreading it. My hands used to know what to do instinctively—how to center, pull, and shape without hesitation. Now? Now I'm not so sure they'll still listen.

As the other students file out, I think about thanking Dr. Hall. He didn't have to support my fellowship application, but he did. He put his name on the line, vouched for me, believed in my work. Thanking him feels like the right thing to do—the professional, respectful thing.

But as I watch him wipe his hands on a towel and glance around the nearly empty room, I hesitate. This is the perfect moment: no students clamoring for his attention, no distractions. And yet, the thought of walking up to him, of saying thank you while my head is still buzzing with everything I've lost, makes me feel a little sick.

I look down at my shoes, avoiding his gaze as I shuffle toward the door. I'll thank him another day—when I don't feel so raw. When I don't feel like the whole world is still watching me fail.

"Birdie."

I glance up to find Nick standing there, hands buried in the pockets of his impeccably tailored pants. "Hey," he says. "You got a minute?"

I grip the strap of my bag tighter. "What do you want, Nick?"

He raises his hands in mock surrender. "Easy, Collins. I just wanted to check in. See how you're doing."

My stomach twists. "You wanted to check in? On me?"

"Yeah," he says, his tone infuriatingly sincere. "I know you were vying for that fellowship, and it's not easy to lose something you put so much into."

The lump in my throat doubles in size. "Thanks for the reminder."

He winces. "I'm serious. Look, I know it probably doesn't mean much coming from me, but your work? It's incredible. The judges said so, too. You're really talented, Birdie."

I blink at him. "Mmhmm, that's why *you* were the winner."

"My work was good, too. But I also have connections. My dad and David were fraternity brothers here at Dayton, and they're still close." He gives a self-deprecating laugh. "Honestly, I just wanted the internship. I wish we could've, like, split the win so you could get the stipend."

The words hit me like a knife sliding between my ribs, hollowing me out. The thing I'd spent months pinning my hopes and future on was just a stepping stone for him—a casual networking opportunity. And the kicker? His father and David, frat bros swapping favors, like this whole process was predetermined from the start.

After all that talk of me having an unfair advantage with Liam, the irony's almost laughable. His connections were baked in from the start while I was over here scrabbling for crumbs, hoping my work would be enough to speak for itself.

"I don't know what you want me to say to that," I snap. "Congratulations? Thank you for taking something I actually needed?"

His smile falters, but only slightly. "I didn't mean it like that. I just—I know how hard it is when you put everything into something and come up short."

"Do you?"

He cocks his head to the side. "I didn't mean to upset you. I just thought maybe we could . . . I don't know, talk. Grab coffee or something. You've been on my mind."

There it is. The real reason he's here. A thinly veiled proposition disguised as a wellness check. How transparent. How audacious.

I stand, slinging my bag over my shoulder, my movements

sharp. "I'm sure you mean well, but I'm not interested. In coffee. Or talking. Or whatever this is."

"Birdie, look—" He leans in slightly, his tone shifting to something overly smooth, like he's reciting lines from a play. "I'm just saying, I think we'd get along if we gave it a shot. You've got this edge to you I really like."

"No," I say firmly, cutting him off before he can spin more nonsense. "Congratulations on the fellowship, Nick. I mean it. But I'm not interested in getting to know you. I already have someone anyway."

His brows knit, and for the first time, he looks genuinely taken aback. It disarms me for a moment, but I don't stick around to see what he'll say next. I push past him and head for the door.

I have someone, is what I'd told him.

And it's true. Liam and I were . . . doing some light kissing before everything blew up. But it wasn't just that. It was trust. It was warmth. It was the feeling of being seen—completely—when the rest of the world felt like it didn't even notice I existed.

But we're not together. We weren't then, and we certainly aren't now. I'm not sure I'm ready to be, even if he wanted that. I'm not in a good place, and I can't be the girlfriend who's constantly falling apart.

I shove my hands into the pockets of my jacket and walk toward the bookstore. There's no time to go back to the apartment and change before my shift, so I'm stuck in this sweater that smells faintly of the studio.

Once I'm there, I pull out my phone while I wait for the manager to unlock the doors. There's a text from Liam waiting for me, sent just ten minutes ago.

LIAM

you survive your first day back? or should I come rescue you?

BIRDIE

> barely. can't talk long—waiting for my shift to start. but nick riordan just tried to "check in" on me after class, and I almost lost my shit

LIAM

> what does "check in" mean? that little bastard didn't hit on you, did he?

BIRDIE

> oh, he absolutely did. tried to "grab coffee" but I told him to shove it

LIAM

> glad you dodged that bullet. guy's got the personality of wet toast

BIRDIE

> you're not wrong

LIAM

> seriously though—you good? want me to swing by after work with snacks?

My chest tightens in the best way, and I bite my lip, trying to keep my smile in check. He's not asking because he feels obligated. He's asking because he cares. Because he's Liam.

But caring doesn't mean he should have to carry me.

BIRDIE

> yeah, actually. we need to talk about something

My fingers hover over the screen, my heart beating a little faster. I want to tell him how important he's become to me, how supportive he's been, how lovely it feels to have him in my corner. But the thought is terrifying. Saying that out loud risks everything —our connection, the comfort he brings, the fragile bond we've built.

Because what if I can't be what he deserves? I'm not steady. I'm not whole. He deserves someone who can meet him where he is, not someone stuck trying to claw their way out of their own mess.

LIAM

okay

really fucking hate that sentence btw

BIRDIE

it's nothing bad. see you tonight x

I stare at the screen, my thoughts swirling. I need to tell him how much he means to me. But I also need to be honest—with him and myself. If I can't give him what he deserves, I have to draw a line. I have to let him go before I drag him down with me.

Still, I hope he'll understand. I hope he'll stay, even if I can't offer him the romantic version of us. Because losing him completely? That would break me in a way I don't think I could recover from.

Chapter Thirty

I CLIMB the stairs to Birdie's apartment, my hands shoved deep into my jacket pockets to keep from fidgeting, silently repeating a mantra in my head.

You're not nervous. She just wants to talk. It's fine. Everything's fine.

But my body isn't buying it. My stomach twists itself into knots, and my pulse hammers like I'm halfway through a penalty sprint. Because let's be real—no one ever says "we need to talk" when it's something good. Those words have a track record, and it's not a great one.

By the time I knock on her door, I've worked myself into a quiet panic. What if this is it? What if she's decided she doesn't want me around anymore? What if—

The door swings open, cutting off my frantic thoughts. Birdie stands there in a striped sweater, her cropped bob tied back on both sides with ribbon. She looks soft and tired and completely beautiful, and my chest does that weird, unsteady flutter it always does when I see her.

"Hey," she says quietly, stepping aside to let me in. The faint scent of clay and lavender drifts toward me, so unmistakably Birdie that it sends my thoughts reeling.

"Hi, Birdie."

She closes the door behind me, her movements careful, almost hesitant, and gestures toward the couch. "Sit?"

I do as she says, and she settles beside me, close enough for her warmth to brush against me but not close enough for our shoulders to touch. The space between us feels charged, like it's holding the weight of everything left unsaid.

I clear my throat. "You wanted to talk?"

She pulls her legs onto the couch and tucks them beneath her. "Liam," she starts, and my stomach sinks. "I just want to say, first of all, how much I appreciate you. You've been so . . . good to me. Better than I probably deserve."

"Look, if this—"

"Let me finish," she says, cutting me off with a small, shaky smile. "You've been this incredible, steady presence in my life, even when I tried so hard to distance myself. And I really want to keep . . . hanging out with you. I do. But I don't know if I can be what you deserve. I don't know if I can be a good girlfriend to you, if that's what you're looking for. Honestly, I'd probably be a really bad one."

She laughs a little, but it's strained, like she's trying to make light of something that's anything but. "What I'm asking is . . . would you stick around? Even if there was nothing romantic going on between us?"

It feels like I've been gutted. She's scared—I can see it in the way her fingers twist in her lap, the way her shoulders hunch like she's bracing for impact. But if she thinks she's doing this for my benefit, then she's not only scared—she's just plain wrong.

Because I don't need her to be perfect or put together or anything she thinks she's not. I just need her to be Birdie.

"No, I don't accept that," I say firmly.

Her head snaps up, eyes wide and startled. "What?"

"I don't accept it," I repeat, leaning forward, my elbows resting on my knees as I face her fully. "I'm not going to lie to you, Birdie. Or to myself. There is something romantic going on between us. There has been since the day I kicked that ball through your studio window and met you. There's a spark there, and it hasn't gone out. Not for me, anyway."

She blinks at me, her mouth opening and closing like she doesn't know what to say.

"And I'm not going to keep being with you and pretending it's something it's not," I continue. "I know you're scared, so if you need time, if you need space, I'll wait. I'll wait as long as you need. But we're not just 'hanging out.' That's not what this is, and we both know it."

For a moment, she just stares at me, like she's trying to process what I've said. Then, to my complete surprise, she laughs. It starts as a small chuckle, then grows into full-on, uncontrollable laughter.

I frown, confused. "What's so funny?"

She shakes her head, still laughing so hard a tear slips down her cheek. I reach out instinctively, brushing it away with my thumb. My hand lingers, cupping her jaw, and she leans into the touch, her laughter tapering off into a soft, breathy sound.

"I just—" She looks up at me. "I didn't expect you to say all that. I thought you'd agree, and we'd just . . . keep things casual."

"Yeah, well, I didn't expect you to sell yourself so short," I say, my tone softening. "You're not a bad girlfriend, Birdie. You're not anything bad. You're just you. And that's all I want."

She stares at me, her eyes searching mine like she's looking for a crack in my resolve. But she won't find one. Not this time.

Finally, she lets out a shaky breath. "You make it sound so simple."

"It is simple," I say. "I want to be with you. You want to be with me. Everything else? We'll figure it out."

Her gaze flickers to my lips. Slowly, she leans in, her hands resting lightly on my chest. And then she's kissing me. Again.

She's kissing me, and I'm sitting here like a fool, completely stunned, completely lost in the way she feels against me. Like everything else has fallen away, and it's just her—soft and warm and perfect.

Our lips meet, and when she deepens the kiss by flicking her tongue against mine, something ignites inside me. My hand slides to the back of her neck, pulling her closer, guiding her until she swings one leg over my lap and straddles me.

"Birdie," I murmur against her lips, my voice rough and unsteady. "Do you—"

She cuts me off with another kiss, her hands threading into my hair. "I want this," she whispers, her breath warm against my mouth. "I'm sure."

Her words melt my hesitation, and I kiss her harder. It's messy and a little desperate, like we're both trying to say a hundred things without pausing to breathe. She pulls back slightly, her forehead resting against mine, her hands cupping my face. Her thumbs trace soft, deliberate circles over my cheeks.

"You were right," she whispers. "I am scared. But you . . . you make me feel like I don't have to be."

My chest tightens, and I let my hands settle on her thighs, squeezing gently. "You don't," I say firmly. "Not with me. I've got you, okay? If you don't want to call me your boyfriend, that's fine. But just know that I'm yours, no matter the title."

She shakes her head, and a small, breathless laugh escapes her. "You can be my boyfriend, Liam."

Relief crashes through me, so raw and overwhelming that it spills into my voice. "Great, I was really hoping you'd say that."

Her laughter bubbles up again, warm and light, and it's the best sound I've heard all day. Then she leans in, her lips brushing against mine, and this time, the kiss is deeper, hungrier, like we've both been holding back for too long.

My hands move instinctively, gripping her waist, sliding up her sides, feeling the heat of her through the soft knit of her sweater.

She's so close, so perfectly here, and I know I'll never get enough of her—of this.

Her fingers tangle in my hair, sending shivers down my spine, every nerve in my body lighting up at once. The way she presses against me, the soft, breathy sounds she makes, the way her fingertips trace the edge of my jaw—it's intoxicating. It's everything.

My hands move to her lower back as she shifts on my lap. A low groan escapes me, and she gasps softly, her lips parting against mine. "Birdie," I murmur, my voice unsteady.

"Mm." Her lips trail along my jawline, down to the curve of my neck. My head falls back against the couch, my eyes fluttering shut as her mouth brushes a spot just beneath my ear, her teeth grazing my skin. A jolt of pleasure shoots through me.

I jerk my hips, unable to help myself, pressing my erection against her, and she lets out this soft, breathy sound that makes my entire body tighten. She shifts again, grinding down, and we both gasp at the friction.

"God, Birdie," I groan, gripping her hips to hold her steady, though it feels like I'm the one who needs grounding. "You're gonna kill me."

Her lips find mine again, the kiss deep and consuming, her fingers threading into my hair as I lose myself in her. My hands slide under her sweater, skimming over the warm, bare skin of her back. She arches into me, her soft moan vibrating against my mouth, and I think I might lose my mind.

I want her—badly. So badly it's all I can think about. But I don't want to rush her. I pull back slightly, resting my forehead against hers, my breathing ragged and uneven.

"Can I touch you?" I ask, my voice low and raw with need but laced with hesitation.

She nods, her teeth sinking into her bottom lip as her eyes meet mine. "Please," she whispers.

That one word nearly undoes me. My hand slides under the

waistband of her pants, hesitating for just a heartbeat before slipping beneath the thin fabric of her panties. She's warm and wet, impossibly soft, and the feel of her sends a shudder down my spine.

"Fuck," I rasp, my fingers brushing lightly over her clit. Her hips jerk, and I can't stop the groan that slips out. "You're so . . . goddamn perfect. So responsive."

She buries her face in my neck, her teeth scraping lightly against my skin as my fingers move in slow, deliberate circles. Her breath is hot and uneven, and I can feel the tension building in her with every movement, every shiver.

Her hips rock against my hand, matching my rhythm, and the quiet, desperate noises she's making have me on the brink of losing control. My other hand slides up her thigh, gripping just enough to keep her steady, to anchor her as she moves.

She trembles, her breath catching. "Oh, God, Liam."

Hearing her say my name like that—breathless, needy—it sends a pulse of heat straight through me. My hips snap up reflexively, pressing against the place where my fingers are working her, and she cries out softly, her hands clutching my shoulders like she's holding on for dear life.

"Birdie," I rasp, my voice breaking under the weight of the moment. I'm so close to losing it, and she hasn't even touched me. But it's everything—how good she feels pressed against me, how beautiful she sounds when she whispers my name, how much I want to give her everything I have, everything I am.

Her movements grow more frantic, her breath hitching as my fingers press harder, faster. She's so wet, so warm, and every tiny sound she makes pushes me closer to the edge.

"I told you I've got you," I murmur against her ear. "Just let go."

Her body tenses, her hips stuttering as a soft, broken moan escapes her lips. She shudders against me, her nails digging into my shoulders as she falls apart, her release washing over my hand.

The sight of her, the feel of her trembling against me, the way she whispers my name like it's the only thing keeping her grounded —it's too much. My hips snap up again, grinding against her, and the tension inside me unravels all at once. A guttural groan rips from my throat as I come, the heat of it coursing through me in waves, raw and overwhelming.

We stay like that for a moment, tangled together, both of us breathing hard and trembling. Her forehead rests against mine, and her hands slide down to cup my face, her thumbs brushing lightly over my cheeks.

"Wow," she whispers, her lips curving into a small, breathless smile.

I press a soft kiss to her forehead before gently easing her off my lap. "Be right back," I murmur, standing and heading to the bathroom.

Once inside, I grab a washcloth, wet it with warm water, and clean myself up first, my hands a little shaky but steady enough to get the job done. My reflection catches my eye for a second— flushed cheeks, mussed hair, and a dazed kind of smile I don't even try to hide.

Shaking my head, I rinse a new washcloth and wring it out before heading back to the living room.

Birdie is still curled up on the couch, looking softer and lighter, like the weight of the world isn't pressing down on her quite as hard anymore.

"Here," I say, crouching in front of her. "Let me clean you up."

Her eyes widen slightly, but she doesn't protest as I carefully help her shimmy out of her pants just enough to reach her thighs. I wipe between her legs with deliberate care, keeping my movements gentle and precise. Once finished, I tie the little drawstring back up securely.

"There," I say as I sit back on my heels. "All good."

She brushes her fingers over my jaw. "Thank you."

I nod, standing to toss the washcloth back into the bathroom before returning to her side. I pull her into my arms again, and she leans into me, her cheek pressing against my chest as I drape a blanket over both of us.

It's obvious something fundamental has shifted between us, like we've uncovered a tiny bit of solid ground to stand on together, even if the rest of the world still feels unsteady.

"I'm sorry," she says softly, breaking the quiet. Her fingers toy with the hem of my shirt, her voice wavering just enough to crack something in me. "For trying to keep you at arm's length. For thinking you were better off."

"Don't be sorry," I tell her, tilting her chin up so I can meet her eyes. They're shining, but not with tears. It's something else— something warm and hopeful that makes my chest ache. "Just . . . don't do it again, okay? Because I'm not going anywhere, Birdie. Not unless you tell me to."

She swallows hard. "Okay."

"Okay," I echo, leaning back against the couch and letting her settle against me.

We sit in the quiet, her hand resting over my heart, her breathing soft and even. And I'm thankful. So unbelievably thankful because right now, it feels like we've found something real, something solid—like we're exactly where we're meant to be.

Chapter Thirty-One

I WAKE up in a great mood. Like whistling-on-my-way-to-the-kitchen kind of mood. The kind where the world seems brighter, the air feels fresher, and everything just . . . clicks. After last night with Birdie, how could it not?

I have a girlfriend, and I only had to beg her a little bit.

I'm practically floating as I shuffle into the kitchen, still wearing my sweats and a faded Dayton T-shirt, thinking about breakfast. Maybe I'll do eggs. Or pancakes. Or both. It's a good day. It deserves both.

When I step into the kitchen, I walk into a surreal little scene I wasn't prepared for. Warren is already sitting at the table, like he's been there for hours. Like this is just a normal, everyday morning routine. He's got a bowl of cereal in front of him, a cup of coffee, and an expression that screams *don't talk to me*.

"Warren?" I ask, blinking.

He glances up briefly, his dark, disheveled hair flopping over his forehead, green eyes sharp and assessing. Then, as if he's decided I'm not worth more than a second of his attention, he looks back down at his cereal. "Morning."

"When did you get here?" I ask, grabbing a mug and pouring myself some coffee.

"Last night."

"And you didn't think to let me know?"

"You asked me to move in," he says, deadpan. "I moved in."

I set the coffeepot down and turn to face him. "Right, but most people would, I don't know, give a heads-up first?"

"Didn't want to bother you," he says with a shrug, shoveling another spoonful of cereal into his mouth.

I stare at him, bemused. In some aspects, he's just like me—*blunt, straightforward*. In others, *he's impossible to figure out—like a book missing half its pages.*

"You're such a little weirdo, you know that?"

"Yeah, I've heard," he says, unbothered.

I shake my head and grab a chair across from him. The guy is a total enigma, but I can't say I'm surprised. My aunt has always been kind of a mystery—grumpy, aloof, and perpetually annoyed by the world. It's no wonder her son would take after her.

Warren's like a cat that tolerates you because it has no choice. He's also infuriatingly neat. His hair looks like he woke up and tried not to fix it, but everything else about him—his posture, his movements—is methodical. Even now, he eats cereal like it's some kind of science experiment. Precise spoonfuls, no stray drips of milk, no slurping.

"So," I say, sipping my coffee, "Everything good with your room? My mom told me your last place had a mold problem."

He shrugs, which I'm starting to realize is his default answer for everything. "Yeah."

"Cool," I say, leaning back in my chair. "You're welcome, by the way."

"For what?" he asks, raising an eyebrow.

"For me being such a great roommate," I say with a grin. "I'm the whole package—great vibes, excellent taste in snacks, and a winning personality."

He snorts, the closest thing to a laugh I've gotten out of him so far.

Normally, I'd hate this kind of chatter. I'm usually the one being prodded for conversation, and I'm not big on meaningless small talk or trying to draw words out of people who clearly don't want to talk. But with Warren, it's kind of fun. Like trying to crack a code no one's solved before, and every shrug or deadpan response feels like a tiny victory.

"So," I say, switching gears, "how's the team? You guys getting ready for the conference championships?"

His expression shifts slightly, enough to tell me I've hit on something he actually cares about. "Yeah. Next month."

"Nice," I say. "What's your event again? Backstroke, right?"

"Freestyle and medley relay," he corrects.

"Ah, I'm more of a doggy paddle kind of guy," I say with a grin. "You think you're gonna take the title this year?"

He shrugs again. "Maybe. Depends on our split times and who shows up for the other teams."

"Right," I say, nodding along like I know what I'm talking about. "Split times are huge."

His lips twitch, just barely, like he's trying not to laugh at my cluelessness. "Yeah. They're kind of the whole deal. But you don't have a clue what you're talking about, do you?"

"Not even a little. I respect the hustle, though. You swimmers have it rough. Early mornings, endless laps, and smelling like chlorine 24/7."

"It's not that bad."

"Sure," I say, taking another sip of coffee. "Tell that to your pruney fingers and your likely even prunier di—"

"Annnd that's enough of that."

"What? I'm just stating facts."

I hold back a laugh and start making myself some pancakes as Warren finishes his cereal. He's acting like I'm not even here, but there's something oddly calming about his presence. Like he's perfectly content with the quiet.

"What's your schedule like?" I ask after a while. "We can do a calendar on the fridge."

He stares at me, brow furrowed like I've just suggested synchronized swimming lessons. "Why?"

"Trying to figure out when I'll have the kitchen to myself."

He pulls out his phone and taps away. "Morning practice, afternoon classes, evening practice. Pretty much the same every day."

"Cool," I say, nodding. "Guess I won't have to worry about hiding the good snacks."

"I'm not interested in your protein bars and sour gummy worms, anyway."

I sigh dramatically. "Ah, a man with no taste. No wonder you're always so serious."

"Right." He stands, washes out his bowl, and sets it back in the cupboard like a robot programmed for efficiency. "See you around, Donovan."

"Later, Flipper."

He disappears back into his room, door clicking shut behind him.

Warren's definitely a little strange. Grumpy, aloof, and way too serious for someone who spends most of his time in a Speedo.

Still, I think I'm gonna like having him around. He's nothing like Chase, miles away from Hayes and James, but there's something solid about him. And I guess, despite the unfamiliarity, change doesn't have to be a bad thing.

It's quiet this time of day, with most students in class or holed up in the library. Birdie walks ahead of me, her cropped bob bouncing slightly as she moves. She's still nervous—I can see it in the way she fidgets with the strap of her bag—but there's a steadiness to her that wasn't there just last week.

"You okay?" I ask, keeping my voice low as we approach the front desk.

She glances at me, her lips quirking in a small, hesitant smile. "Yeah. I think so. Thanks for coming with me."

"Anytime," I say, and I mean it. If she asked me to haul these pieces to the moon, I'd probably find a way. But we're just at the Ellsworth, picking up her artwork. And standing here beside her is no big deal, really.

The receptionist barely glances up as Birdie explains why we're here. Her pieces from the fellowship showcase are stored in the back, and she hasn't been by to pick them up yet. She felt too awkward before—too sad, she told me last night—but today, there's a quiet determination in her.

"This way," the receptionist says, motioning us through a door that leads to a storage area.

The back room is dimly lit and packed with everything from towering canvases to delicate glass sculptures, all labeled and stacked neatly. Birdie scans the space, her expression softening when she spots her work.

"There they are," she murmurs, stepping closer to a set of ceramic pieces arranged on a low shelf. Her fingers hover over one of the larger vases, brushing lightly against the glaze.

"They're beautiful," I say, and it's not just a line. They are. The colors, the shapes, the way they catch the light—it's all Birdie, through and through.

Her cheeks flush. "Thanks."

I pick up one of the smaller bowls, running my fingers over the smooth, cool surface. It's a deep, glossy blue, like staring into the heart of an ocean. The craftsmanship is undeniable—perfectly balanced, flawless in execution, and yet brimming with something deeply personal.

And yet, even as I admire it, there's this nagging thought I can't shake. I'll never know if I'm the reason she didn't get chosen. If my so-called "help" backfired. If my dad docked her points because he thought I gave her an unfair advantage.

Or worse—maybe she really wasn't the best candidate, though I can't bring myself to believe that. The idea that Birdie—who breathes life into clay in ways that feel like magic—wasn't enough? That's harder to swallow than any of the other possibilities.

"I still can't believe they didn't pick you," I say, my voice low.

She glances at me, her brow pinching slightly. "Liam, don't bother—"

"I'm not harping," I say quickly, carefully setting the bowl back on the cart. "I'm just saying . . . my dad's a loser. He should've chosen you."

"He wasn't the only deciding factor," she says, grabbing a blanket from her bag and draping it over one of the larger pieces. "But Nick told me something interesting," she adds lightly. "Apparently, your dad and his were fraternity brothers here at Dayton."

I blink, then laugh—a dry, humorless sound. "Of course they were. Should've guessed."

She cuts me a sharp look. "I'm not saying that's why Nick won. Nepotism maybe gained him some points, but he's a brilliant artist, too."

I shrug, not in the mood to dissect my dad's choices any longer. We'll never know what really happened because that man is an enigma of business strategy and ego, and trying to understand his decisions is like trying to catch smoke.

"Maybe," I say. "But that doesn't mean you weren't just as deserving. If not more."

Her smile is small and doesn't quite reach her eyes, but she doesn't argue. Instead, we focus on gathering her pieces, wrapping each one carefully in blankets and loading them onto a cart.

"You sure you're okay with this?" I ask, watching her secure the last piece. "I can drive everything over to your place, then circle back and walk home with you."

"No, it's freezing." She straightens, brushing her hands on her sweater, and nods. "And I trust you. Just . . . talk to me the whole way, okay? Distract me."

"Done," I say without hesitation. "You're not gonna have a second to think about the car."

She smiles, something soft and grateful. "Good."

I close the trunk with a satisfying click and step over to open the passenger door for her. Her smile stays firmly in place, and I silently promise to do whatever it takes to keep it there for as long as she'll let me.

Before I can shut her in, her fingers curl around the front of my shirt, tugging me in. She presses a soft kiss to my lips, her hand sneaking up to ruffle my hair before pulling back, leaving me dazed.

I blink, shaking off the haze, and catch sight of her fingers dropping back into her lap. That's when I realize what's missing. My hat. Damn it.

"Hold on," I say, straightening. "I left my hat inside."

Birdie leans back in her seat, giving me a teasing look. "Don't take too long," she murmurs, her voice carrying just the slightest edge of humor. "I don't trust these drivers to not ding your bumper while we're out here."

I grin, closing the door gently. "Good to know you're looking out for my precious car."

She smirks but doesn't say anything else as I jog back toward the gallery, retracing our steps to the storage room. My hat's sitting right on the counter where I left it—typical—and as I grab it, the door behind me creaks open.

"Liam?"

I turn to see Claire Mahler stepping out from the back, her cropped auburn hair catching the light. She's taller than I remember—or maybe it's just the way she carries herself, with a self-assured ease that feels magnetic.

"Ms. Mahler," I say, startled.

"Please," she says, a small smile tugging at her lips. "Call me Claire."

"Claire," I correct, fumbling slightly. My brain is already bracing for some mention of my dad, but she doesn't go there. Instead, she tilts her head, her green eyes sharp and curious.

"You're friends with Bridget Collins, right?"

"Yeah, actually," I reply, surprised. "Birdie's just outside, loading her pieces into my car."

Her smile deepens, her eyes softening. "Good. Can you give her something for me?" She reaches into the pocket of her blazer and pulls out a sleek white business card, extending it toward me.

I hesitate for a second before taking it, glancing down at the embossed letters. *Claire Mahler, Ceramicist.*

"Of course. Is everything okay?"

"More than okay," she says, her tone deliberate yet warm. "I'd like her to call me when she has a moment. I have a proposition for her."

My heart skips a beat, the significance of her words sinking in. "A proposition?" I echo, trying to keep my eagerness in check. "I can grab her now if you want. She'd love to talk to you."

Claire shakes her head with an elegant flick of her hand. "I'd rather not put her on the spot. I suspect she's had enough surprises lately. Just let her know I'm very interested in her work."

"Yes, ma'am," I say automatically before grimacing at myself. "I mean, Claire."

She chuckles softly, already turning back toward the storage area. "Thank you, Liam. And tell Birdie she has remarkable talent. Truly."

I stand there for a moment, staring down at the card in my hand like it's solid gold. When I finally make my way back to the car, Birdie looks up from her phone, her brow furrowing at the look on my face.

"What?" she asks, sitting up straighter.

I slide into my seat, pull the door shut, and hold out the card. "Claire Mahler wants you to call her."

Birdie's eyes widen, her fingers trembling slightly as she takes the card. "What? Why?"

"She didn't say," I admit, grinning now. "Just that she has a proposition for you and that she thinks you're a fantastic artist."

Birdie stares at the card like it might dissolve in her hands, her mouth opening and closing as she tries to process the words. Then, slowly, a smile spreads across her face—small at first, then growing until it lights up her entire expression.

"Liam," she breathes, her voice shaky with disbelief. "This— this is—"

"Yeah," I say, cutting her off with a grin. "It's a big deal. And you deserve it."

She looks over at me, her eyes shining, and for a moment, neither of us says anything. Then, before I can react, she leans across the console and throws her arms around my neck, the awkward angle doing nothing to diminish the warmth of her embrace.

"Thank you," she whispers, her voice muffled against my shoulder.

"For what?" I ask, laughing softly as I hug her back, my hand resting lightly on her arm for balance. "I didn't do anything."

"You always show up," she says simply, pulling back just enough to meet my eyes. Her cheeks are flushed, her smile softer now but no less radiant. "That means everything."

My chest tightens, and I give her a crooked smile. "Always," I promise.

She settles back into her seat, still clutching the card like it's her ticket to another world, and I start the car. As we pull out of the parking lot, I can't stop glancing at her—the way her excitement glows quietly beside me, like a sunrise breaking over the horizon. Gorgeous and so unapologetically herself.

Chapter Thirty-Two

THE VOICEMAIL WAS EXCRUCIATING. Three minutes of me trying to sound breezy and confident, stumbling through my name, and then immediately second-guessing if I should've started with "Hi, this is Bridget Collins" instead of just "Birdie." Or maybe, "Hey, it's me. The girl who nearly puked on your shoes at the Montrose opening." Too late now.

Still, I did it. I called *Claire freaking Mahler's* personal number and left a voicemail. And now? Now I'm pacing around the apartment with entirely too much nervous energy and a stomach that feels like it's been taken hostage by a swarm of anxious bees.

To distract myself, I've taken all my fellowship pieces out of their blankets and set them up around the living room. It's ridiculous—like I'm hosting a miniature art exhibit for an audience of two, and one of them just dragged herself out of bed wearing mismatched socks.

"Wow," Sena says, her voice laced with awe as she studies the collection. She's holding a coffee mug shaped like a cat, and her bun of curls is threatening to collapse under the weight of all her hair. "They're even better out here. Like, in the wild."

"You make it sound like they're endangered."

"Well, they kind of are," she says, taking a sip of her coffee. "Rare, valuable, beautiful. You're lucky I don't try to steal one for my room."

I laugh, but her words hit somewhere deep. *Rare. Valuable.*

Beautiful. I haven't let myself think of my work like that since the rejection, even with Liam's insistence. But maybe I should. Maybe I'm allowed to.

"Thanks," I say softly, stepping back to take it all in.

The vases, the bowls, the little sculptural pieces. Each one feels like a piece of me—my anxieties and hopes, my late-night break-throughs, the stubborn globs of clay that refused to cooperate until they suddenly did.

"You know," Sena says, settling onto the couch, "I was half expecting you to bury these in your closet forever. But this?" She gestures to the display. "This is cool. It's like you're reclaiming them."

I glance at her, surprised by how much her words mean. Sena has this way of saying the right thing without making a big deal about it. It's one of the reasons I like her so much.

"Yeah," I admit, sitting down next to her. "I guess I am."

She leans back, her gaze still on the pieces. "So, any updates from Claire and her mysterious proposition?"

"Not yet," I say, trying to keep the nerves out of my voice. "I left her a voicemail this morning, so now I'm just . . . waiting."

"Well, obviously, she's going to offer you something great," she says confidently. "I mean, you're amazing. And she knows it. Otherwise, why would she give you her number?"

I nod, fiddling with a loose thread on my sweater. "So, how's your directing class going?" I ask, shifting gears. "Has Maxxine still been giving you a hard time?"

She groans dramatically, throwing an arm over her eyes. "Don't remind me. We're doing scene workshops right now, and it's not just Max. My whole group has zero chemistry. Like, imagine trying to direct a romantic scene between two bricks."

I snort. "That bad?"

"Worse," she says, lifting her arm just enough to give me a

pointed look. "If one of them forgets their blocking one more time, I might actually combust."

"Sounds like a great learning opportunity," I tease, and she throws a pillow at me.

Sena mutters something about "creative differences" while I stare at one of my bowls—the deep blue one Liam loves. Just thinking about the way he looked at it yesterday makes my chest warm, a quiet flutter settling beneath my ribs.

"Hey, do you want to come watch Liam's scrimmage with me? It's at three."

There's a beat of hesitation, and then she makes a face. Not a bad face, exactly—more like someone just offered her a bowl of lukewarm oatmeal.

"Oh God," I say, cringing. "Am I not supposed to invite you to my boyfriend's games? Is that, like, against roommate code or something?"

She bursts out laughing, nearly spilling her coffee. "No, no, that's not it. It's just . . . sports."

"Sports," I repeat, raising an eyebrow. "You hate sports?"

"With the fire of a thousand suns," she says dramatically. "And it's freezing outside. Like, I'll go if you really want me to, but I'll be miserable and probably complain the whole time."

I laugh, feeling a little ridiculous for not knowing this about her already. "Okay, no worries. I can go by myself."

"No, no, wait. Scratch that. I'll go with you," she says, quieter now. "I like spending time with you."

The words hit right in the softest parts of me. Sena's always been the one dragging me into things—bars with her friends, movie nights, random trips to the farmers' market for overpriced candles. She's the reason I have any kind of social life at all.

But this? Her offering to step out of her comfort zone for me? It makes me feel unexpectedly seen, like maybe I'm just as important to her as she is to me.

"You don't have to," I say quickly. "Really, I'll be fine."

"I know I don't," she says, her lips curving into a small smile. "But I want to. As long as you're okay with my running commentary about how annoying sports are."

I laugh. "Deal. But you have to promise not to heckle Liam."

She winks. "No promises."

We spend the next hour lounging around, sipping coffee. Sena tells me about an improv class she's taking on the side (how she has time for that, I'll never understand).

"I know, I know," she says, throwing her hands in the air. "It's overdone. But they're adding puppets. Like, full-on sock puppets. I don't know if it'll be brilliant or a hot mess, but I'm dying to be a part of it."

"Of course you are," I say, grinning. "You thrive on chaos."

"So true."

There's a lull in the conversation, and I glance at the mugs between us, twirling mine idly on the table. "So, uh, Liam did this thing the other day," I say casually, though my cheeks heat just thinking about it.

She narrows her eyes in mock suspicion. "Define 'thing.' Is this a *weird* thing or a sex thing?"

I chuckle. "Uh, neither?"

She perks up. "Okay, then spill."

I rest my chin on my hand. "He made me this list. Two columns—Glad and Bad. And he wants to double down on all the Glad."

"Oh my God," she murmurs. "What does that mean?"

"It means he thinks sour gummy worms can fix everything," I say, rolling my eyes but unable to stop smiling. "Really, he just wrote down a bunch of things that make me happy on a bowling alley napkin."

She nearly chokes on her coffee. "Aw, I sorta love him."

"Me too." It's the first time I've admitted to it, and the truth of it settles over me like the comfort of an old, favorite sweatshirt. "It worked, by the way. For, like, five minutes, I forgot how miserable I was."

"The man is willing to immortalize his bad jokes in list form to make you laugh. Seriously, B, that's adorable. And you deserve adorable. Don't mess this up."

I blink, swallowing the sudden lump in my throat. "I don't plan to."

"Good. Because if you do, I'm stealing him."

"Oh, please." I swat at her. "Liam wouldn't survive five minutes with you."

She gives a dreamy, teasing smile. "But what a glorious five minutes it would be."

I roll my eyes, but the warmth of the moment settles deep in my chest, like the glow of sunlight after a long storm. It feels good, natural—one of those rare times when life slows down just enough to let you breathe.

When it's time to leave, she pulls on three layers of clothing and mutters something about frostbite, though there's a playful glint in her eye that says she doesn't mind. Not really.

I'm happy that things are shifting—not just with Liam or Claire, but with me. I'm finally starting to let people in, to believe that I deserve the kind of connections I've always been too scared to reach for. That despite life's setbacks—the accident, the loss—I can still find joy in these quiet, fleeting moments that remind me I'm still here, still moving forward.

THE COLD BITES through my layers as Sena and I make our way across campus to the practice field. I can see my breath every time I exhale, and the frosty air clings to my cheeks, numbing them.

Sena has her beanie pulled low over her ears, scarf wrapped tightly around her neck, and her puffer jacket zipped all the way up. "I hate this already," she mutters, her gloved hands stuffed into her pockets.

"You're the one who insisted on coming," I remind her.

"Yeah, because I'm a good friend," she shoots back, her tone dripping with mock resentment. "Don't let it go to your head."

I laugh, nudging her as we approach the field. The players are already out there, jogging around to warm up, their breath misting in the cold air. Liam's easy to spot, even from a distance—tall, confident, and utterly in his element. He's wearing a long-sleeved black compression shirt under his practice jersey, his blond hair a messy halo under the floodlights.

Sena follows my gaze and groans. "How is he still attractive in this weather? It's like twenty degrees out, and your man looks like he's shooting a Nike ad."

I roll my eyes, but warmth spreads through me despite the cold. *Mine.*

We find a spot along the sideline, close enough to see the action but far enough back to avoid stray balls—or worse, colliding players. Sena pulls out a travel mug from her oversized tote and takes a sip, her breath curling in the cold.

There aren't many people here—just a handful of friends and girlfriends, bundled up like us, braving the chill to show their support. It's practice, not a game, so there's no crowd or pressure, just the low hum of chatter and the occasional laugh as the players warm up.

It's not long before the scrimmage begins. The team splits into two squads, their jerseys marking the difference—white for one side, red for the other. Liam's on the white team, playing his usual position on the wing.

Sena leans in close, her voice low. "So, do I cheer like a supportive friend or heckle like a chaotic neutral?"

I snort. "Please don't heckle. He'll just use it as fuel to show off, and then I'll never hear the end of it."

Her grin is mischievous, but she raises her mug in mock solemnity. "Fine. I'll keep it classy—for now."

It doesn't take long for Liam to get into the rhythm, weaving around defenders with that effortless speed that makes him look like he's gliding across the field. Even in practice, he's magnetic to watch. The way he moves, the sharp focus in his eyes, the sheer control he has over the ball—it's mesmerizing.

"You know," Sena says after a while, breaking the quiet, "this isn't as bad as I thought it'd be. It's kind of fun, seeing you like this."

"Like what?"

"Happy," she says simply, her tone softer now. "You've got that look, you know? The one people get when they're completely smitten."

I duck my head, my cheeks burning. "Shh."

"It's true," she insists, grinning. "And it's cute. Gross, but cute."

We both laugh, the sound muffled by the layers of scarves and coats. For the next hour, we alternate between cheering quietly and complaining. Sena's commentary is relentless and hilarious—she calls the goalkeepers "big bumblebees" and spends a good five minutes trying to figure out why soccer doesn't allow tackling.

"That guy just pushed Liam," she says indignantly, pointing at one of the defenders. "Why isn't there a penalty for that?"

"Because they're technically on the same team," I explain, though I'm not entirely sure I understand the rules myself. "And because this is an intra-squad practice scrimmage. Besides, it's not a foul unless someone actually gets taken out. I . . . think?"

"Annoying," she declares, sipping her coffee. "Let me at him. I'll foul him."

The scrimmage winds down, and Liam's team finishes strong with a 3–1 win. The final goal is a thing of beauty—a gorgeous assist from Liam that sets up his teammate perfectly.

"Okay, I'm officially frozen," Sena announces, standing and rubbing her gloved hands together. "I'm gonna go thaw out somewhere warm. Maxxine wants to run lines, so I'm gonna head to hers. You good?"

"Go ahead," I say, pulling my scarf tighter around my neck.

"Thanks for coming, though. I know this wasn't exactly your vibe."

She waves me off with a grin. "Anything for you. But next time, you owe me a bar night—or something equally indoors. With heaters. And no running."

"Deal."

Sena gives me a quick, tight hug before heading off, her steps crunching in the frost-covered grass. I watch her go, warmth spreading through me. Having two people—Sena and Liam—who I'm close to, who I trust, who I really gel with, is so much better than trying to keep up with a big group of shallow friendships.

It's not about quantity; it's about connection. And with them, I feel it in a way I haven't before.

The players pack up their gear, shaking hands and chatting as the scrimmage officially ends. I spot Liam jogging toward me, his breath misting in the cold air, his face still flushed from exertion. His lopsided grin grows wider as he gets closer, and I can't help but smile back.

"You were amazing!" I say as he reaches me, bouncing on the balls of my feet to stay warm.

"Thanks," he says, running a hand through his damp, messy hair. "You survived the whole thing. Color me impressed."

"Barely," I tease, wrapping my arms around myself. "But you looked great out there."

"Yeah? You weren't bored out of your mind?"

"Not even a little," I say honestly. "You make it fun to watch."

His expression softens, and he takes a step closer, resting a hand on my arm. Even through my coat, I can feel the warmth of his touch. "You ready to head back? Or do you want to hang out here and freeze a little longer?"

I laugh, shaking my head. "Let's go. My toes stopped working like ten minutes ago."

"Come on, then. Don't want you to lose 'em."

He drapes an arm around my shoulders as we walk toward the parking lot. It's a firm, steady touch that radiates warmth, and I lean into him, letting the moment settle. Watching him play, seeing him so at ease out there—it felt like catching a glimpse of a world that's entirely his. A world full of confidence, quiet determination, and joy.

And somehow, he's letting me be part of it.

I feel lucky that he's opened his circle to me, that he's invited me into this part of his life. Into every part of his life. That he trusts me enough to let me exist in all the spaces where he feels most like himself—and that, somehow, I've become one of those spaces, too.

Chapter Thirty-Three
LIAM

We pull up to the house just as the porch light flickers on. Birdie cradles a half-empty travel mug Sena made her take, her cheeks pink from the cold.

She's more at ease in my car now, though her fingers still grip the edge of the seat like we might launch into orbit at any second. She avoids watching the road, her eyes following the sky, the buildings sliding by, anything but the glare of oncoming headlights. It's a quiet shift, but it's there.

I'm ridiculously proud of her and honored that she trusts me.

She catches me looking and smiles—a small, tired curve of her lips that warms me all the way through. "That was really fun," she says softly, her voice carrying over the low hum of the engine. "I want to come to more of your practices."

I grin, shifting the car into park. "Yeah?"

Her nod is subtle but sure. "Yeah. I like seeing you like that—doing what you're good at. What you love."

I shut off the engine, the soft click of the key cutting through the quiet. "You're welcome anytime."

Inside, the smell of coffee and toasted bread greets us first, warm and familiar. Then we spot Warren, sprawled across the couch like it's his personal throne. His physics textbook is open on one knee, a half-eaten sandwich balanced precariously on the armrest, and he's wearing the same vaguely annoyed expression that seems permanently etched onto his face.

"Donovan," he says without looking up, his tone flat. "Your door squeaks."

"Nice to see you, too, Warren," I reply, kicking off my shoes. "Glad you're making yourself at home."

"Well, I do live here," he mutters.

Birdie muffles a laugh beside me, her eyes dancing as she watches our exchange. "Is he always like this?"

"Always," I say with mock resignation, gesturing for her to follow me to the kitchen. "And yet, somehow, he grows on you."

Warren shuts his book with an obnoxious amount of force and stretches, his movements unhurried and deliberate. He looks at me, then at Birdie, his green eyes narrowing like he's trying to solve a math problem. Then, he stands, grabbing his plate.

"Don't worry," Warren says, voice deadpan. "I'll clear out. Looks like you two need some privacy."

Birdie turns crimson so fast it's almost impressive.

"Warren," I groan, dragging a hand down my face. "Please spare my girlfriend."

It's funny because that's exactly the kind of thing I'd say to Hayes or Chase. But the fact that he's embarrassing Birdie makes me feel weirdly defensive—like he's stepping on some invisible boundary I didn't know I had.

Warren shrugs, completely unfazed. "Should I stay and watch the show?"

Before I can respond, he grabs his coat and leaves the house, the front door closing behind him with a quiet click. Birdie lets out a laugh, the sound somewhere between amused and mortified.

"Your roommate," she says, still laughing. "Wow."

"Yeah," I mutter, running a hand through my hair. "He's a special kind of angry."

She grins up at me, and just like that, the awkward tension evaporates. "Angry, but not hateful. He just seems . . . I don't know, like a grumpy old man trapped in a swimmer's body."

She's not wrong. I've started to figure Warren out better now. He doesn't hate me—he's just rough around the edges, carrying this worn-in energy like he's lived ten lives already. Like he's seen it all and doesn't have the patience for much more.

"Yeah, you're probably right," I say, eyeing her with a smirk. "But enough about him and his *swimmer's body*. Come on." I tilt my head toward the hallway. "Let me show you the rest of the place."

When we reach my room, my pulse does this weird, jittery thing. It's not like she hasn't been over before, but this feels different. She's stepping into my space. My room. The one place that's really mine, where I don't have to worry about keeping up appearances or filtering out the messy parts of me.

"Here we are," I say, pushing the door open.

She steps inside, her eyes sweeping over the space like she's trying to piece me together from the things I keep around. The walls are bare except for a few soccer posters and a framed photo of my team from last season. My desk is cluttered—laptop, a few notebooks, a half-empty water bottle—and my bed's not exactly pristine, but it's made. Sort of.

"It's . . . cozy," she says, her lips curving into a teasing smile.

"Cozy?" I close the door behind us, leaning back against it. "That's a compliment?"

"Yes, it's . . . very you."

She steps closer to the desk, picking up one of the notebooks and flipping it open. Her eyes scan the page, and I realize too late that it's filled with notes on plays and formations. Nothing too embarrassing, but still—this is *my stuff*.

"Do you ever stop thinking about soccer?" she asks, glancing at me over her shoulder.

"Yeah, of course," I say, shrugging. "But it's kinda my thing."

She sets the notebook down and turns toward me, her smile softening. "I like it. Your thing."

"That's good," I say, clearing my throat and pushing off the door. "Now you've seen my not-so-cozy room. What do you think? Could use a lava lamp, right? Or maybe a beanbag chair?"

She laughs, and it's the same light, musical sound I've grown to love. "I think you're good without it." She sinks onto the edge of my bed. "I like being here," she says after a moment. "With you."

Her words hit like a soft punch to the chest—not painful, but unexpected and full of weight. Not because I didn't think she felt that way, but because hearing her say it out loud makes it feel real. Tangible.

"Me too," I say, and I mean it more than I've ever meant anything.

She tilts her head back, catching sight of the shelf above my bed. It's lined with knickknacks I've collected over the years: a miniature soccer ball, a goofy picture of me and James at a theme park, and, right in the middle, a gray Jellycat bunny with one ear flopped over.

Birdie zeroes in on it immediately. "Wait, is that yours?"

I shrug, my cheeks heating. "Yeah. Got it when I was six. Haven't had the heart to get rid of it."

She turns to me, delighted. "I love Jellycats. I have a whole collection back at my apartment."

I blink. "I've never seen them."

She shifts, suddenly bashful. "That's because I keep them stored away. It's . . . kind of an embarrassing amount."

"How many are we talking?"

"Too many," she says, laughing. "You'd judge me forever."

"Probably."

I move closer, sitting beside her as she picks up one of the smaller trophies from the shelf and turns it over. My hand settles lightly on her back, and I lower my chin to rest on the top of her head.

"You're so cute," I murmur, my voice soft against her hair.

She freezes for a half second before relaxing into me, her fingers brushing over the trophy. "Because I like stuffed animals?"

I snort. "Exactly."

She sets the trophy back and turns in my arms. There's something unguarded in her expression—open and vulnerable in a way that makes my pulse stutter.

"Hi," she whispers.

"Hi," I whisper back, leaning in as her hands slide up my chest.

When our lips meet, it's soft and slow at first. Gentle. Her hands curl into the fabric of my shirt, pulling me closer, and my fingers flex against her back, steadying her.

She tilts her head, deepening the kiss, and my heart trips over itself. Her touch grows more confident, her hands cupping the back of my neck, her nails grazing my skin in a way that sends shivers down my spine.

"Birdie," I murmur roughly. It's all I can manage because my brain is officially mush.

"Hmm?" she hums back, her breath warm and teasing as she pulls away just enough to meet my eyes.

"I—" My hands move instinctively, skimming over the curve of her waist. "Do you want this? Me? Tonight?"

"Yeah," she says without hesitation, then, "It's what I'm here for."

I laugh softly, a mix of relief and disbelief, and close the distance between us again. This time, the kiss is deeper, hungrier, and I savor the way she presses into me, her warmth sinking into my skin like she's becoming a part of me.

She swings a leg over to straddle my lap, and her sweater slips off one shoulder, revealing a divot of soft, bare skin. My fingers trace over it, marveling at how perfect she feels. At how she's letting me have this moment with her.

She tugs at the hem of my shirt. I pull it over my head in one swift motion, and nimble hands immediately explore the planes of my chest, fingertips tracing over the hard ridges of muscle and faint line of my sternum. When she skims lower, following the defined line of my stomach to the deep V at my hips, my breath catches.

The look in her eyes—wide, curious, and a little awed—sends a rush of heat straight through me. "You're unfairly attractive," she mutters, cheeks flushing.

"Yeah?" I slide my hands under the hem of her sweater and tug it upward. "Have you seen you?"

Her laugh turns into a gasp as my hands move up her sides, brushing over warm, impossibly soft skin. She raises her arms, letting me pull the sweater off completely, and I take a moment to just look at her, my pulse racing.

Her skin is flushed a delicate pink, and the soft lighting in the room gives her this glow, like she's something out of a dream. The curve of her shoulders, the line of her collarbone, the way her chest rises and falls with each quickened breath—it's all so perfectly her.

"You're the most beautiful person I've ever seen," I say, the words coming out rough and unfiltered, like they've been pulled straight from my chest.

Her cheeks flush deeper, and she ducks her head, her hands resting lightly on my shoulders. "You're just saying that because I'm sitting on top of you, ready to have sex."

"No." I tip her chin up so she's looking at me again. "I mean it."

She holds my gaze for a moment, her expression softening, and then she leans in, her lips brushing mine in a kiss that's somehow even sweeter than the last. Shaking hands tangle in my hair, pulling me closer, and I let mine drift down her back, mapping every inch of her.

She pulls away slightly, forehead resting against mine. "I feel really safe with you," she whispers, so quiet I'd miss it if I weren't hanging on her every word.

My chest tightens. I wrap my arms around her, holding her like she's the most precious thing in the world. "You are," I say, full of conviction. "You always will be."

Her finger trails down my jaw, a touch so light it sends a shiver down my spine, and then she kisses me again, soft and slow. I let my hands wander, brushing over her ribs. When my thumbs skim the edges of her bra, I pause, glancing up to meet her eyes.

"Okay?" I murmur, my voice low.

She nods, her breath hitching, and I take my time, sliding the straps down her shoulders and unhooking it with careful fingers. Her bra falls away, and I stare at her perky, rounded breasts, her rosy pink nipples.

She's perfect. Soft and flushed and so goddamn beautiful it makes me weak.

"You're stunning," I whisper, brushing my lips over her collarbone before trailing lower. I kiss the swell of her breast, then take her nipple into my mouth, rolling my tongue over the hardened peak.

She gasps and arches into me. "Liam."

I move to her other breast, giving it the same attention, licking and kissing and sucking until she's squirming in my lap, her thighs tightening around me. Her soft whimpers spur me on, my hands skimming over her hips, pulling her closer.

"Want these off, too," she says breathlessly, tugging at the waistband of my sweats. I grin, shifting just enough to let her push them down. My boxers go next, and we fumble together, laughing when the fabric gets caught on my heel.

She sits back, gaze falling between us, and her cheeks flush again as her hand reaches for my cock. Five fingers wrap around me, firm but hesitant, and I let out a low groan as she strokes me. "God, baby."

She bites her lip, her thumb brushing over the tip, and I swear I'm about to lose it already. "You're so big," she says, her voice filled with wonder.

I laugh, the sound rough and proud. "Not what you were expecting?"

"Haven't had much time to picture it," she teases. "Though it's quite perfect, I think."

I swallow roughly. "Oh, I have."

Her head tilts, eyes curious and sparkling. "Have what?"

"Had plenty of time to picture it," I rasp. "How we'd be together when we're like this. What you'd feel like suctioned around my cock. How I'd pump into you until you shudder and come apart. How fucking good it'd feel to come while I fisted my hands in your short hair."

I rake my fingers through her hair now, gently grabbing hold, and she gasps softly. "Liam," she murmurs, her whole body flushing.

"Sorry," I say, though my hand stays where it is, holding her close. "Wanted you to know you've been on my mind."

Her lips curve into a shy smile. "Apparently, in many different ways."

"Mmm," I hum, nuzzling into the curve of her neck, pressing a soft kiss there. "And which way appeals to you tonight?"

She hesitates, thinking for a moment, then says, "Me on top. I think it might make me feel . . ."

"Powerful," I finish for her, my hands bracketing her hips. "You are. You have so much fucking power over me."

Her smile turns radiant, and she leans in to kiss me again. Then she shifts, her hands sliding to the waistband of her panties, and she tugs them off. I follow suit, grabbing a condom from the drawer and rolling it on as quickly as I can.

We're both naked now, her body pressed against mine, and I can barely think straight. I grip her hips and lift her, scooching us until I'm leaned back against the headboard and she's still on top of me.

She takes my cock in her hand, aligning me with her, and I hold my breath as she sinks down, inch by inch.

"Fucking hell," I groan, my head falling back as the heat of her surrounds me.

Her breath hitches, her fingers gripping my shoulders as she takes me deeper. "Liam, honey, want you so bad."

I tighten my grip on her hips, helping her find a rhythm as she starts to move. It's quick and jerky at first, but soon, she settles, her body rising and falling over mine. I slide one hand to the back of her neck, the other cupping her hip as I guide her, pushing and pulling, bouncing her in my lap.

"You feel so fucking good," I rasp, my voice raw. "Riding me like that."

Her head falls back, her hair already damp with sweat, and the sight of her—flushed and radiant, completely lost in the moment— is pure magic. I can barely keep my composure as I watch her fuck me, her body moving with a raw, unrestrained sort of desperation.

I thrust up to meet her, matching her pace, and the friction, the heat, it swells in my cock, radiating through my entire body. Every bounce of her hips, every breathless moan that slips past her lips, pushes me closer to the edge.

Her nails dig into my shoulders as her thighs tremble against mine. "Liam," she whimpers, her voice breaking, "I—I'm—"

"I've got you," I murmur, my voice hoarse with need. "I want you to come."

Her body tenses, her movements stuttering as she shatters around me, a soft cry escaping her lips. She tightens, pulses, squeezes on my cock, and the sensation is so overwhelming, so all-consuming, that it pulls me right over the edge with her.

I come hard, my release slamming into me with a force that steals my breath. My vision goes white, and for a moment, I swear I'm seeing a whole galaxy of stars. I think we both are.

Her body collapses against mine, trembling, her forehead

resting on my shoulder as we try to catch our breath. I wrap my arms around her, holding her close, my fingers brushing gently over the damp skin of her back.

"Birdie," I murmur, pressing a kiss to her temple. My voice is soft now, reverent, like saying her name is some kind of prayer. "Was that as good for you as it was for me?"

"Mmhmm," she says, too spent to form words, and I grin from ear to fucking ear. Whatever this is between us, whatever we're building together, it's everything. It's infinite.

Chapter Thirty-Four
BIRDIE

Claire calls back on a quiet winter's afternoon. The sun is spilling through the windows like warm honey, and I'm trying not to bite my nails as I pace the living room. I answer so quickly it's embarrassing, the phone almost slipping out of my clammy hands.

"Hello? This is Birdie—Bridget Collins." *Bridget,* because we're being professional today.

"Hi, Birdie. It's Claire Mahler."

Her voice is smooth, confident, a little raspy—like someone who's spent years laughing too loud and working with clay dust in her lungs. I stop pacing and grip the back of the couch for balance. "Hi, Claire. Thanks for calling me back."

"Of course." I hear the faint clinking of tools in the background —she's probably at her studio, mid-project. "I wanted to talk about that proposition I mentioned."

"Yeah?" I sound too eager, so I clear my throat. "I mean, yes. I'd love to hear more."

"I've been following your work since we met at the Montrose, and I think you have real potential. The fellowship winner will be working with me during the second half of the summer, but I'd like to offer you the opportunity to intern with me during the first half."

My heart leaps into my throat. Claire freaking Mahler wants me to intern with her. This is huge. This is what I wanted from the beginning. Not David, not a random name on some committee, but someone who truly inspires me to create.

But.

But I need money. Not inspiration, not exposure, but actual, practical, survival-level money.

My stomach twists. "Claire, I—I can't tell you how grateful I am. That sounds incredible, really, but . . . I need to focus on a paid position this summer. My tuition and, well, everything else—it's kind of nonnegotiable."

There's a pause on the other end. For a split second, I'm sure she's about to tell me never mind—that I've blown it, turned down the opportunity of a lifetime.

"Well," Claire says finally, "I happen to have a spot open at my studio."

I blink, not sure I heard her right. "What kind of spot?"

"Receptionist. It doesn't pay much—minimum wage, plus a little commission for any pieces you sell in the shop—but you'd get to work alongside me and see the day-to-day. You'd help with the shop, assist in classes, and have full access to the studio to work on your own projects."

My breath catches. A paid position and an internship with Claire Mahler? The tears prickle at the edges of my vision before I can stop them.

"That—" I swallow hard, my voice coming out wobbly. "That would be amazing. More than amazing. Thank you. Thank you so much."

"Good," she says, warm and sure. "I'll send over the details this week, and we'll get everything lined up. I look forward to working with you, Birdie."

When I hang up, I just stand there, phone clutched in my hand like it might evaporate if I let go. Claire Mahler is going to be my boss. My mentor. Holy shit.

And then I'm crying, because of course I'm crying. Big, happy, overwhelmed tears that I wipe away with the sleeve of my sweatshirt as I stumble into my room. For the first time in a long time, I feel like the pieces are clicking into place. Like the universe is holding out a hand, saying, *Here. Keep going.*

It's late when I finally pad out of my room to find Sena. The apartment is glowing with the warm flicker of candles and incense. She's in one of her witchy moods—an oversized black sweater, a messy braid draped over her shoulder, and some kind of ritual bowl clutched in her hands as she moves around the room.

"What are you doing?" I ask, watching her light yet another candle and mutter something under her breath.

"Cord cutting," she says matter-of-factly, setting the bowl on the coffee table. "Symbolic release of all the lingering negativity. Bad vibes, fair-weather exes, imposter syndrome—you name it."

I snort, sinking onto the couch with my phone. "Sounds ambitious."

"Let me live," she says, flashing me a grin. "Speaking of—" She gestures at the notebook and phone spread out in front of me. "Did I hear you on the phone in there earlier?"

I bite back a smile. "Yeah. Claire Mahler called me back."

Sena freezes mid-candle placement, then straightens, turning to me with wide eyes. "Claire Mahler as in *Claire Mahler*?"

"Yes," I say, grinning like a fool. "She offered me a paid summer position at her studio. Receptionist slash artist intern, basically. I'll get to help with classes, work in the shop, and have full studio access. Plus, I get a commission for anything I sell."

Her jaw drops. "Are you kidding me?"

I shake my head, the grin still plastered to my face. "Not even a little. I left her a voicemail this morning, and she called me back to offer the job."

"Oh my God, Birdie!" She practically launches herself onto the couch next to me, grabbing my arm and shaking it. "That's huge. You're going to be, like, the next big thing. I'll get to say I knew you when!"

"Please," I laugh, swatting her away. "This is not the life of the rich and famous."

"Not yet," she says, wagging a finger at me. "But this is where it starts. Paid work, access to the studio, commissions—Birdie, this is everything."

"It really is."

"Does Liam know yet?" she asks, flopping back against the couch cushions and beaming at me.

"Not yet," I say, tucking my phone into my lap. "I'll tell him later. I just . . . I needed to sit with it for a minute, you know? Let it feel real."

She gives me a knowing smile. "I get it, and you deserve this, B. You really, really do."

I glance around the room—the flickering candles, the faint curl of incense smoke, Sena perched cross-legged like the little hedge witch she is—and I feel a tightness in my chest that isn't fear or sadness. It's gratitude.

"Thank you," I murmur, letting my head drop back against the cushions as the moment settles over me. It's strange how much I suddenly believe it. That I deserve this, all of it. The good things, the small wins, the chance to build something from the brokenness.

I'm not just surviving. I'm starting to live again.

It's late—almost ten—and the campus studio is empty, save for me and the giant eight-pound monstrosity I've been working with for the past hour.

I exhale through my nose, pressing my ribbon tool into the spinning mass on the wheel. "Come on," I murmur to it, my voice low, coaxing. "Work with me here."

It's almost meditative, the way I work—tools trimming, fingers coaxing, a quiet give-and-take between me and the clay. My jeans are streaked with gray smudges, my sweater sleeves rolled up past my elbows, and I've already pushed my hair back three times.

I've missed this feeling. The quiet focus, hands deep in the grit of something I can control. My spark is back—that little drive that pushes me to sit here for hours on end, spinning and shaping until my back aches and my hands feel raw.

It's funny how one phone call could change everything. Claire's voice, so certain, so sure, still rings in my ears: *I think you have real potential.* I told my dad the next day, and for the first time in a year, his voice was thick with something other than worry-laced caution. Pride. He said he wants to shake hands with Claire himself, like she'd done him a personal favor.

And Liam—oh God. I didn't even get to finish telling him before he spun me around the kitchen like I'd just won the lottery, his laughter loud and reckless, his smile so big it made me dizzy. "I told you, Birdie. I told you you'd get there."

That moment, the pure joy in his face—it stuck with me, wedged somewhere warm and unshakable inside my chest. It's been fueling me ever since. My hands are steady, my focus sharp as I carefully apply my trimming tool to the nearly finished piece.

I'm so absorbed in the work that I don't hear the footsteps until they stop a few feet away.

"Don't let me interrupt the magic."

I jolt, my hands slipping slightly, and glance up. Liam stands near the door, his hair damp from practice, wearing sweatpants and a Dayton Soccer hoodie. Just as handsome and effortlessly self-assured as the day we met but somehow even more familiar now—like he belongs here.

"How long have you been standing there?" I ask.

"Long enough to know you talk to clay when you think no one's watching," he teases.

"I'm coaxing it," I reply defensively. "It's called encouragement."

"Sure." He raises an eyebrow, still grinning. "Does it ever talk back?"

"Only when you're not here to scare it into silence," I shoot back, rolling my eyes as I focus on the wheel again.

Liam pulls out one of the old wooden stools from under a nearby table, the legs scraping against the concrete floor as he drags it closer. He sits, leaning his elbows on his knees as he studies me.

"I didn't think you'd still be here," he says after a moment, his tone softer now. "You didn't answer my text."

"Phone's over there," I say, jerking my head toward the far corner where my bag sits, abandoned. "I needed a break from screens."

"Everything okay?" he asks, his eyes narrowing slightly in concern.

"Yeah." I glance up, surprised by how serious he suddenly looks. "Better than okay, actually. I just needed to make something, you know?"

His expression softens. "I get it."

And I know he does. For him, it's the field—those endless hours of drills and scrimmages, the repetition, the precision, the rhythm of something he's mastered. For me, it's this. The clay, the wheel, the messy, beautiful process of turning nothing into something.

For a while, he just watches, quiet and still, as I work the clay into shape. The silence between us feels easy, natural. Like it's enough just to be here, in the same space, breathing the same air and existing alongside each other without needing to fill the quiet.

When I finish, I sit back on the stool and wipe my hands on the towel draped over my knee, letting out a long, satisfied breath. It's not perfect—not yet—but it's close. The shape is there, sturdy and clean; it just needs a few minor tweaks.

Liam whistles low, leaning back as he looks at it. "That's impressive, and huge."

"Thanks," I say, feeling the familiar ache in my arms and shoulders. It's the best kind of exhaustion—the kind you earn.

"You ready to go?" he asks, standing and stretching.

I glance at the hunk of clay still spinning lazily on the wheel. I'm trimming the piece for Hall's class, and usually, I wouldn't dare step away from something when I'm in the zone. But I'm trying to be reasonable these days. Trying to be better to myself.

Obsessing and overworking hasn't done me any favors in the past—it's burned me out, left me picking through broken shards of what could've been. So, maybe for once, I'll let this small amount of progress be good enough.

"It'll still be here tomorrow," he says gently. "Come on, let's get you home. I don't want to have to wrestle you out of this studio."

I huff out a small laugh. "Fine."

A few minutes later, we're in his car, and the engine hums beneath us as we pull onto the road. I have one hand locked in a tight grip on the edge of the seat—my fingers probably leaving permanent indentations—and the other is curled in Liam's.

It's been easier lately. The car rides. The weight of being a passenger. Fewer flashbacks, fewer sharp jolts of fear. But it's still there, lingering in the corners of my mind, waiting for the wrong turn or a sudden brake.

"You're okay," he murmurs, glancing at me briefly before turning back to the road. "Hey, we can go over the list if you want. What's next on your Glad side?"

I squeeze his hand in silent gratitude. "Socks," I tell him. "The expensive ones that don't slide down."

His thumb brushes over my knuckles. "Solid choice. Nothing ruins a bad day faster than shitty socks."

When we pull up to the apartment, the weight of the day starts to ease. The anxiety of the drive fades, replaced by the familiar stillness of home.

We trudge inside, kicking off our shoes in the doorway, and head straight to my room. It's still cozy from the last time he was here—blankets half-folded, fairy lights glowing softly along the walls.

Liam stretches out on my bed like it's his own, his arms flopping over his head as he sighs dramatically. "So, what's the verdict?" he asks, staring at the ceiling. "In terms of Otis."

"Who?" I ask as I rifle through my closet.

He sits up like I've just committed the ultimate betrayal. "Our turtle. I've been thinking, and we've not been visiting him nearly enough."

"I saw him literally yesterday."

I've been dropping by the fountain between classes every now and then. Liam and I talked about giving him a better home, but it would mostly be for selfish reasons. It's likely that Otis has adapted to his odd little world—the algae-covered stones, the still water, the scattered leaves that collect in the corners of the fountain. Removing him might be more disruptive than leaving him where he is, even if it's not the life we'd imagine for him.

His jaw drops, and he clutches his chest like I've wounded him. "You went without me?"

"All the time," I reply, trying not to laugh.

He narrows his eyes, pushing up onto his elbows. "That's why he's been so aloof with me since winter break. You've clearly stolen Otis, and now he's mine in name only."

I roll my eyes, grinning as I grab an armful of Jellycats from my shelf and turn back to the bed. Liam's still rambling about how he's the picture of excellent company when I unceremoniously dump the stuffed animals beside him.

He freezes mid-sentence, his eyes going wide as he takes in the mountain of Jellycats now surrounding him. "Wait, wait, wait," he says, holding up his hands like he's trying to process the situation. "This—this is the collection?"

"Yup." I plop down on the edge of the bed, smug as anything. "Meet my Jellycats."

His expression shifts to pure amazement as he sifts through the pile, pulling out a brown bunny and a green bunny, each with one floppy ear. He inspects them like they're precious artifacts, carefully turning them over in his hands. Otis is long forgotten.

"This is . . . more impressive than I expected," he says finally, his voice filled with mock reverence.

"You thought I was kidding?"

"No," he admits, holding up a tiny fox with an embroidered scarf. "I just didn't realize you had a whole *society* of them. These ones are my favorite," he declares, gazing lovingly at the bunnies. "They're us."

I blink, bemused. "The bunnies?"

"Of course, the bunnies." He gives me a deadpan stare, completely serious. "Can't you tell?"

I laugh, shaking my head as I lean back to prop myself on my elbows. "You're so weird."

He grins mischievously, and before I can move, he grabs me around the waist and pulls me down onto the bed with him. "Liam!" I shriek, half laughing, half squirming as I try to escape his grip. "Stop! I'm all messy from the studio."

"And I'm so pristine?" he teases, wrapping an arm securely around me to hold me in place. "You've seen me post-practice—I'm practically a swamp creature by comparison."

I roll onto my side, panting and trying to catch my breath, my hair sticking out in all directions. Liam's grinning up at the ceiling, one arm draped lazily across his chest, the other casually tucked behind his head.

"Annoying little gremlin," I mutter, half-heartedly swatting at him.

"You're cute when you're mad," he fires back, turning his head to look at me. His gaze softens slightly, flickering over my face like he's memorizing every angle, every smudge of clay. He gently brushes a strand of hair behind my ear.

"I like you so much," he says softly.

I swallow, my heart doing that fluttery thing it always does when he looks at me like this. "Yeah," I whisper back. "I like you, too. And I plan to stick around as long as you let me."

Something swells in my chest—this fragile, beautiful thing I don't quite know how to name. Love, probably. Hope, definitely.

I glance at him, his face lit with a warmth that's so achingly Liam. "I'll hold you to that."

"Good," he says like it's the easiest promise in the world.

When we're together like this, I feel light—giddy, even—like all the broken pieces of me are finally starting to fit back together. One soft, silly moment at a time.

Chapter Thirty-Five

THE BANQUET HALL is buzzing tonight. It's the end of March, and the air outside is just starting to feel like spring, all soft breezes and budding trees. Inside, though, it's fluorescent lighting and formal-wear—soccer cleats traded for dress shoes, jerseys for button-downs.

Birdie's beside me, her hands fidgeting with the edge of the emerald-green dress. It's formal but understated, the rich color making the gold in her hazel eyes glow. Her heels—a modest two inches because she insisted on not towering over me—tap a quiet rhythm against the floor.

She looks stunning, obviously, but there's a tightness to her posture, the kind that says she'd rather be anywhere but here.

"Hey," I whisper. "You doing okay?"

She nods quickly, but it's not convincing. Her hands tighten around the fabric, her eyes darting around the room like she's mapping out potential escape routes. "It's just . . . your parents."

Ah, yes. My parents. The immaculately dressed, judgmental elephants in the room.

"They're not that scary," I tell her, keeping my tone light. "Annoying? Sure. Overbearing? Absolutely. But scary? Nah. They're just two people who think being rich makes them more fascinating than they actually are."

She gives me a look—half-amused, half-exasperated. "That's not helping."

I reach over and take her hand, giving it a gentle squeeze. "Okay, listen. They're not judging you for who you are." She raises an eyebrow, skeptical, and I add, "They're judging you for wanting to be with me."

Her mouth drops open. "Liam! Why would you say that?"

"Because it's true," I say with a self-deprecating laugh. "They've never really warmed up to the whole autistic thing, you know? It's like they think they got dealt a bad hand with me or something. They'd rather I—" I pause, considering my words. "Blend in better. Be quieter. Basically, not be myself."

I say it casually because that's how I've learned to deal with it. The blunt honesty makes it easier to swallow. I'm not ashamed of who I am—it's the rest of the world that tries to make it feel like something to apologize for.

When I glance at Birdie, her brow is furrowed, her lips pressed together in this way that tells me she's working through how to react. How to balance between sympathy and outrage without making it weird. Then she tilts her head slightly, studying me like she's trying to see past the words. Finally, she squeezes my hand back.

"Well, screw them," she says fiercely.

A startled laugh bubbles out of me, warming the tightness in my chest. "Yeah. Screw them."

The corner of her mouth twitches upward, but the tension hasn't fully left her shoulders. I fumble in my jacket pocket, feeling the cool, waxy skin of what I'm looking for, and pull it out with a little flourish.

"Here," I say, holding it up between us.

Birdie blinks at the lemon in my hand, then at me, like she's waiting for the punchline. "What . . . what am I supposed to do with that?"

"Sniff it," I say, completely serious.

"Sniff it," she repeats flatly.

"Yeah." I roll the lemon between my fingers. "My brother told me that sniffing lemons or limes can help with anxiety. Thought I'd give it a shot. You know, start carrying one around for you. Combat tool."

She stares at me for a long moment, her lips twitching like she's trying not to laugh. Then, out of nowhere, she loops her arms around my neck and pops a kiss on my cheek.

"The strangest brand of sweet," she murmurs, her voice warm and amused.

"Maybe," I say, grinning. "But you're not panicking anymore, are you?"

She huffs out a small laugh and shakes her head. "You win, Donovan. Pass me the lemon."

I hand it over, and she brings it to her nose, inhaling deeply like she's humoring me. "I hate to admit it, but it actually smells . . . calming."

"Told you."

She rolls her eyes but slips the lemon into her bag, her lips quirking into a faint, reluctant smile. Just like that, the tension in her shoulders softens, and the restless tapping of her foot comes to a stop. For a moment, we sit together in easy silence, her hand still nestled in mine. Then I catch sight of the clock on the wall and let out a quiet sigh.

"Time to face the music," I say, standing and offering her my hand.

She takes it, and we make our way back to the table, where my parents are already seated alongside two of my teammates and their families. My dad is mid-conversation with Amir's mom, his expression polite but distant. My mom, on the other hand, is scrolling through her phone, her perfectly manicured nails clicking against the screen.

"Liam," she says when she notices us, cool and composed. "There you are."

"Hi, Mrs. Donovan," Birdie greets. "So nice to see you again."

"Bridget," my mom replies, offering her a polite smile that doesn't quite reach her eyes. "You as well."

We sit, and I slide my palm over Birdie's thigh, a small, grounding gesture meant as much for me as it is for her. Her hand brushes mine in response, her fingers warm and reassuring.

"How was the drive in?" my dad asks, his tone as formal as ever.

"Uneventful," I say, reaching for the water glass in front of me. "You know, cars, roads, the usual. Though, there was a squirrel that looked like it was plotting something sinister at a crosswalk. Pretty sure it made direct eye contact."

My dad doesn't laugh, but I catch the faintest twitch of my mom's lips, like she's fighting a smile. Small victories.

Birdie taps the back of my hand lightly. "How was your day, Mrs. Donovan?"

"Oh, you know," she says vaguely. "Busy. But nothing terribly exciting."

Birdie nods. "Well, you look wonderful tonight."

My mom raises a perfectly arched brow. "Thank you, Bridget. You look . . . nice as well." Her gaze sweeps briefly over Birdie's dress, lingering just long enough to make the compliment feel pointed, like an afterthought carefully disguised as civility.

My dad, meanwhile, seems focused on Amir's mom, leaning slightly toward her as he murmurs something I can't hear. It's a classic David move: making polite small talk with the people who matter to him professionally while the rest of us might as well be furniture.

Birdie tries again, her gaze shifting to my dad. "Mr. Donovan, I wanted to say thank you for introducing me to Claire Mahler. She's been so kind and supportive."

My dad glances at her briefly. "I'm glad it worked out for you."

"Yes, I'm really excited," Birdie continues. "Did Liam mention I'll be interning with her starting in May?"

My dad gives a tight nod, his gaze flickering briefly to the bread basket before shifting back to Amir's mom. He offers no follow-up, no acknowledgment of her excitement. Doesn't inquire about her work or even feign polite interest. Just moves on like she didn't say anything at all.

I bristle, my jaw tightening as I glance between them. "Did you hear my girlfriend?"

My dad's brows draw together. "Of course I heard her," he says dismissively. "And I responded."

"No, you brushed her off," I counter. "She's trying to make conversation with you guys, and you can't even pretend to care for five seconds?"

"Liam," my mom interjects lightly. "Quit being a bug."

"No, no, it's fine," Birdie says calmly. She places a hand on my arm and taps it twice. "Really, Liam. It's fine."

But it's not fine. Not to me. I want her to feel comfortable around them, even if I'm not. You'd think they'd be excited—proud, even—that I've finally found someone I love. Someone incredible, who has more in common with my dad than most people.

If it were just me they were dismissing, I'd let it go, like I always do. I've learned to let their passive disapproval slide off my back, a habit born out of years of necessity. But when it comes to Birdie? I can't stand the thought of them brushing her aside, their indifference or subtle digs chipping away at her confidence.

She deserves better—better than this, better than them.

It's probably a good thing, I guess, that Coach Harris steps up to the microphone before I can say something I might regret. "Good evening, everyone. Thank you for being here tonight to celebrate another successful season," he says, his voice steady and commanding.

The room quiets, all eyes shifting toward the podium, and I

force myself to inhale deeply. The simmering anger in my chest doesn't vanish, but it dulls just enough for me to keep it in check. Birdie's hand stays on my arm, her fingers moving in slow, soothing patterns against the fabric of my sleeve.

I glance at her, and she offers me a soft, understanding smile. It's enough to remind me why I'm here—and why making a scene, as satisfying as it might feel, wouldn't be worth it. For now, I let it go.

Coach launches into a speech about the team's achievements this year, highlighting key moments and players. My name comes up a couple of times, but I barely hear it, too distracted by the simmering tension I'm trying to tamp down. The noise of clapping and laughter blends into a dull hum, my focus scattered like leaves in the wind.

When the awards are announced, I zone out completely, nodding absently at the names and clapping along with everyone else. It's not until Birdie squeezes my leg under the table—her nails digging just enough to snap me out of my head—that I realize something's happening.

"Liam," she whispers, her voice urgent but still low enough not to draw attention. "They just called your name."

"What?" I blink, looking toward the stage. Sure enough, Coach is standing there, holding up a plaque with my name etched into it. The room erupts in applause, and the weight of every pair of eyes in the room presses down on me like a spotlight I didn't ask for.

Birdie grins at me, her face glowing with a mix of pride and amusement. "Go," she says, giving me a nudge. "It's the Scholar-Athlete Award."

I stand, my chair scraping loudly against the floor, and make my way to the front of the room. Coach claps me on the shoulder as he hands me the plaque.

"This young man exemplifies what it means to be a student-athlete. Not only has he been a force to reckon with on the field, leading the team in assists this season and being a relentless presence on the wing, but he's also demonstrated remarkable commitment to his studies, balancing the rigorous demands of civil engineering with his dedication to the sport."

There's a smattering of applause, and I glance back toward our table. Birdie is beaming, her hands clasped together, pride radiating from across the room. It feels good—grounding, even—to have her here for this moment, her confidence in me making it feel a little less daunting.

"But it's not just stats and academics," Coach continues. "Liam is the kind of guy you want in your corner. He's dependable, hardworking, and always willing to put in the extra effort for the good of the team."

The applause grows louder, and I shift awkwardly, my grip tightening on the plaque. Compliments are great and all, but standing here in front of everyone is overwhelming.

"And," Coach adds with a grin, "he's also the only player I've ever seen trip over the ball, recover, and still manage to make an assist."

Laughter ripples through the room, and I duck my head, a smile tugging at my lips. Okay, that one was fair.

"Congratulations, Liam," Coach says, shaking my hand firmly. "The Scholar-Athlete Award is well-deserved."

"Thank you, Coach," I manage, my voice steady despite the nerves crawling up my spine. I nod to the crowd, murmuring a quick "Thanks, everyone," before heading back to my seat.

When I sit down, Birdie leans in, her eyes sparkling. "So proud of you."

"Thanks," I murmur. Her hand finds mine under the table again, and I cling to it like a lifeline.

The rest of the banquet passes in a blur. My parents congratulate me on the award, though it's more of a measured acknowledgment than a celebration. A quick "Nice job, son" is about all I get.

By the time the event wraps up, I'm more than ready to leave. As people gather their things, I help Birdie into her coat, brushing a stray curl from her face. She murmurs a quiet thank-you, her cheeks still faintly pink from the warmth of the room.

We stand to say our goodbyes, and my dad steps forward, extending a handshake to Birdie. "Good luck with your work."

Birdie hesitates for the briefest moment before shaking his hand firmly. "Thank you," she says steadily, her voice unwavering. There's no shrinking back, no falter, and I feel a flicker of pride watching her hold her own.

My mom, ever the polished diplomat, offers Birdie a faint smile as we turn to leave. "It was nice to see you again, Bridget," she says. "Perhaps you can join Liam for dinner at our place soon."

Birdie blinks, surprised, but recovers quickly. "I would love that."

I raise an eyebrow, caught somewhere between shock and amusement, but I don't say anything. As we walk toward the parking lot, Birdie exhales a long breath, her shoulders relaxing slightly.

"Well," she says, glancing up at me with a small, tired smile. "That was . . . something."

I laugh quietly, slipping my hand into hers. "You did great."

"I'm sorry about tonight," I say, my voice low as I shove my free hand into my pocket. "My dad—he's just—"

Rigid? Impossible to please? A laundry list of traits I've spent years trying to navigate without losing my mind.

"Don't," Birdie interrupts, her tone firm. "Don't apologize for him. You're not responsible for how he acts."

"I just hate that he was so rude to you," I say, my jaw tightening. "You didn't deserve that."

She squeezes my hand, her smile soft but resolute. "I've dealt with worse. Besides, I'd sit through an entire evening of tense small talk and sideways comments if it meant supporting you, my prized Scholar-Athlete."

The way she says it—with unwavering pride, like she truly believes it—stirs something deep inside me, a warmth that spreads slowly and roots itself firmly. It feels like she's my biggest fan, standing in my corner no matter what. And maybe she's right. Maybe I've earned this.

All the grueling practices, the sleepless nights, the constant balancing act—it wasn't just about proving something to everyone else.

It was about proving something to myself.

Chapter Thirty-Six
BIRDIE

I'VE BEEN HOOKED on throwing big pieces lately. Something just clicked during those first weeks in Hall's mastery class—like I finally cracked some secret code. There's this rhythm to it, a kind of hypnotic pull when you let the wheel guide you and trust the clay to respond.

The biggest piece I've thrown so far is twenty-eight inches tall. It's not perfect, but it's huge and commanding in the way I wanted it to be. There's this rush in pushing the limits, testing what I can handle. And seeing how far I can go without it collapsing feels like its own kind of victory.

I've been toying with submitting them to the Ellsworth, but they need to feel finished—not just big. That's why outside of Hall's class, I've been working with Professor Tanaka, too. His ideas are inspired—sculptured additions that elevate the forms into something alive.

I feel like I've hit my stride with this. It's not about impressing anyone or proving I belong anymore. It's about the love of creating something that feels like an extension of myself. In just a few weeks, I'll be working in Claire's studio, and I'm eager to take everything I've been learning to the next level, to experiment without limits.

Right now, though, I'm in Liam's room, sprawled out on his bed like a starfish. He's at his desk, flipping through the photos he took of my pieces. Some of the prints are already developed, scattered across the desk in a haphazard display.

"Did you ever think about taking photography more seriously?" I ask, rolling onto my back and propping myself on my elbows. "Like, classes or an internship or something?"

He doesn't even look up. "Nah. Too good at too many other things. Wouldn't be fair to the rest of the world if I monopolized photography, too."

I snort. "Right. Such a humanitarian, keeping your talents to yourself."

"It's a heavy burden. You wouldn't understand."

I grab the nearest pillow and chuck it at him. He catches it one-handed, like it's nothing, and tosses it right back. We're both laughing when a muffled thud and low grunts come from the other side of the wall. Liam freezes mid-throw, tilting his head like a confused golden retriever.

"Is that Warren?" I ask, sitting up straighter.

He squints at the wall. "Sounds like he's wrestling a bear."

We both stay silent for a minute, listening intently. Warren's been living with Liam for three months now, and I've barely gotten to know him. He's like a silent enigma—gruff and intense, with this perpetual storm-cloud expression that makes connection feel impossible.

I've seen him exactly twice outside of this apartment: once heading to the gym with a duffel bag slung over his shoulder and another time at the coffee shop, ordering a medium black coffee in the flattest monotone I've ever heard.

"Warren, buddy, you good?" Liam calls, just loud enough to carry. There's another beat of silence and then—faintly—laughter. A girl's laughter.

My eyes go wide. Liam's expression mirrors mine, and for a second, we're just sitting there, locked in stunned disbelief.

I didn't even know Warren was capable of being intimate with anyone. He's so closed off, like he's built an impenetrable wall around himself. The idea of him laughing with someone, let alone sharing something as vulnerable as this . . .

"Oh my God," I whisper.

"Yup." Liam's lips twitch. "Not a bear."

We sit there, frozen in some weird mix of horror and amusement, until we hear footsteps—two sets, hurried and unsteady—followed by the front door slamming shut. Liam raises an eyebrow at me, and I clap a hand over my mouth to keep from laughing out loud.

"Well," he says after a moment. "Guess we mind our own business now."

"I feel bad. He just . . . left."

"Good for him," Liam says. "Man's got his priorities straight."

I stare at him for a moment, processing everything before an idea strikes. "Come here," I say, grabbing his hand. My voice dips, teasing, like I'm about to share some grand conspiracy.

"What are you up to?" he asks, one eyebrow quirking as he lets me pull him up from the chair.

"Just come here," I insist, dragging him closer until he's standing in front of me. Then, without warning, I flop back onto the mattress, pulling him with me. He stumbles, barely catching himself as he lands beside me, his weight shifting the bed beneath us.

"Birdie," he says, his tone caught somewhere between a laugh and a groan. "What the hell are you—"

"I didn't know Warren had sex."

His laugh bursts out of him, loud and unfiltered. "Seriously? That's what this is about?"

"Yes!" I exclaim, rolling onto my side to face him. "I mean, did you know Warren was having sex? Do you think he's, like, secretly a wild card?"

His laugh morphs into a groan as he drops his head dramatically. "Nope, nope. Don't like that. Those two words should not be coming out of your mouth together."

"What? Warren and sex?" I tease, dragging out the words just to watch him squirm. I shift so I'm straddling him now, my fingers tracing lazy patterns on his chest. "You're acting like it's scandalous."

"It is scandalous," he retorts, looking at me with mock seriousness. "Warren is basically a cryptid. Cryptids don't—" He gestures vaguely, his cheeks tinged pink. "—do that."

"Maybe he's a sexy cryptid," I say, biting back a grin. "Have you ever read monster romance?"

"Oh my God, stop," he groans, covering his face with his hands. "You're ruining everything."

"Am I, though?" I tease, leaning down to nudge his hands away. "Because you're laughing, and I know you love it when I make you laugh."

His hands drop, and he looks up at me, his grin softening. "Yeah, I do." His fingers trail up my sides, settling at my waist as his gaze flicks between my eyes and my mouth. "Even when you're being ridiculous."

"Because Warren—"

"Birdie, baby, say the man's name. One. More. Time."

His hands are gripping my hips like he's torn between stopping me and letting me keep going. "Warr—"

Before I can finish, he surges upward, cutting me off with a kiss. I squeal in surprise, but it's muffled by his lips. Warm and insistent, they steal the breath right out of me. His laughter melts into the kiss, and mine does, too, until it's just us, lips moving together.

Liam flips us over with surprising ease, rolling me beneath him as his weight presses me into the mattress. His hands are on my waist, then in my hair, threading through the strands and tugging lightly as his mouth deepens the kiss.

It's slow and teasing at first, but then he shifts, his hips settling against mine, and a sharp jolt of heat shoots through me.

"Liam," I whisper, the sound caught somewhere between a gasp and a plea.

My hands clutch at the back of his shirt, fisting the fabric as he leans into me. Every inch of him feels solid and overwhelming in the best way—his broad shoulders, the strong line of his torso, the way he fits against me so perfectly.

His lips leave mine to trail along my jaw, then down to my neck, where he presses kisses that make me shiver. "You're . . . very distracting."

"Good," he mutters against my skin, his voice low and rough. "Don't want you thinking about *anything* else."

His hands slide down to my hips, gripping firmly as he grinds against me. My breath catches, and I arch up into him instinctively, the friction sparking something primal and needy inside of me. I'm wet, aching for something to fill me up.

He feels so good, so solid and warm, and I want more. My head tilts back against the pillow, my body moving against his as if it has a mind of its own.

"Birdie," he murmurs, his voice thick with want as he presses his forehead to mine, his hands tightening their grip on my hips. "I want to taste your pussy."

Heat rushes through me, flooding from head to toe, and I wriggle beneath him, my body reacting before my brain can catch up. I want that. I really want that.

But my thoughts spiral, pulling me out of the moment. I've only ever done that twice, and honestly, it wasn't that good. Both times were awkward, rushed, and left me wondering if I'd built it up too much in my head.

I liked to save that kind of intimacy for boyfriends, and before the car accident, I had plenty of them—casual, surface-level relationships that never went anywhere. Nothing that mattered, nothing that felt even close to this.

Now, with Liam above me, his lips brushing mine and his hands gripping my hips like he can't get enough, I'm torn between the raw pull of the moment and the overthinking that's always been my worst enemy.

"You're in your head," he murmurs, his voice softer now, cutting through the storm of my thoughts. He pulls back just enough to look at me, his blue eyes scanning my face with a mix of patience and mischief.

Then he flashes me that lopsided grin, the one that always makes my stomach flip. "I don't have to eat you out if you don't want me to. I was just thinking it could be really good. For both of us."

A nervous laugh escapes me, and I lift my hands to his shoulders, gripping them as if I need the anchor. "No, I want that. I really do."

He cocks his head, feigning innocence. "Want what?"

I flush even deeper, biting my lip as I try to muster the courage to say it. "You to . . . eat me out. I just . . . don't know if I like it."

That perks him up immediately, and his brows rise with exaggerated delight. "Boy, do I love a challenge."

His playful tone pulls a startled laugh from me, and I relax a fraction, my fingers slipping from his shoulders to the back of his neck. "What if I'm terrible at it?" I blurt, my voice smaller now but still laced with humor.

He shakes his head, his smile softening into something reassuring. "Birdie, baby, I promise, you won't have to do anything but enjoy it. If it's not good, we stop. No pressure."

I stare at him for a beat, his words sinking in. He's so calm about it, like he's completely certain this is going to work, that I'm going to love it. His confidence should be obnoxious, but instead, it settles something inside me, easing the nervous energy bubbling in my chest.

"Okay," I say, my voice steadier now. "But if you're bad at this, I'm making fun of you forever."

He lets out a low chuckle, leaning down to press a kiss to my forehead. "Deal. But spoiler alert—I'm not bad at this."

He shifts, trailing his hands down my sides and settling between my legs with a wicked grin that sends a fresh wave of heat surging through me. Every nerve in my body is on high alert, anticipation coiling tight.

His hands are quick, tugging at the button of my jeans and peeling them down my legs. My panties go next, a fleeting press of his fingers before I'm bare beneath him, utterly exposed. He pauses, his gaze dragging up my body, and the way he looks at me— like I'm art, like I'm something to be savored—makes my heart stutter in my chest.

He pushes my shirt up, baring my stomach, and leans in, his breath hot against my skin. I shiver as he blows a puff of warm air just above my navel, his lips brushing over the spot. Then he works his way lower, kisses trailing a path down my stomach and along the inside of my thighs, where his teeth nip gently at the sensitive skin.

When his lips finally press against me, I gasp. It's like everything sharpens at once—every nerve alive and begging for more. He licks, lavishes, kisses, and sucks with a focus that makes my head spin.

It's not just good—it's overwhelming. He's quite literally making out with my pussy, and it feels like . . . magic. Like fireworks detonating behind my eyelids, like I'm floating and sinking at the same time, like nothing else in the world exists except the way he's making me feel.

I grab at the sheets, my knuckles white as my head falls back against the pillow. My hips buck against him, completely out of my control, chasing every press of his tongue. His mouth moves to my clit, and I cry out.

Then his fingers join in—two of them, sliding inside me with the same ease as his tongue, pushing and pulsing in rhythm with the swirling heat building low in my belly. One flat hand presses firmly against my lower abdomen, anchoring me as his fingers curl just right, hitting that spot that makes me see stars.

The combined pressure—the way he's everywhere at once—is too much, too good, and I instantly shatter. My whole body tightens, every muscle locking up before releasing in a powerful wave as I come. I'm exploding into his mouth, my body trembling with the force of it as he keeps going, coaxing every last aftershock from me.

And then he's licking me clean, gentle now, his tongue soft and soothing against oversensitive skin. I think I've just died. Truly, honestly. There's no way I'm still alive, not after that.

My chest heaves as I try to remember how to breathe, how to think, how to exist. Liam looks up at me, his mouth curling into that smug, lopsided grin. His lips are shiny, and I should probably feel embarrassed, but I'm still too blissed-out to care.

"So," he says, his voice low and gravelly as he rests his chin on my thigh, looking entirely too pleased with himself. "Still not sure if you like it?"

I manage a shaky laugh. "Oh, I like it. I definitely like it."

"Good," he says, leaning forward to press a soft kiss to my hip. "Told you I wasn't bad at this."

And for once, I can't argue.

Chapter Thirty-Seven

LIAM

It's the first week of May, and school's finally out.

It's warm enough to ditch a hoodie but not so hot that I'm melting under the sun. The park is quiet today. Quiet but alive, like everything's waking up at once. Kids are laughing in the distance, birds are chirping in the trees. Birdie's curled up next to me on the blanket, her head on my shoulder, and the smell of spring—fresh-cut grass, faintly sweet flowers—wraps around us.

I close my eyes for a second, letting the moment settle. I don't think I've ever felt like this before. So content, so steady, like I'm exactly where I'm supposed to be.

"Do you think Warren ever takes a break from scowling?" I ask, cracking one eye open to glance at her. "Because I swear he's been practicing it like it's a sport lately."

Birdie hums, her fingers lazily tracing patterns on my knee. "He might. But only when no one's watching."

I laugh because she's not wrong. "I wonder if he'll finally loosen up next year."

We'd talked about it briefly—a quick exchange in the middle of unpacking finals stress—and decided to keep the same living arrangements for senior year. It wasn't some huge, dramatic decision. It just made sense. Warren's quirks are more than manageable, and I think I've started to grow on him, too. Slowly.

"You two are like an old married couple already." She smiles up at me, and it does something to my chest, the way her face softens in the sunlight, her hair a little messy from the breeze. "Sena's gonna drive me up the wall, too. Ever since I started inviting her to more things, she's been talking about themed wine nights and a murder mystery dinner party."

"You'll survive the company." I press a kiss to her temple. "And I'll be close by to rescue you if she starts singing show tunes at two in the morning again."

"Deal." She cups my jaw, her thumb brushing lightly over the stubble I forgot to shave this morning. "It feels good, doesn't it? Knowing what's next."

"It does. Because this time, I've got an unfair advantage."

I've got a clear sense of direction now. Soccer preseason kicks off in a few weeks, and I'm more than ready—ready to push my limits and see how far this journey can go. The draft is looming in the back of my mind, but it doesn't feel like an insurmountable obstacle anymore. It's just the next step forward.

And Birdie's a big part of why it feels manageable.

She raises an eyebrow. "Oh yeah? What's that?"

"You."

Her cheeks flush, and she ducks her head, pretending to fix the edge of the blanket like I didn't just make her all soft and flustered. I let her have a moment before I reach for her hand again, lacing our fingers together.

"I mean it. This year was strange, but you . . . you make everything feel solid. Like I can handle whatever's next."

"Even if 'whatever's next' is you getting drafted to some team on the other side of the country?"

"Yeah, even then," I tell her earnestly. "Wherever I end up, I want you to be a part of it."

She blinks, her lips parting like she wants to say something but isn't sure how. I can see the wheels turning in her head, that little furrow between her brows that shows up when she's overthinking.

"Birdie," I say softly, giving her hand another squeeze. "We'll make it work. No matter what."

She lets out a breath, her shoulders relaxing like I've said exactly what she needed to hear. "Okay."

"Okay?" I echo, grinning.

"Yeah, I'm easily convinced when it comes to you."

I lean in, brushing my nose against hers before pressing a quick kiss to her lips. "Good. You're stuck with me."

She rolls her eyes, but the way she tucks herself closer to me says she doesn't mind. We sit there for a while, the sun dipping lower in the sky. Pink and gold and all sorts of perfect.

"What about you?" I ask after a while, my voice quieter now. "The gallery job, Claire's studio—you think it will tide you over for the year?"

Her eyes light up. "Yeah. Claire already said she'd introduce me to some people who might want to show my work, so . . . we'll see. If I can sell a piece or two every few weeks, I should scrape by without dipping into my savings too much."

"You're gonna crush it."

Her laugh is soft, disbelieving. "You always say that."

"But human beings are fascinating. Like, why does Warren own a single pair of swim goggles for every day of the week? That's a whole sociological study waiting to happen."

She shakes her head, but she's smiling, her cheeks pink again. "You're goofy."

"And you're brilliant," I counter, resting my cheek against the top of her head. "Perfect match."

She settles against me, and I watch the way the light filters through the trees, the breeze rustling the leaves, and wonder how I got so lucky.

"Liam?"

"Yeah?"

"I love you." Her voice is soft, almost hesitant, but there's no mistaking the weight behind it. "A whole lot. More than I thought was possible. Before I met you, I was in a rut. I was lost and drifting, and you turned my whole world around."

I swallow hard, her words hitting me with all the force of a tidal wave. "Wow."

She blushes, looking down. "I know. I didn't think I'd be the one to say it first, but I just couldn't hold it in anymore."

I tilt her chin up gently and kiss her, slow and deep, letting everything I feel pour into the moment—the gratitude, the awe, the overwhelming certainty that she's it for me. She's my forever.

When we pull apart, her eyes search mine, and I murmur, "I love you, too. So much. I didn't think someone like you existed until you came crashing into my life. But now, I can't imagine it any other way."

She wrinkles her nose, trying not to smile. "You're the one who came crashing. You literally kicked a ball through the studio."

"It's a metaphor, baby. And whichever way you spin it, all I know is that I can't picture doing life without you."

Her laugh is quiet but radiant, her fingers threading through mine. "Good. Because I'm not going anywhere."

And with her reassurance, I know we've got it figured out—whatever comes next, we're facing it together. She's the steady rhythm in the noise that drowns me, my matching Jellycat in a sea of worn-out plushies. My everything.

Epilogue
LIAM

IT'S COLD IN CHICAGO, the kind of chill that creeps into your bones no matter how many layers you wear. The snow hasn't started falling yet, but the weather app says it'll hit by midnight.

Birdie walks beside me, her gloved hand tucked into the crook of my elbow as we make our way through the streets. The city's all decked out for the holidays—twinkling lights in every window, wreaths on lampposts, and the faint sound of a street musician playing "Jingle Bells" on a saxophone somewhere in the distance.

She nudges me with her shoulder. "Stop looking like you're about to storm the field. We're going to a gallery, not a game."

"I'm not," I protest. "I'm just . . . taking it all in. Did you know that Chicago dyed the river green for St. Patrick's Day so many times they had to check if it was killing fish?"

Her smile grows, and she squeezes my arm. "Yes, I did know that. And no, it didn't, Mr. Fun Facts."

I lightly slap her ass, and she gasps, her eyes narrowing in mock outrage before breaking into a soft laugh. By the time we arrive at the gallery, she's giving me side-eyes that are equal parts amused and exasperated.

The one she picked is tucked into a quiet street, all minimalist lines and big windows. Inside, the warm glow of recessed lighting highlights an array of ceramics—everything from impossibly delicate teacups to bold, abstract sculptures that look like they belong in a history museum.

Birdie's face lights up the second we step inside, and I swear, watching her take in the space is better than the art itself.

"You picked a good one," I say, trailing behind her as she moves from piece to piece.

"Of course I did," she replies, her fingers hovering just shy of a vase with swirling blue and white glazes. "I always do my research."

I watch her for a moment, the way her eyes linger on every curve and texture, and for a second, the weight of tomorrow presses just a little less heavy on my chest. The MLS draft is less than twenty-four hours away—everything I've worked for, dreamed about, is almost within reach.

And Birdie has been by my side every step of the way, grounding me when my thoughts spiral, celebrating every win, no matter how small.

"Do you think your stuff will look good here?" I ask, leaning against a display case.

She pauses, her lips pressing together like she's trying not to smile. "Maybe. It's no Metropolitan Museum of Art, but it'll do."

"Just wait," I say, my tone certain. "People are going to be lining up just to get a glimpse of your work."

She shakes her head, but there's a faint blush creeping up her neck. "You always know how to make me sound way cooler than I am."

"Not possible," I reply, straightening up and stepping closer. "You're the coolest person I know."

She turns back to the display, a soft laugh escaping her. "You're biased."

"Damn right I am," I say, sliding my arm around her waist. "And I can't wait to be even more obnoxiously biased when your name is displayed in galleries across Chicago—or New York—or wherever else people are smart enough to show your work."

It's not just a dream, either. She's been working with Claire nonstop this semester, experimenting with larger pieces, more sculptural forms, and finally gaining the confidence to show them off.

Her ceramics were part of the Ellsworth showcase in the fall, and one of her pieces even made it to the Montrose Gallery student exhibition—a huge step for someone who spent last year doubting her place in the program.

She tilts her head. "And when your name is up on stadium lights tomorrow?"

I smile, my fingers tightening slightly around her hip. "We'll celebrate. No matter what happens, we'll celebrate."

She leans into me. "Deal."

The weight of tomorrow presses a little less heavy, and as we leave the gallery, the first snowflakes start to fall. Birdie lifts her face to the sky, her eyes bright with wonder, and I know without a doubt that whatever happens tomorrow, I've already won.

THE NEXT MORNING, nerves hit me hard.

The Chicago Convention Center is massive, all glass and steel, with banners for every MLS team hanging from the ceiling. Snow flurries dance outside the windows, but the cold doesn't follow us in. Inside, it's all heat and energy, a steady buzz of excitement and anticipation.

Birdie walks beside me, her green coat a pop of color against the sea of dark suits and jerseys. "You okay?"

"Yeah," I say, even though my stomach is doing flips. "Just feels . . . big."

"It is big," she replies, smiling. "But so are you."

I snort and waggle my brows. "I know what you mean, but I'm trying really hard not to make a dirty joke right now."

She smirks, giving my hand a squeeze. "I think you can keep it tucked up in your noggin'. Just this once." She tugs me toward the doors, the green of her coat standing out against the muted tones around us. "You've worked for this your whole life, Liam. You're ready."

I want to believe her, and maybe a part of me does. But as the doors slide open and we step into the lobby, the sheer size of it all threatens to knock the air out of me. The space is sprawling, filled with banners, booths, media stations, and clusters of people talking in hushed but excited tones.

Birdie stays close, her hand warm in mine as we check in and head toward the main ballroom where the draft is taking place. My agent, Ben, is already inside, texting updates and telling me to "stay loose."

"Stay loose," I mutter under my breath, my lips twitching. "Right. Sure."

Birdie glances up at me, her eyes shining with quiet amusement. "You're already killing it at pretending to be calm. Very convincing."

"Thanks."

She digs into her pocket and pulls out something small and bright yellow. "Here. I thought this might help."

It's a lemon.

The tightness in my chest eases as soon as I see it. I take it from her, bringing it to my nose and inhaling the sharp, citrusy scent. The absurdity of the gesture—of us—makes me grin.

"Thanks, baby. But sniffing lemons at the MLS Draft isn't exactly gonna help my street cred."

"Right. Because you're always so worried about your reputation."

"Exactly. I'm a pillar of seriousness and dignity."

"You're lucky," she says. "I almost brought our Jellycat bunnies for emotional support, but then I was worried they'd get lost in transit."

I laugh, leaning down to kiss her, and it's enough to make the nerves quiet for just a second. She smells like coffee and something sweet, and it's the only thing that feels real in this huge, over-whelming space.

We find our seats near the middle of the room, surrounded by other prospects, their families, and agents. The stage is front and center, decked out with MLS logos and a massive screen cycling through highlights of the top-ranked players.

"You were right," Birdie says after a moment, her voice quieter now. "This is . . . a lot."

I nod, my gaze fixed on the stage. "Yeah."

"But it's also kind of amazing."

I glance at her, my lips quirking. "You just like the banners, don't you?"

"They're very well designed," she admits, grinning. "Someone here has artistic vision."

The first round starts, and the tension in the room is electric. Names are called, players walk to the stage, and applause fills the air. Each announcement feels like it stretches forever, but also like it's over too quickly.

Birdie stays close, her hand resting on my leg, her thumb brushing soothing circles against my knee. Every time the commis-sioner steps up to the podium, I hold my breath.

"With the fourteenth pick in the 2025 MLS SuperDraft," the commissioner announces, his voice echoing through the room, "FC Cincinnati selects Liam Donovan, winger, Dayton University."

For a second, the words don't register. Then Birdie's hand tightens on my leg, and her voice cuts through the haze. "Liam."

I turn to her, and she's grinning, her eyes bright with pride and something softer, something steady.

"That's you," she says, her voice cracking just a little.

I stand, my chair scraping against the floor as applause rises around me. Ben claps me on the back, and I manage to give him a quick nod before heading toward the stage.

The lights are blinding, and the cameras feel like they're aimed straight at my chest, but the moment I shake hands with the coach and hold up the FC Cincinnati scarf, it hits me.

I did it.

One of the staff members hands me a jersey—bright orange and navy with my name on the back—and someone else points me toward another round of interviews. The reporters' questions blur together: "What does this mean to you? How does it feel? What are you most excited about?"

Ben's at my side, guiding me through the chaos like he's done it a hundred times before. Cameras flash in every direction, and my face hurts from smiling, but every few seconds, I catch glimpses of Birdie at the edge of the crowd, her presence a steady anchor in all the madness.

Later, when the buzz finally dies down, I find Birdie waiting for me in the lobby. She looks up, sees me, and her smile widens, lighting up her entire face. It's the kind of smile that makes everything else fall away.

"You did it," she says, launching herself into my arms.

I laugh, catching her easily. "*We* did it."

She pulls back, hands resting on my shoulders. "I didn't kick a single ball, Donovan. This was all you."

I shake my head, my grin softening. "You were there every step of the way. I couldn't have done this without you, Birdie. You know that, right?"

Her eyes shimmer. "Okay, maybe I was a little helpful."

I chuckle, pressing my forehead to hers. "Just a little?"

"Fine, a lot."

"Then it's settled," I say, leaning in to kiss her, soft and slow. "This is ours."

Her lips twitch, her cheeks flushing pink. "So, Cincinnati, huh?"

"Looks like it."

"You ready for it?"

My grasp on her hand tightens. "Yeah. Are you?"

She tilts her head, pretending to think. "Am I ready to visit my boyfriend in the middle of Ohio? Sure. I'll bring snacks."

I laugh. "We're gonna make this work, Birdie. No matter what."

She presses one last perfect kiss to my lips. "I know we will."

Acknowledgments

First and foremost, to my husband and baby girl—thank you for being my greatest cheerleaders and the heart of everything I do.

To my mom, for always being there and believing in me.

Sandra at One Love Editing, thank you for your sharp eye and for making sure this book was as polished as possible.

Megan, my wonderful alpha reader and the only other person to have read this book in its earliest form—your feedback and encouragement meant the world to me.

To the book bloggers and influencers who pour their passion into sharing stories, thank you for making books like mine come alive for readers.

And to every single person who has ever picked up my work, thank you for being part of this journey.

About the Author

Ki Stephens is a romance enthusiast who finds comfort in the happily-ever-after . . . with just a little bit of angst along the way. She has a special interest in works that include neurodivergent characters like herself. When she's not daydreaming about books, Ki enjoys working with kids, creating art in her backyard studio, and spending loads of time with her baby girl, her husband, and their three pets.

She released her debut novel, Spring Tide—Book 1 in the Coastal University Series, in December of 2022.

www.kistephens.com